THERE WON'T BE ANY MORE

Best Wishes

Keith

THE ASKENES TRILOGY: BOOK 3

KEITH POLLARD

Published by Keith Pollard

ISBN 9781685832476

First published in 2022

Design and typesetting by Hawk Editorial Ltd, Hull

I would like to thank Sam Hawcroft at Hawk Editorial for all her help and patience with me while proofreading and editing my trilogy, for without her help this would never have happened.

Once again I would like to thank my wonderful wife Jacky for all her love and patience during my time creating the trilogy; it has at times been frustrating and how she puts up with me I will never know.

I would like to thank the following, who helped me in my research on the history of the fishing industry:

Ken Platten: ex-Hull bobber
Ray Hawker: The Hull Bullnose Heritage Group
Jerry Thompson: The Hull Bullnose Heritage Group

CHAPTER 1

LEIF

Another Job

After putting Mum to bed, Billy came back down. He still had a funny look on his face, a kind of embarrassed look, and it was bothering me what Mum had said about her son coming home from Australia.

'Is she all right, mate? She hasn't thrown up or anything? Those snowballs always send her over the edge – why she drinks them I will never know.'

'Yes, she is fast asleep now. You are right; when she drinks them, she gets fucking delusional. I think that's the right word – she starts talking rubbish.'

'So this stuff about her son from Australia is a load of shite? What do you reckon she means by it?'

'I don't know, son. Your guess is as good as mine; I know she went through a bad time when you went. You might not like what I am going to say, son, but you broke her heart, you leaving her like that; I know – I was there. She could be thinking about those days, I don't honestly know, but I wouldn't worry about it. She won't even know she has said it in the morning, so don't you go reminding her, dragging up bad times, OK?'

'Yes, sorry, Billy, you are right; must have been those memories flooding back. OK, I won't say another word on the subject. Thanks for telling me – I never knew; she never let on.'

'Well, she wouldn't, would she? Her fucking blue-eyed boy could do

5

no wrong, but I got it in the fucking neck. That's why I'm telling you now. Let's leave it at that, OK?' 'Mmm, OK.'

It was back to finding a job now, as I'd used too much of my savings. I wasn't getting greedy, just careful; I had done all right from my pay-off, but I was ready to get back to work.

February 1987

I had been home a couple of weeks. It was bloody cold and windy. As the old saying goes, about March coming in like a lion – I was hoping it was going to start the lamb bit a few weeks earlier, as I was missing the sun. Those few days in Tenerife had spoiled us.

Martin had been moping about like a lost puppy; he was missing his friend Juliette. I was sure she had taken his cherry and made a man out of him – lucky bastard.

I was watching Match of the Day when the phone rang. 'Who the hell is that at this time of night?' Connie said, as she got up to answer it.

'Hello? Who? Yes, he is here – do you want to speak to him?'

What a question. No, silly twat, that's why they have rung up; what else do you do on the phone? The stupid things people say.

'It's some bloke called Einar; I think he said he wants to talk to you.' She handed me the receiver.

'Hello, Einar, how are you? For what do I owe this pleasure? How did you get this number?' I could not ever remember giving him Connie's number. 'What do you mean you have your contacts?'

'Listen, Leif, I heard you were looking for work, and I know of someone who could use your capabilities. I know of a company looking for a project/contracts manager, someone with experience in South America. They have worked in that area before and are in for quite a bit of work with one or two countries, Brazil being one of them – would you be interested? I know the situation with Caporal did not work out, but between you and me, they were pissing in the wind; it was never going to work.'

He went on to tell me they were a Dutch company. Why could they not be a UK concern – why did I have to travel to Holland again? Not that I did not like the Netherlands and the people. I just wanted to be home for a while. I was getting used to getting in my own bed every night, even if it was at Connie's house, as I seemed to be here now more than my pad. I enjoyed going to bed with the same woman, cuddling up with her and waking up with a belly full of bum every morning; I must have been getting old.

'When are they looking for someone to start? What do you mean, yesterday? That quick? But what about an interview?

'A phone interview?'

'When?'

'Tomorrow?'

'What time?'

'Noon UK time?'

'Where and how did they get my number?'

'Don't ask…'

'Einar, you never fucking change; what do you mean?'

'Don't swear at me, or I won't give you any more details.'

'OK, I will make sure I am there; what is his name again?'

'Jan Verboom.'

'OK, got it – I look forward to hearing from him. Good night, Einar.'

'What was that all about? It sounds like you have a job away again. Am I right, or was I just imagining it?'

Connie was looking a bit pissed off; I suppose it was knowing that I was going away again.

'Yes, sorry, but that's the sort of business I am in. They just don't build oil refineries in Pickering Park or even in the Humber; sorry to say, it's the nature of the job. Let's just see what they have to say tomorrow; it won't be a bad job, not if Einar has anything to do with it. If he has put my name forward and contacted me, he knows I won't take a shit job. Before you say it, the last one did not work out, I know, but the idea was right; it just did not bear fruit.'

I was up early. I couldn't sleep, running through my mind what questions they might ask. No doubt Einar had given them the lowdown on me and maybe even given them a copy of my CV that I had given him just in case. I had often done this whenever I had met people who were in positions of power.

Bang on noon, on the phone rang. I was sitting there with sweaty palms; Connie went upstairs – I did not want her to poke her nose in, or maybe come out with some comment, as often women do.

I picked up the phone. 'Good morning; how are you, Jan?' It was a girl's voice. 'Oh, sorry, is Jan there, please?'

'No, sorry, I am his PA, Kaira. Jan is just on another call; he asked me to ring you as he had stated a time. I will put you through; he is just finishing a conference call and can't get away, which is why I have called.'

'OK, no worries, do you want to ring me back when Jan is free? I don't mind chatting to you, Kaira. What a lovely name, by the way – where does it originate from?'

'Oh, thank you, Leif, you are so kind – it is Scandinavian and, before you ask, the name means pure.' She giggled as she said it.

'Mmm, it sounds nice. What a beautiful name,' I could almost see her blushing as I said it.

'Oh, thank you so much; your name, Leif, is also from Norway, I believe – is that correct?'

'Yes, my forefathers came over to the UK on the way to America during the great famine in the 1800s.'

'Yes, I am aware of that time in our history; my great-great grandparents came to Holland around the same time. We should get together sometime to discuss our genealogy; I find it fascinating… oh, hang on, he has finished. I will put you through now; great talking to you, Leif – bye for now.'

With that, she was gone, and a male voice took her place, 'Sorry, Leif, to keep you waiting, I could not get rid of them, but I do hope Kaira did not bore you. She is such a lovely girl but does tend to go on when given free rein. Well, down to business.'

'No, she was quite charming, and sounded very knowledgeable. We have a lot in common – both our ancestors came from Scandinavia many years ago. But yes, you are right – down to business. I believe you have been talking to Einar Hegdahl; he rang me last night to tell me you would be contacting me. I believe you are looking to take on some more staff, is that correct?'

'Yes, we are, Leif, and you come highly recommended not only by Einar but other, what shall I say, "People in the game," to use an English phrase. I believe your CV reads very well, and it seems you could be just the man we are looking for, dependent on terms and conditions, obviously. I won't beat about the bush – another one of your sayings. I believe you were with a new company, Caporal, that Vanderries, one of our competitors, set up. Also, I heard it did not quite work out as they had hoped it would, but that is another story. May I ask what salary you were on, and the office was based in the Bahamas, I understand?'

'Yes – may I speak frankly with you? I have nothing to hide, and I do hope that this conversation can be strictly confidential.'

'OK,' Jan agreed.

'I was paid in US dollars or any denomination I asked for into my bank account in Switzerland, equivalent to £130,000 a year, completely free of any tax liabilities – that was down to me. Also, I had a company Amex card, with no limits, within reason, which had to be backed up with receipts. I also was given a per diem payment of $75 to cover incidentals and other items that did not require receipts. On top of that, all hotel bills were paid by the company; all flights were first-class or no less than business class, with car hire, fuel, etc., all reimbursable.'

A whistling sound came down the phone. 'I can understand why you would be gutted that did not work out; you had a good thing going there, Leif. I don't know if it's even worth offering you the position with us; our managing director is not on that sort of salary.'

'I know it was a hell of a package, and yes, it was a bit of a letdown, to say the least, but don't think that I don't know that. I know what the current rates are, and I am willing to listen to any offer that you would like to put on the table.'

'OK, I understand. Well, it's like this, the position we can offer you with Noroil carries a basic salary of, and I will give it to you in sterling. You would be employed on a contract basis; all taxes and insurances are to be paid to your account, OK? We would be paying £500 per day for all days worked, including travel days, and we would cover all flights – in economy only, though, sorry to say. You would pay all hotel bills yourself, and they would be fully reimbursed monthly, paid in arrears. We do not pay for public holidays or annual leave. Nor do we pay for any days off; for instance, if you were to go offshore for us on a two on, two off, you would not receive payment for the two off, but having said that, if you were to come and work in the company offices, you would still be on your rate of £500 a day. Along with the same scenario on expenses, Amsterdam's offices are not far from the central station.

'We are quite willing – if you are based in Holland, and you will be initially – to let you work a four-day week and travel back on a Sunday night ferry. It would be handy living in East Yorkshire; by travelling home on a Thursday night, you can work it to leave early to catch the night ferry, which usually leaves around 7pm. You would then get Friday, Saturday, and all day Sunday at home. We would pay the ferry costs; just put it on your expense sheet as travel costs. Is that OK? That would give you £500 for more or less nothing.

'We also pay a per diem payment of £50 per day, no bills required; we have an account at the American Hotel in the city centre on the Leidsekade, only ten minutes on a tram from Central Station. Does that sound attractive enough to tempt you to join us?'

It sounded good to me; I had no questions at this time, and Jan continued with his sell.

'Let me put it this way – for a full year, forty-six weeks per year, this would give you £115,000 plus £9,200, which equals £124,200 per year paid into your offshore account. The company pays all other outgoings, which will not show on any invoice. All we require from you is a timesheet signed by me or your immediate supervisor or manager. As a project manager, it would be me. You would need insurance to cover public liability – yourself, and company liability. We in the Netherlands do not recognise UK limited company status. Therefore you would not have to file any company records to anyone, and payments can go into an account anywhere in the world. The insurance is just to cover, as you say, our arse.'

'Jan, you certainly make it an attractive proposition, and I am truly tempted. Is it OK to sleep on it and let you know my decision in the morning? I'm just trying to take it all in; it's a lot of information all in one go.'

'Oh, I forgot to add that at the end of every twelve months you stay with the company, we pay a 20 per cent bonus; how stupid of me to forget that. That would take it to nearly £150,000 per year, or £149,040, to be exact, all completely tax-free – as long as you don't declare it, that is. We do have other ways of paying our staff from overseas – we pay you in two stages: a monthly payment going into your UK account for, say, £400 per week or £18,400 a year. This way, it will keep the taxman happy; you would be paying normal tax rates and National Insurance from a UK agency. Fully covered by invoices and payment slips, showing you are a self-employed consultant working from home. This will mean you get £2,425 tax-free, so you would pay NI At nine per cent on £16,000, which equals £1,440, then the remaining £14,560 at twenty-seven per cent, which is £3,932, giving a full liability of £5,371.20p – not bad on £150,000. I hope you have a pen to write all that down, Leif.' I heard him chuckle as he said it.

'No, I had worked it out in my head.' I was lying, of course – I had been jotting it down, and he was spot on; I had a calculator by my side just in case he quoted figures.

'I will ring you in the morning, Leif, OK? The same number, if that is all right with you? I will let you go now; we have talked quite enough for one day. Is there anything else you want to know about the company? I do assume Einar filled you in on our background and who we are, etc. Should you think of anything, leave it until tomorrow. With that, I will say goodbye and look forward to hearing your decision.'

He was gone. Wow, I could not believe it; one of the top offshore and onshore construction companies in the world wanted me.

Did I want it? Too fucking right I did; there was no doubt about that. I was mulling over the figures when Connie came down.

'How did it go? You have a smile on your face like the proverbial Cheshire cat; it must have gone well.'

I told Connie everything he had told me; she smiled and said, 'Money isn't everything, dear. Will you be happy working away again? You won't have me, don't forget.'

'Yes, I will be in Holland. I will be back in Hull every weekend; I'll only be working four days a week.'

'Leif, did you notice you did not say home? You said Hull.' Women don't miss a trick do they, I thought. How to make you feel bad without even trying, just twisting words? It was a masterclass. OK, I did not want to cause a fuss. I had been thinking 'home', but if I said that now it would look as if I was patronising her.

'You know what I mean, Connie.'

'Do I? You know I love you, don't you?'

This was the first time she had ever said those three little words without me being inside her, in the heat of passion. I knew she had her serious head on.

'I don't want to lose you, Leif – you are the best thing that has happened to me for years. Apart from that, Martin thinks the world of you; you have been like a father to him, ever since you first met. He adores you, never stops talking about you; he will miss you something awful. I have been alone for far too long, losing both my parents early on in my life and being the only one – it has been hard. Then getting married so young, and that failed… life has been hell at times – then you came into it. You have changed my life, and I can't lose you – I just can't.' She started to cry.

What could I say? No one had ever been so close to me in all my life, only my mother. She was correct; we needed each other.

'Connie, I have to get a job soon, and I'm afraid ones like this don't come by every day; I don't want a job in Hull. There is nothing here for me.' Whoops – now that was the wrong phrasing. 'Work-wise, I mean, before you think otherwise. I will miss you both, but it will only be four days a week when I am not away, either offshore or abroad.'

I had not asked about working overseas in places such as South America, for that was what I was supposed to be taken on for; Jan had not mentioned that at all, which seemed strange, thinking about it now. I made a note to ask him in the morning.

We discussed it most of the rest of the day; I knew Connie was only working part-time after Christmas as things were a bit slack. I think she was getting a bit sick of it and was looking for a change herself; itchy feet syndrome – I had had it all my life.

Martin came home from school; there was a letter from Juliette, so he disappeared upstairs and was not seen again after tea. Oh, such was young love.

We were in bed by ten. I was reading my book, and the leg came across mine, and a smooth hand stroked my belly. I tried to make out I was not interested, but the old fella stood to attention in a flash. Her head disappeared under the covers. We had not made love much since our holidays, and even then that was when Martin wasn't around.

I could feel her body pressed against my side; she moved a little, then she was on top of me; her leg appeared out of the covers; I pushed against the bed head and slid us both down the bed. We were both lying full length, she on top. I was licking the sole of one of her feet as she worked on me; I was in heaven. I only got as far as Leeds and could not hold it any longer; she never came up for air, her lips firmly wrapped around me. I went limp, and she just continued. Oh god, she had never done this before. As most men will tell, once you have reached the happy end, it starts to tickle; just a touch makes your balls crawl up your belly – it's the weirdest feeling, like you don't want to be there.

Now a woman was clamped on to me like a limpet, and did not want to unleash me. It was not only good, it was beautiful. On the other hand, I just wanted her to stop... but then again, I didn't.

Oh my god, it was an unreal feeling. She just kept him in her mouth; her tongue was rolling around me. She was working up and down until he started to like it, we both did, he got stiff again, mmm. Connie still had not come up from under the covers; I had not touched her or anything. She must have orgasmed four times to my one, up to now. Connie opened her legs wider and slid up the bed, and pushed her lower lips to mine. Oh my god, she left what she was doing under the bedclothes and then more or less sat on my face. I was drowning in her sap, and with that I reached Workington – the lot just gushed out of me. What a session. I'd never had sex like it. Could this be a way of trying to keep me at home? It would kill me first.

She rolled off me; I was soaked in both of our juices, 'OK, baby? Enjoy that, did you?'

'Where on earth did you find that position? You've never made love like that before; what got into you? You're an animal. God, it was so good, Connie.'

'I read it in a book I got from the library a few weeks ago. I knew I was not that experienced and wanted to please you. To thank you for being you – and the only way was to learn how to seduce a man. Not just fuck him, but make love to him. Good, wasn't it? I have never felt like that either. Want some more? I do!'

We fell asleep in each other's arms, well and truly shagged, the pair of us.

It was 10am when I woke up; I got out of bed. Jesus, I ached in some places I did not know I had. I went into the bathroom and turned on the shower. That felt better already; the hot water was cascading down my head, down to my body. I lathered the gel into my hair and body, washing the aches and pains away. I was towelling myself down when I looked in the mirror. I had not noticed the love bite on my chest next to my nipple on my right side. She had gone to work, leaving me in the land of nod. There was another one lower down on my belly; I'd never seen one on a stomach. One on my thigh… holy hell, I was riddled with them. I took the small shaving mirror off the shelf; my inner thigh and groin were covered in love bites; I counted about six. The woman had tried to eat me alive. She was a cannibal. I never felt her sucking the blood to my skin; I had never had a love bite since I was at school.

I had to find this book she had borrowed to find out what else she had in mind. I went back into the bedroom and looked in all the drawers, the cupboard, the wardrobe, under the bed, but nothing. Where the fuck was it?

Then it dawned on me – under the mattress, it had to be there. Bingo, I was right. It was not so much a book, but a magazine – glossy pages with loads of pornographic photographs, and written in French. Now I knew how she got her ideas. I could not read the instructions, so to speak, but the moves were laid out in numerical order, exactly how Connie had done them.

There was one that alarmed me; it was a woman with a strap-on cock. I had seen one used in Amsterdam but never seen any for sale in the UK, not that I had looked – but what alarmed me more than anything was she had written comments alongside each picture, such as, 'Leif will love this. I want him to know what it's like the other way – I want him to feel just like I do, must get one.' Oh my god, she intended to rape me.

I put the book back where I found it, got dressed, and went downstairs. It was almost noon, and Jan Verboom would be calling soon. I had a coffee and some toast and was sitting at the table when the phone rang.

'Oh, hi Leif, it's Kaira, Noroil – good morning. I am afraid Jan will be late back in the office; he had to go out. Can he ring you back in an hour, no later – is that OK?'

'Yes, of course, no problem, I will be here.'

With that, she said goodbye and the phone went dead.

CHAPTER 2

LEIF

Part of My Life

The longest hour passed, and the phone rang again. It was Jan. 'Hello, Leif – sorry about the delay. I was called to meeting in town, a bit of an emergency, but all OK now. So have you decided on your answer, yes or no – or any further questions before you decide? Before you tell me your decision, after we finished speaking yesterday, I realised that we should have discussed South America. We, or should I say I, had got carried away with the offshore industry here in Europe and the North Sea, particularly along with the Amsterdam office; we never touched base on Latin America.'

'Yes, that was going to be my first question this morning.'

'OK, fire away. What did you want to know?'

'Well, one thing for a start – will it be the same day rate we discussed yesterday, £500?'

'Yes, the same rate, but we will double the per diem rate to £100, only paid when you are working onshore. If you are offshore, you do not get any payment as, well, you can't spend it anyway – there are no shops or bars offshore, is that OK?' He laughed.

'Yes, that's fine. One other question – how long would I be expected to be away from home? What is the rota, if any?'

'It depends on where you would be working. There are three scenarios, considering that the continent is that vast. At some time you could be working in the jungle environment. We would expect you to job-share the position, working a month on, month off rota, but you would be on the same rate both home and away, as you work seven days a week in the jungle. The second scenario would be working in offices in a big city, such as Rio, Caracas or Lima, for example, then we would expect you to be there for a minimum of six months, with a month's leave in-between. The third and final scenario would be for offshore work, and that would be the same as the first scenario – a month on, month off, with one week off working in Amsterdam on full rate with the other three on leave, on half the rate. It may sound a bit harsh, but you would be getting paid seven days a week when offshore and twelve hours a day; we feel that this is a fair deal.'

I tried to work out the different options in my mind, and it seemed OK at first.

'Leif, you have gone quiet. Is that all OK, or do you need more time to make your mind up? We will not rob you; we feel we are one of the leading players in this industry. We pay accordingly – don't forget the twenty per cent annual bonus applies to all salary earned over the year, not just on worked hours. Therefore it is a tidy sum, at the end of the year, paid on the anniversary, if you started on, say, March 1, then on April 30 next year, twenty per cent of what you have earned would be paid into your nominated bank account. We intend on keeping our much-valued staff.'

That sold it to me – that bonus payment, I could not work it out. There were too many twists and turns to knock the rest back.

'OK, thank you so much, Jan. I will accept your offer; when do you want me to start?'

'Next Monday in our Amsterdam head office there will be a week's induction and a getting to know each other period. You will be on a three-month trial period, which works both ways; once the period is over, we will sit and discuss our options. If we decide that you do not fit the bill, your contract will be terminated, and we will pay you the bonus on the period worked. Should you decide that you do not like it, then you can walk away, but unfortunately, you would not receive the bonus. Is that understood?'

'Understood – that seems fair enough to me. Thank you for giving me the opportunity of working for Noroil, and I will say you will always get 110 per cent from me. Thanks, Jan.'

'No, thank you, Leif! I look forward to meeting you next week. Bye for now.'

It was a done deal. I was like a dog with three dicks. I had to admit I was looking forward to getting back to Holland, and Amsterdam particularly. I just loved the place.

I went out and bought some best fillet steak, along with a bottle of champagne to celebrate my new job and our good fortune. I had something else I wanted to ask Connie, which was going to be a big surprise. I had decided to ask her to marry me, but with a condition.

Connie arrived home along with Martin. I had set the table along with candles and napkins. 'Bloody hell, you have been busy,' she said. 'What's going on here, Leif? Why the fuss?'

'I want it to be a special evening. We could have gone out to a restaurant, but I wanted to do it myself. Come on, sit down, the pair of you, it's almost ready.'

I had also got a bottle of rioja to go with the steak, along with coke for Martin. We sat and had the meal; the steak just melted in your mouth perfectly – medium, no blood, just the way it should be cooked. Martin said he preferred a Wimpy, but kids are like that. The chips were big thick home-cooked ones with onion rings and a side salad; I had even sprinkled watercress on the top. Once we had finished, I went into the kitchen and brought out three glasses and the champers.

'Right – and now for the final touch.' I opened the bottle with the usual bang. The cork hit the ceiling, bouncing down and hitting Martin on the head.

'Fuck, that hurt.'

'Stop swearing!' said Connie.

I poured the wine and handed them a glass each, 'Here, Martin, you can have one to toast my good fortune and the future.'

I put my glass in the middle. 'The future,' we all said, touched glasses, and took a drink.

'Mmm, that's nice,' said Connie. 'Tastes expensive.' Typical woman's comment.

We went into the living room to finish the champers; Martin finished his off with one swig and said, 'I am off to bed. Thank you, Leif, for a lovely night.'

He stood up and gave me a hug, which quite surprised me. It was the first time he had showed affection towards me. I looked at Connie over his shoulder, and she had tears in her eyes.

'Night, son, see you tomorrow.' It was the first time I had called him 'son'; it just seemed right, and sounded it too.

I sat next to Connie on the sofa, 'Right, now for the news on the job.' I went through what we had discussed that day and that I had accepted their offer, and that I would be leaving and going to Amsterdam to start working a four-day week for the next three months.

Connie did not say a lot during my sales pitch. She just listened intently, and then said, 'OK, I can understand why you want the job, what with the money and travel; it's been your life for so long, but I have my reservations about it – what about me? How do I fit into all of this? Are you expecting me just to sit back and wait for you to come back, as and when you choose? I am your girlfriend, we are not even engaged, and that is not a proposal. I have a life and a son to think about.

'What if you find someone else while you are away, and then just blow me out when you get back or maybe even never, ever return. You could decide to stay in some far-off land and never come back to me; you have told me you knew a couple of guys who went out to South Africa, left their wives and families, and just never came home. I do not want that to happen to me, Leif. You have altered me; you have turned me into something I never was, and you taught me how to enjoy sex. I was a virgin when I met my first husband; we had sex, but not as we do – it was wham, bam, thank you, ma'am, with him. I then went a long, long time before I went with another man, or men. Yes, I had a couple of flings but nothing like the relationship with you. We have come such a long way in a short time. I now enjoy it, even to the extent of saying I need it – but I need you Leif… no one else, you.'

Fucking hell, what a statement of intent. I would have had a heart to heart with her, but she had said it all.

As I said earlier, I was going to ask her to marry me, with one condition – that we give it a year's trial, to find out if we could live apart for weeks at a time or put up with me being away four nights a week, or two weeks at a time. Or at the worst, away for six months at a time – that would be the hard one. The whole thing would be a tester that she had never had to put up with, for she only did it for a short time with her first husband, and then they split for reasons I was not a party to. There was one thing for sure – this sort of life would either break a marriage or make it a lot stronger.

'Connie, I had made my mind up before I accepted the job – that I would put a proposal to you. I have had many relationships over the years with many women of different types. I was engaged to one, but that did not work out for reasons I will not go into. But I need to work, and the only work I know means me being away for periods. Not a five-day, nine to five, home every night existence – for me, that is what it would be; we would not live, we would only exist. I need to live, and I want you to be part of that life with me – and, yes, Martin as well, as part of my life. Please marry me, get engaged, be a couple, but with the condition that we try this life that we will be living together.

'I will be away, that is no doubt – but also I will be back home in our house, for I want us to move into a bigger, better place. We can pool the two – your house, my apartment – and get somewhere better, but we have to give this a trial before that. I am on a three-month trial with the job to see if we both like each other. I want us to do the same, but for a year, to see if we need each other as much as I think we do. I have loved and lost; I am not going to say I have never loved anyone as much as I love you, Connie, but the difference this time is I not only love you, I need you in my life. So, what do you say, Connie Winterton – will you be my wife?'

'I do not know if this is going to work, Leif, but I am damn sure I will be giving it my best shot. Of course I will marry you – oh, baby, I love you so, so much – thank you.'

She threw her arms around my neck and kissed me. I can't explain the feeling I had inside me at that moment. I had thought she was the one from the first night I met her in King Eddie, but I knew she was the one right now.

She ran out of the living room and shouted up the stairs. 'Martin, come down right now, please – no arguments – get your arse down here.'

Martin appeared. 'What's up? What's going on? I was just about to go to sleep. My head aches from that wine you gave me.'

'We have something to tell you, love; Leif is going to be your dad; we are getting married. What do you think about that?'

'Oh, Mum, that's great; when are you going to do it?'

'It will be in about a year; we are not going to rush into it, but we are going to get engaged soon and then get married later, is that OK?'

Martin came over to me and put his hand out. 'Congratulations, Leif, I am so pleased you want to be my stepfather – thank you so much.' He then hugged me and left the room.

'I am pleased you did not mention the trial period, Leif; it may have put doubt in his mind. He does not need more stuff to think about. Let's just be positive, eh?'

'Connie, I am confident, or I would never have asked you to be my wife, but as I said, it's a big step for both of us. Let's just make sure it's what we both want – you agree?'

That night we slept and made love, time and time again, until we were both drained. The last time, we both climaxed at precisely the same time, coming into Workington – perfect.

The following Sunday, I took the night ferry across to Rotterdam. A car was waiting for me and took me straight to Amsterdam and the Noroil offices. I had a bit of an induction, signed all the contracts, and met my new boss, Aart Van De Berg, along with the guys I would be working with; everything looked great.

*

I'd been about two months working on a regular four days in Amsterdam, with three at home, when Aart called me into his office.

'Hi, Leif, come in – take a seat. How are you today? OK, I hope?'

'Fine, thanks, Aart – what can I do for you? What's the problem?'

'Oh, no problem – I was talking with Jan yesterday about you and your progress within Noroil, how you had settled down, what a conscious worker you are, all that good stuff. He was wondering if you would be willing to change tack a bit. When you were first taken on it was as a project manager. Well, since you have been here you have shown, to me, that is, that you would be of more benefit to the company as a contracts manager, more on the proposals negotiating team – what do you think about that? I have read your CV, and you have been involved with that side of the industry as much as you have been involved on the construction side, which is something we lack in our negotiating team, and we think that you would fit in well with them. You would still come under my supervision. Another point – you would also be involved with your old friend Einar Hegdahl, as he acts as our head liaison with our clients in both North and South America. As we are pushing SA, we think you would make a great team – what do you think Leif? Would this interest you?'

I wondered what input Einar had into this change of direction. I knew he had said earlier it was a projects or contracts man they were looking for, but it had never been spelled out what role I was taking on.

'Yes, OK, whatever you think I can help Noroil with, I will do it. I like it here, and if you think I will be of more use to you in that role, and if it means working with Einar, then, great, count me in.'

I had never actually worked with Einar and was very interested in gaining some experience from him. He seemed to know the oil game inside out, and gathering his knowledge could do nothing but help me in my career.

I went home that weekend and told Connie about my move and, as usual, she wanted to pick the bones out of it. The main worry she had was the fact that I would be away from her for more extended periods, as the four on, three off would go out of the window, but she understood me wanting to further my career, and this would do just that.

We discussed the future and what it would bring; we had had a good three months or so of our trial year. I enjoyed coming home to my wife. I did like being away; there was no doubt about that, but I loved coming back. I had not been with another woman, not even tempted, which was a first.

*

Another month had passed, and I was once again called to a meeting with Jan and Aart to discuss my trial period. They had extended it a few weeks to see how I fitted in the proposals estimating team.

'Welcome, Leif. You know why you have been called to this meeting today – it is regarding your trial period.'

'Yes, Jan, I do. Can I just say before you give me your thoughts on my past few months, I am very pleased that you asked me to join the new team. I feel that I have found my place in the organisation. I love doing what I am doing. I find the work so stimulating and fulfilling. Every day is a new challenge, working on clients' requirements, liaising with their process and design teams – it is the best thing I have ever done.'

'That's great, Leif,' said Jan. 'I was just saying before you came in how the lead estimator was praising you just the other day; the guys in the team are pleased with your progress – like a duck to water, was one comment. Therefore we need not go on any further; as far as we are concerned, the trial period is over, and we want to confirm that we will be keeping you on. Is that OK with you?'

'Of course, Jan, thank you very much. I have no intentions of going anywhere else.'

'Great, that's settled then. There's not much need to go on with the meeting, and seeing we have much to do between us I will call it to a close,' said Jan, 'Now, if you will excuse me, I have to be over in Rotterdam later this afternoon.'

*

After a few more months had passed, something out of the ordinary occurred. It was a Monday morning. I had been home that weekend but had gotten late into the office as Hull's ferry back was late docking. The crossing had been a bit rough, to say the least; the weather had been terrible, with hurricane-force winds.

As I walked through the door, Aart spotted me. 'Ah, you are here. I need to speak to you, OK?'

'Sorry I am a bit late, but the ferry was held up – it could not berth due to bad weather.'

'Oh, don't worry about that, that's no problem, but I need to speak you – come with me.'

He took me aside in one of the meeting cubicles; they were set up with large screens, telephone/speakers for conference calls, and sound-proofed so no one could listen to conversations. He had my attention straight away, for this was a new one on me. We cut out the small chat, and he got straight down to the nitty-gritty.

'Right, I have had a request from up above for you to go and see the top man on Thursday evening after work. Is that OK? You have nothing on, have you?'

'Er, no, nothing.'

'Now, this is not a request; it is an order – you have to be at the head office at around 7.15pm, as he is away out of the country and will not be back until then.'

'Right – any idea what it's about?'

'No, even I am not a party to it, so it must be important – don't be late.'

It all seemed rather odd. Although it was a Norwegian company, quite a few of the top management were from the Netherlands. I think it was company policy to employ as many locals who knew the right contacts, if you know what I mean. It was on my mind all through the day. What the hell did they want from me that was so secretive?

Thursday finally arrived. Aart had not mentioned it again; in fact, I thought he was trying to avoid me, but maybe I was getting paranoid about it. I left work at the usual time and went for a coffee in a bar just around the corner to kill time. When I went back, the doors were all locked. I had to use my card to get in; swiping the lock, then pressing in my security code, I entered the building.

I took the lift up to the top floor where the managing director's office was, knocked on the door, and heard, 'Come in, Leif.' I walked in, and Diederik Bakker met me halfway across the office.

He greeted me with a warm handshake and a smile. 'How are you, Leif? I hope you are well. You may be wondering what and why is going on – why the intrigue, meeting me here after office hours, etc.?'

'Well, yes, I suppose so, but whatever – I don't have that much to do on an evening, as it is you that pays my salary. I will do anything you request – within reason,' I laughed nervously.

'Good, good, thank you, Leif – I have been getting useful reports back about you, and I hope we will be able to work together and further your career with us. We are looking at a contract in South America, a country with which we have done quite a few large projects. Now, I believe that the commercial side of the business is made for you, and I have an idea that will benefit both of us.'

I was confused about why were they asking me. I was already working in the commercial department, and had been for four months now.

He carried on. 'As I said, your immediate supervisor Aart Van Den Berg has taken a shine to you. He has always been an excellent judge of character; we are going to follow his instinct. It seems we believe you have had the experience of both estimating and cost engineering previously. Is this correct?'

He had not been fully briefed about my past working life, so I stopped him before he went any further and explained what had gone on over the period since I started with Noroil. I gave him the complete history, and he listened intently, then said, 'The reason I have asked, and now knowing even more details about you, the thing is – our head of that department is retiring next year, and we want you to fill his position. I feel that after a year of working as his number two, you will eventually take over from him.'

My mind was working overtime. Once again – why me? I was relatively new to the company, and yes, I had done some estimating for the previous employer, although on smaller projects. Having said that, I had developed an estimating package based on Excel for developing estimates from FEED through to installation. I remember telling Aart about it one time, and even showed him a copy of my programme. He must have been impressed and passed it on to Jan.

CHAPTER 3

LARS

Arrival in the UK – September 1988

Having left Denmark, we arrived at Harwich on September 10. The trip had just flown by, and I'd really enjoyed it up to now; Maya was getting a little homesick, which surprised me as I thought she was enjoying too. She said she was, but was just missing home a little, whereas I was not missing it at all.

We picked up the hire car, which would be ours for the next three weeks, and set off up north; we picked up the A14. On the way we had passed Newmarket, famous for its horse racing, but had decided to travel just that bit further as far as Cambridge, where we stayed for a couple of nights. I could not believe how old everything was; mind, I had said the same everywhere we had been. It just blew my mind how the buildings had stood so long; the modern facilities I had been involved in would not be standing in, say, 500 years, that was for sure.

After a couple of days there, we set off to drive to Newcastle, bypassing Hull, as we had decided to go there on the way back to London. We had a couple of nights in Newcastle, and then up to Edinburgh – a week had gone already. After Edinburgh, we drove up across to Glasgow for two nights, then we stayed at Cameron House, an old house on the bottom of Loch Lomond, for two nights. Then we spent the next eight days staying in Fort William, Inverness, Aviemore and Pitlochry, before heading back to Edinburgh, then across to Gretna and Perth. It was getting a bit much, all this driving. If we were to come again we would cut down on mileage, that was a certainty.

Then it was down to Manchester, where my parents came from, across to Blackpool, where I was allegedly born, then Liverpool, before heading over to Hull. In total, we had been away three weeks – a lot of travel, but we were thoroughly enjoying the UK.

It was now into Yorkshire and Hull. I was in two minds about finding my brother. Could I locate him quickly? Or was it going to be hard? I had his full name, Leif Askenes-Daniels; it should not be too hard to find. Indeed, only time would tell.

We had booked into the Station Hotel, assuming it was in the city centre, but never having been to the place we were only guessing. It was smack bang in the centre, and Hull was a lot bigger than I had imagined – quite a modern city, but I had read there had been a tremendous amount of damage to the area during the Second World War, and a lot had to be rebuilt.

The concierge had given us a map of the city and told us where the places of interest were, such as the Old Town pubs, Queen Victoria square and the museums; we were impressed. I knew it wasn't my hometown, but being here felt like it was. We decided to call in a pub for lunch, and picked one down High Street – Ye Olde Black Boy. Now, there was an unusual name, and small wasn't the word, but it was very quaint – all it needed was sawdust on the floor.

I was reading a plaque on the wall. It stated the building dated back to 1336 – now, that was old in anyone's language – and the pub was first opened in 1729. Its first landlord was a William Smith, and the current hosts were William and Blanche Leighton, who had been in since 1976. Some of the tales on this notice were unreal; when you saw things like this, you realised how bloody young Australia was.

What a spot – and to top it off, the tucker was simple, but OK, although this Pommie beer was getting a little hard to get used to. It was not cold enough for me, and even what they called lager was not as chilled as back home, but when in Rome, do as the locals do, I supposed. We spent most of the afternoon in there until they threw us out at 3pm – another Pommie custom.

There was a dock that had been filled in to make a park, and a memorial thing about Hull, telling that, in 1642, the king had tried to enter the city and this guy named Sir John Hotham refused him entry. We had to get used to all this old stuff – it was amazing.

We wandered back down a place called Whitefriargate. At the end of this street was the gate where old Sir John told the king to get to fuck; he wasn't coming in, and it was reckoned that this started the Civil War.

I was beginning to warm to this place; there was heaps of history in Hull and things to see. I wondered if a week would be long enough. After we got back to our hotel, we crashed out for a couple of hours; the traveling was getting the better of us, for sure.

We got changed and went out around eight o'clock, looking for a feed. There were plenty of Chinese restaurants around, but we fancied something different. The guy on the desk suggested a place about a ten-minute walk away, Mustafa's. 'Try the halibut. It's the best you have ever tasted – if you like fish, that is.'

We did, and he was right – the food was fantastic. We came out of there and wandered along the street, until we came to a pub where you went upstairs, which we thought we'd try because it was unusual. As I walked up to the bar, a couple of guys nodded and said, 'Hiya, all right?' I acknowledged them, thinking they were just friendly, then one said, 'Nah then, Leif, been away again, have you? Where to this fucking time – you ever going to stop working away?'

He thought I was Leif, my brother. I had cracked it. I did not say anything, just smiled and nodded.

I ordered the beers, and the barman looked at me oddly; he too must have thought I was my brother, but with a funny accent.

Maya went to the bar the next time. The barman asked her where she was from. He knew she was Aussie by the accent, and she told him Sydney. Giving her a funny look, as he gave her the change, he said, 'Mind if I ask you a question, love? But that guy you are with – has he got a brother or relation that lives in Hull? He doesn't half look like a lad that comes in here pretty regular.'

'We were looking for some distant relations – maybe you could help us?'

Maya came back to the table with a big smile on her face.

'What have you been talking to the barman about? He looked keen on you, and you were talking a lot,' I said. Then she told me the good news. 'Jeez, are you sure he will help us, Maya? That's unreal.'

A few minutes later, we spotted the barman talking to the group of guys standing at the bar. They kept turning around and looking at us as they spoke, and then one of them came over.

'Hiya, are you looking for Leif Askenes, by any chance? You are the spitting image of him; you could be fucking twins – whoops, sorry about swearing.'

'That's OK, no worries, and yes we are looking for a guy, and yes, his name is Leif – do you know him at all? Do you know where he lives, his address or phone number? That would be a great help to us, mate.'

'Yes, I am Billy, an old mate of his – I don't know them; I know where she lives but not the address offhand. But I will find out for you if you want to come back tomorrow night; hopefully, I will have the information for you.'

'Any idea when you will find out? Not being pushy, but it would mean so much to us. We think – well, more than think, we know – he is my brother that I have never met.'

'I will try and get back tomorrow. I will do my best. Great meeting you – fuck, you are Leif's double.'

'I am over the moon to speak to you. I promise we will be back tomorrow night at around eight o'clock?'

'Right, see you tomorrow then.' And off he went back to his drinking buddies.

'What do you think about that, Maya? Unreal – didn't think we would find him that easy. Fuck, I'm so made up.'

'Don't get too excited, babe. We haven't got the information yet, but it sure looks good to me; let's hope the guy is good to his word.'

The following night we were there bang on 8pm, and Billy was standing at the bar. He waved as we entered and came over. 'What's your poison, guys? What can I get you?'

'Oh, I will have a lager, please, and Maya will have a white wine.'

'Go get a table. I will bring the drinks over.'

I could hardly breathe. I would find my long-lost maternal mother and brother after forty years – I could not believe it.

Billy returned. 'There you go – one beer, one wine, no worries. Now, I suppose you want to know what I found for you? Well, his mother Christine lives up near Hessle with her boyfriend Billy, and Leif lives not far away from her – when he is home, that is. He works abroad a lot, in Holland – in fact, anywhere he is a right industrial gypsy. I don't know if he is home or not.'

Billy gave me a piece of paper with addresses on it and a phone number for Christine.

'I don't know how to thank you, mate,' I said. 'You have been more than helpful; I owe you one for sure.'

'How come you look so alike? Are you his brother? He has never mentioned he had a brother in Australia; that is where you are from, right? I have known him years and not once has he ever let on about you.'

'I am not sure he knows about me, and it is a very long story and would take too long to tell you it all now, but that it will all come out one day.'

We had a few more beers on me, and we left the pub at the closing time, going back to the hotel. I could not sleep, tossing and turning all night. Should I ring Mum up or just turn up on the doorstep? I kept reading the address time after time. I was going to meet my real mother.

There were only two lines on the paper Billy had given us.

23 Pickering View, Hessle High Road, Gipsyville Hull Tel 323561
Leif Askenes-Daniels, 2a The Birches, South Boulevard Hessle 262521.

CHAPTER 4

LARS

Calling a Stranger Mum –1988, aged 42

I was up at 7am, had breakfast, and was out by 8.30am. Maya did not want to come – not the first time, anyway; she thought it best I went on my own.

I stopped at a white – yes, a white – phone box on the way to ring and see if anyone was home. I could always put the phone down when they answered… if they answered.

I dialled the number and waited; a voice answered. 'Hello, 323561? Hello?'

I put the phone down; my heart was running. I could not breathe. She was home – my mum was at home. Oh god… what should I do? Pull yourself together, you fucking galah, get your act together – you have to go now, this voice was telling me in my head.

I just had to speak to her. I called again. 'Hello, 323561 – can I help you?' I did not reply; I could not talk. I was numb. I just wanted to listen to her voice, weird as it seems.

'Hello? Who's there, please? Hello? Hello? Will you answer?'

I did not answer; I could not… I haven't a clue why. I just couldn't.

'Will you fucking answer? Oh, fuck you.' The phone went dead.

OK, you fool, go round now – you have come all this way, now have some fucking balls, I told myself.

I pulled into Pickering View; it was a small cul-de-sac of eight houses. They had the number wrong. There was no number 23; oh fuck, which one was it? There was a number 3. I went up to the front door, held my breath, and knocked. No one came. I knocked again – no answer. It can't be that one, I thought… oh Jesus, which one was it – someone had just answered the bloody phone. I was walking away halfway down the garden path, and the door opened.

'Hello, can I help you?' I turned, and it was Mum. I just knew it was her. 'Oh my God, why didn't you come round the back door? You know we never use the front, you stupid twat, Leif. When did you get home?'

She did not know the difference; my mother did not know me. Or did she not know her other son had not died in childbirth? 'Hello, Mum,' I said. 'It's not Leif; it's me, Lars, your other son.'

'Lars! Oh, fuck, Lars… oh, fucking hell… Lars! How? Why? It can't be!'

She ran down the path and hugged me. Tears were rolling down her face – tears of joy.

'Come in, come in… oh, I can't believe it is you; after all these years, how did you find me? Oh, god.'

We went into the house; she was going on with question after question. She kept breaking down and crying, then she was OK again.

A couple of hours passed. We discussed Mum being lied to all those years ago in Blackpool. My birth father's entire story was a big shock to me; my grandfather was my real father – nothing like keeping it in the family. We talked about Leif and how well he had done with his life, but he was away again, working in Holland. Sometimes he was even in South America. She did not know when he would be home; they did not keep in touch that much.

She pulled some photographs out; it was like looking at myself in another world from being a child; it took some sinking in, I can tell you.

I looked at my watch; it was after three. I had to get back to Maya to give her the good news.

'Listen, Mum.' It sounded odd calling a stranger Mum. 'I will be back tomorrow. I have my fiancée, Maya, with me; I will bring her, OK?'

'Yes, great – come for tea. My Billy, my boyfriend, will be home – he would love to meet you. Make it six, OK? It will be great to meet Maya.

You will come for tea, right?'

I told her we would and would ring her to confirm it, but could not see a problem.

One thing that bothered me was she had never mentioned her husband – where he was, or anything. She told me she had met a guy over in Lancashire. He came over to Hull, but then nothing else. I had not asked even when she mentioned Billy, her boyfriend; I just assumed they had got married when he came to Hull.

I told Maya the news about meeting Mum. There I went again, calling her Mum; it seemed so natural, and I suppose it was – she was my birth mother. Maya was pleased for me, or so she appeared; she was a bit hesitant when I said we had been invited for tea the following day, but she agreed to go anyway. I supposed it was going to be odd for her as well.

We arrived at six as requested, and were introduced to Billy. He seemed like a decent guy – quite different from what I expected, but having said that I don't know what I expected; he just didn't seem to look right together with Mum, I don't know why, but that's just me. She put a great spread on – something I had never eaten: braised steak, mashed potatoes and green runner beans, with onion gravy, which was unreal, and there was apple pie and custard to follow. I was full as a boot when we finished.

We went into the living room, as the Poms call it, as we had eaten at the kitchen table. I could not get my head around how tiny the houses were, especially in the North of England. Billy offered us a beer, but I was too full of drinking beer, and hot ones at that.

I had to ask. 'Mum, you never mentioned what happened to the guy who came from Lancashire with you when you came back with Leif. Whatever happened to him? What was his name?'

A distinct silence came over. Nothing was said. I noticed Mum look at Billy, and he looked down to the ground; they were hiding something, I could tell.

'Oh, him… we don't talk about him, Lars. He was a bastard to Leif and me for eleven years. He gave us hell. I got rid of him – I told him to get out, as we had had enough. He left one night to go away to sea – he was a fisherman, you see – and we never saw him again.'

'Oh, I'm sorry, Mum, I didn't want to upset you. I just wondered, that's all. No worries, I won't mention him again.'

The conversation carried on into the night, talking of the past four decades, and what all of us had got up to in the past. Billy was interested in my rugby career, as he was a black and white bastard – his words, not mine. He told me about the rivalry between the two Hull clubs. I know he was not amused when I told him I had heard of Hull Kingston Rovers but did not know there was another team in the city, Hull FC. I was quite surprised at his reaction. It was like telling him the Pope wasn't a Catholic when I said, 'Rovers are the better team, though, aren't they?'

It was getting late, and we were going to York the following day for a look around there, so we bid our goodnights and said we would see them over the weekend.

When we got back to the hotel, Maya looked a bit sheepish, very quiet, and didn't pass much of a comment.

We were sitting in bed reading when she said, 'There is something they are not telling you, Lars. Did you see their faces when you asked about the guy who came with Christine to Hull? They never even mentioned his name. Something happened, and they are not telling you. I don't like it, babe.'

CHAPTER 5

LARS
York

The next day we went to York as planned; what a place – again, it made us realise how young Australia was. I could not believe it; the old buildings went around an area called the Shambles, an old cobblestone street with overhanging timber-framed buildings, some dating back as far as the fourteenth century. It was once known as the Great Flesh Shambles; they think the name came from the Anglo-Saxon 'Fleshammels', which means the shelves on which butchers used to display their meat. They told us that there were in 1872 around twenty-five butchers' shops along the street, but they had all gone, and it was all independent little jewellery, souvenirs, cafés, that sort of thing.

There was so much to see – including the railway museum, and the Minster, where we walked around the old city walls. The place had more tourist attractions per square mile than any other city in the UK. One place we went to was Clifford's Tower, a bloody high solid stone building right in the centre of the city. It was a symbol of the power of England's medieval kings. The tower took its name from one horrible incident in its long history when Roger de Clifford was executed for treason against Edward II and hanged in chains from the tower walls. I could not believe the view of York and the surrounding countryside. It wasn't hard to see why Clifford's Tower played such a crucial role in northern England's control. We ran out of time; it was getting dark, so we decided to head off to Hull. We were both rooted from the walking; we had had enough for the day.

We stopped on the way back for an early meal at a small country pub called the Windmill. It was heaving, but we managed to get a table. Looking around, everyone seemed to be eating a meat pie. Unlike Aussie meat pies, this was square and about two inches thick, with lumps of meat hanging out of it, with a suet crust, whatever that was; it looked delicious. We both ordered one; it came with what the Poms call 'proper chips' as thick as your finger cooked in beef dripping, with peas, and loads of onion gravy. I had never tasted anything so good in my life. I will never eat a pie at the footy again, I vowed. It never even had ketchup on it.

We got back to the hotel, had a shower, and that was us knackered. We were lying in bed, and Maya came out with a gem. 'Lars, you know we planned on getting married in London... why not get married in Hull? It would be nice – after all it is your home town?'

'Great idea about my home town... well, it's not, really, but Mum is from here. Why not?' I had not even thought of it, but it seemed like a good idea. I needed to look into it; how and where would we get married in such a short time?

The next morning we were up and about. I gave Mum a ring asking her if she fancied going out for lunch. We wanted to give her the news of our decision; the only worry we had was could we get married in the UK? We were Australian citizens. I was born in the UK, but as far I knew, I did not have a birth certificate. We had planned to get married in London, but to be honest, we had not made any enquiries about it; we just took it for granted that we could.

Before we said anything to Mum, we decided to determine the protocol for getting married. I went down to see Michael, the concierge in the hotel. Concierges knew everything; it was their job to. He said he would make some enquiries. 'Just give me an hour or so – I will get back to you, OK?'

We had not yet booked our flight back as we had an open ticket, so we could alter our travel details to suit our movements.

We left ringing Mum until we got an answer from Michael, so we went to do a bit of shopping for a couple of hours. Michael stopped us in the hotel foyer.

'Hi, Lars – I have been in touch with the registry office, and they have suggested you go down and see them; they have a vacancy for a type of interview at 4pm if you wanted to go, but I will have to ring them to confirm it.'

'My bloody oath we will – where is it? How far is it? Do we need to drive or get a cab?'

'No, you can walk it – just go out of the front of the hotel and keep walking straight. Do not leave the main road, and it is on the left, just before you get to North Bridge. You can't miss it – if you go over the bridge you have missed it.'

We got to the office just before four; as Michael had said, it was not far from the city centre. A few people were waiting to go in and tie the knot. Others were in the small garden outside, having photos taken after their ceremony.

We went in, and this lady, Mrs Jackson, asked us to take a seat. 'Now what can I do for you? Michael at the Station Hotel told me you were over here on holiday from Australia and were looking to get married. I know Michael; I am a friend of his mother's. We go back a long way.'

We told her the story about how I had just found my birth mother, but I did not mention being sold as a baby; I thought that might cause some problems. I said I had been adopted years ago and taken out to Australia, and was an Australian citizen, as was Maya; she was born in Oz. We both had Australian passports and wondered if we could get married in the UK while we were here.

'Well, yes, you can; there are a couple of ways it can be done. The only problem is there is no quick fix, so the earliest I can fit you in is around a month?' She looked at her diary, biting her bottom lip and putting her tongue on the side of her lips as she talked. She looked over her glasses, which were on the end of her nose. 'The ninth of November. Is that manageable?'

'Wow, yes – we have brought the relevant marriage visas we obtained from the British Embassy in Sydney, giving us six months to get married in the UK. We know we have to give seven days' notice of marriage once we pick where we are going to get married, which is now Hull.'

'That's very good. So you have no limit on your stay, no flights booked home?'

'We can do that – we will just have to alter our trip a little and come back to Hull in a month. It will mean extending our trip, but that does not matter as we are on an open ticket. A week here or there does not make much difference.'

'Very good, then – I will put you down for the ninth.' She wrote in her diary.

Now we could let Mum know she was going to a wedding. We went straight round to her house to give her the news. She hadn't a clue what we were going to drop on her as we walked in.

'Hi, Mum, you there? Hello?'

'I'm upstairs – won't be a min… put the kettle on.'

'OK, don't be long. I have got something to tell you; where is Billy, still at work?'

'Yes, he is working late tonight; got an all-nighter or something – he rang earlier.'

Mum came back down after about ten minutes, 'Now, what is it you've got to tell me? You're having a baby? Go on, tell me.'

'No, Mum, not yet – but we are getting married in a month, OK? On November 9, but in Hull, what do you think about that?'

'Oh, Lars, wonderful!' She hugged and kissed me, and did the same to Maya. 'Oh, that's so wonderful – to think you are getting married here for me, after all these years. I so wish Leif could be home; it's just getting hold of him – it could be six months before I hear from him again. You never know where he is; he's very secretive about his life and work, and never tells me anything. If he isn't here, he isn't here, that's all I can say.'

'We will be leaving tomorrow to go to London for a few days, then over to Cornwall and Devon to show Maya the surf down there.'

CHAPTER 6

LARS

Trip Down South

After a long drive, we had an overnight stay in Gloucester before heading further south. We found a small B&B on the city's outskirts, which was only cheap, but all we needed was a bed for the night. It was clean, and the old lady who owned it was very kind. She offered to cook a meal, as we had not eaten since stopping for a snack at a transport cafe around lunchtime.

We took her up on her offer and were so pleased we did; she laid on a beautiful meal. We then decided to go for a quick run into Gloucester for a beer and a look around the place. We hadn't realised it was an inland port; I had never heard of such a thing. We learnt that the docks were first built at the end of a new canal that was created to bring ships inland from the Bristol Channel in 1827. Some of the engineering in those days was out of this world; I could go on, but Pommie history got to me, I loved it.

Back at the B&B, we were ready for bed after a long day. Driving was a lot more tiring here; I supposed you were concentrating more with so much traffic on the roads; back home it seemed a lot more relaxed. Maya suggested it was about time we rang home, as we'd not been in touch with anyone for a month or so at least.

'Yes, you are right – will ring home tomorrow. I'll find a place to call home. I believe you can use some post offices.'

The next morning we were up early for breakfast. 'Have you got a minute, Mrs Mills? Have you any idea if there is a post office we could use nearby to call home?'

'You don't have to do that, dear – you can use ours as long as you either reverse the call or book it through the operator and find out the cost and pay me the cash, no problem.'

After breakfast, we went into the private lounge, and Mrs Mills kindly went into the kitchen to give us some privacy. I could not believe how friendly folks were in the UK. I organised a reverse-charge call and dialled my parents' number in Maitland; it rang for quite a while, then Mum finally answered.

'Oh, hi, Mum, how are you? It's Lars calling you from England; how're things? How's Dad? Everything OK?'

'Where the hell have you been? It's been six weeks since we heard from you. Why haven't you called before? And what do you think you are doing reversing the charges?'

'Whoa, Mum – hang on, slow down. What the hell is wrong with you? I am on holiday, you knew we were coming to Europe for a couple of months; what's wrong?'

'What's wrong? I will tell you what is wrong; it is your father, he had a bad stroke five weeks ago. No one could get hold of you. We don't know if he will survive, as he had a blood clot on his brain. Why haven't you rung before, Lars? You just don't give two hoots about your old parents, do you? They operated on him that night in Newcastle, and the doctors said they did not think he would make it, but he did. He is in a coma – I just don't know what to do, Lars…' She started crying. I felt so useless; there was nothing I could say to ease the pain.

'Mum, please stop crying now… calm down, please, Mum,' I said, but I could not console her. 'Mum, please, now listen to me – we will come home. I will try to get a flight back as soon as I can.' Maya flashed a look at me and mouthed, 'What?'

'Will you, Lars? Oh, please, will you come home? I think it would be for the best. She suddenly stopped wailing, as if a tap had been turned off; had I been conned there? No, she would not do that… or would she?

'OK, Mum, I'll be in touch when we organise a flight. Must go – give our love to Dad. If you can, that is?'

'OK, Bye, love, see you soon; get home as quickly as you can.'

I turned to Maya and shook my head. 'We have to – I'm sorry, Maya, but I could not live with myself if Dad died, and I was not there. Mum has no one but me.'

'OK, you are right. I agree we must get back home. We can postpone the wedding. We must get in touch with Christine and tell her that the wedding is off, and get in touch with the registry office too, while we are at it.'

I picked the phone up again and dialled Mum's number in Hull; it rang once, and she answered. 'Hello, can I help you?'

'Hi, Mum, sorry to phone you.'

'Hi, Lars, what's wrong? Why are you ringing so early in the morning?'

'Sorry, Mum – got some bad news. There is no easy way of saying this, but we have to get back to Australia. My father is gravely ill; they have been trying to get in touch with us for weeks. He had a massive stroke and blood clot on his brain, and he may not last much longer. The wedding is off. Sorry, Mum, but there's nothing we can do – it's just bad luck.' There was silence at the other end. 'Mum, you OK? You still there?'

'Yes, I am here. You are right; you must get home, but I am so disappointed. We have just met and now this – that's the story of my fucking life. Oh well, never mind. It was good while it lasted. Will you be coming back to Hull or going down to London to get a flight?'

I hadn't thought about it. We were nearer to London, so it made sense to fly from there. 'We will be going down to London,' I said. 'I will ring the airline later today to see when we can get a flight. So sorry, Mum. Oh, if Leif does get in touch, please do not tell him we have been over. I want it to be a surprise when we do manage to get back for the wedding; another few months will not hurt him, I am sure?'

'OK, baby, just let me know; I will contact the registry office for you; no worries, it will be OK, I am sure. Safe journey, babes, give my love to Maya – tell her I love her, OK.'

With that, she was gone.

I turned to Maya; she was in tears. Her wedding just blown away, as quickly as that. I felt so sorry for her, but she would get her marriage once this was all blown over. I would bring her back to Hull, and we would get married there, I promised myself. I did not want to say anything to her right now, as it would sound too condescending, but it would happen, I was sure of it.

CHAPTER 7

LARS

Back to Australia

We were lucky that we managed to get a flight back on Sunday 14th, arriving back early Monday morning. We went back to our place. It was decided that Maya would not come up to Maitland with me. She could not go through the turmoil. I know she was my fiancée, but to be fair, seeing she did not know my parents and considering the situation, we thought it best she stayed at home.

I drove up to Maitland the following day, my head still spinning, what with the long flight and everything else that was going on. I could not think straight; once again, the journey was murder. It was a good job we lived on the north shore as driving out through the city to get on to the Pacific Highway was horrendous.

Three hours later, I arrived at Mum's house. 'Oh, Lars, thank you – thank you so much for coming home. I know how much it means to you, but your father needs to see you.'

'How is he? I thought he was in a coma? Can he see me, Mum? How is he now?'

'He is still in a coma; he is still very ill. It will be a time before he is awake.' She broke down in tears again; her eyes were red raw with crying. I felt so sorry for her; she must have been through hell these past few weeks, with no one to turn to; she was never one for making friends, what with always moving with Dad's job and everything. It used to upset her so much when she had to say goodbye to people she had got close to. Eventually, she stopped making friends, and everyone became just acquaintances.

We had lunch and then left to go to the Royal Newcastle Hospital. The place was built in 1817 when the city was founded as a penal settlement and coal port. Just a bit of useless information, but I thought I would throw it in after being in Pommie land with all its history.

We went into the private room, where Dad was. He looked so peaceful lying there that you would not have known he was ill apart from the tubes running out of him. I held his hand and spoke to him; no reaction. He did not know who was there. 'Hi Dad, it's me, Lars; how are you?'

What a stupid question. I felt so dumb after I had said it. I talked to him, but it was a one-way conversation. I was not cut out to be a nurse; I hated hospitals, just the smell put me off, but I had to be there.

I left Mum with him and went to see if I could find someone who could enlighten me on his situation. I wanted the truth, not just Mum's interpretation of how he was. I found a nurse. 'Hello, you must be Lars. I've heard a lot about you. When did you get back from overseas?' Why did Australians always say overseas, I wondered; they never named the place you had been to, like England or France, it was still 'overseas'.

'Monday. It was a long trip, and I'm still bit groggy from the flight. Anyway, can you tell me what the prognosis is, please?'

'As you can see, he is very poorly; we are waiting for him to come out of the coma. Until then, we can't say one way or the other. I am sorry, Lars, but that is being honest with you. He had a massive stroke, and, to be frank, he is even lucky to be still with us, that's all I can tell you. The doctor will be here in about a half-hour if you would like to speak with him. I am sure he can elaborate more than me, OK?'

I thanked her for being so honest with me, and went back to Mum, who was still sitting there talking to Dad. It's such a sad time when anyone is ill, like he was; it's the ones who are left behind that suffer more than the ones who are dying, for that was what my father was doing, dying.

The doctor arrived and said hello; he took me aside and more or less told me the same as the young nurse had said. I asked him what were the chances my father would come out of the coma.

'He will never be right; that's my opinion. I have seen this too many times; the blood clot he had in his brain was one of the biggest I have ever seen. It did a lot of damage. Even if he comes out of the coma, which I doubt, he will be technically brain dead. Only the machines will keep him alive. That's the worst scenario, Lars. I am sorry, but you wanted the truth. We were hoping he would come out of the coma before we operated, and he has been responding to certain things, but we are just giving him a bit more time. We will have another look at him in the morning. Just pray that the treatment we are giving helps, and I will talk to you tomorrow, OK?'

The next day we went back to the hospital after we had had a call from them to go in early; we feared the worst. We got up on to the ward, and the sister asked us into a private consultation room. The doctor I had spoken to the day before came in. 'Good morning, Lars, Mrs Mellows; well, we have some good news. He has come out of the coma. Your father opened his eyes this morning, and they are working OK. We have decided to operate on him today. That is why we asked you in early to sign the forms for us to go ahead – you agree?'

'Yes, of course,' Mum said as she looked at me.

'Yes, I agree with Mum – but what is the chance he will pull through?'

'Fifty-fifty, I should think. Yesterday I would not have given the same odds, but this morning I have changed my mind. I must go now. I'll will be back later to tell you how he is.'

With that, he left us; we looked at each other, both thinking the worst, I guess, but as the doctor said, fifty-fifty was good odds if you were a betting man.

It seemed like a lifetime, sitting in the private visitors' room; I was pacing up and down.

'Sit down, for God's sake Lars; that won't do any good. You will just wear your shoes out. Now sit down, please, you are making me feel tired.'

I sat down, and picked up a magazine that was about four years old; some things never changed. I went for another coffee, and brought one back for Mum.

Three hours passed, then five; at last the door opened, and the doctor came in. 'Hello – well, that went well. It was not as bad as we imagined when we got inside there. It had not done as much damage as we first thought. We got all of it out, and I can now say it's 80-20 that he will recover. It will be a long job, mind, but I think he will be OK.'

Mum burst out crying, more in joy and relief than anything.

'Thank you, doc; we appreciate what you have done,' I said.

'Don't thank me yet, Lars. He is not out of the woods, not by a long chalk, but he is looking a lot better than yesterday.'

'Can we see him please?' Mum asked.

'No, not just yet; we have put him back into an induced coma until things settle down a bit. Give him a couple of days, maybe a week, then we will know. We don't want to rush him now, not after all he has been through. It seems hard, but it's for the best. You may as well go home and get some rest yourselves. There's nothing you can do here – he is in good hands, believe me; now get yourselves off.'

We left the hospital and got back to Maitland a lot quicker than we went. I rang Maya straight away to keep her in the picture. 'Hi babe, good news – Dad's going to be OK, we hope. He had an operation, and it all went well; the doctors seemed to be pleased with the outcome. Great isn't it?'

'That's wonderful news – thanks for calling me; when will you be back home, babe? I miss you so much.'

She sounded a bit subdued; then it dawned on me. I'd never asked how Maya was. I'd just gone straight in with the news about Dad. She must have thought I was a right bastard, not thinking of her, my fiancée, the girl who had just had her wedding taken away from her because of my family.

'You OK, babe? You sound a bit tired; sorry I haven't been keeping you up to date every day, but it has been hectic here.'

That also sounded wrong, as if she did not matter. Don't say any more, Lars, you are digging a big fucking hole for yourself, I thought. 'OK, babe, I will ring you a bit later when I know how things are here. Hope to be home tomorrow, OK?'

'OK, babe, ring when you can. Bye.'

She was gone; things were not right. I knew I had to get home asap, or my marriage would not happen. She was seriously pissed off.

After having another consultation with the doctors and staff at the hospital it was decided Dad should be kept in for another ten days at least, under observation, in the ICU. He had a long way to go, for he needed round-the-clock care. He could not get that at home or the Maitland Hospital. They would keep him in an induced coma for another week at least just to be on the safe side.

I told Mum I had to get back to Sydney. 'Listen, I have a business to run; Maya needs me home; it will be hard trying to catch up with work after being away so long – I need to get home.'

'But what about me and your father – don't we count? You need to be here with your family; we come first, surely. You don't love your work and Maya more than your family. They always come first.'

I was not going to argue; Mum was under a lot of stress. I dismissed the statement she came out with, but to put it like that was nothing short of selfish; I was appalled, if I'm honest.

'No, Mum, I am going. I am leaving now. I spoke with Mrs Kelly next door – she has offered to be available as and when you need her. She can drive, and don't forget she has been through a similar scenario with her husband when he passed away; it will be good for her to be able to help you through this time. Now, I must go.'

'But what if he comes round, he –'

'Mum, I have to go.'

With that, there was a knock on the door, and Mrs Kelly walked in. 'Hello, anyone home? Oh, you are; how is Jon today, any better?'

'Mrs Kelly, thank you for coming round. As I explained to you the other day, I have to get back to Sydney; if you need me, just call, OK?'

I arrived home around 2.30am after a hell of a journey; traffic was nose to tail coming down from Newcastle. There had been yet another accident on the Pacific Highway. How many more people were going to be killed and maimed by going too fast? The roads were just not good enough for the speed of the cars using them.

Maya was in bed when I got back. My head was pounding; that many things were going through it. I went straight into the kitchen to make myself a coffee. I did not want any confrontations, not tonight. Let it wait until morning.

I knew Maya was not happy with us having to cancel our wedding, curtail our holiday and then me shooting off straight up to Maitland. With her having to go back in to work on her own, finding numerous problems, it had been all too much. I decided not to wake her and went to sleep in one of the spare rooms.

I slept in, and when I got up, I found a note from Maya. 'Ring me at work.' No 'please'. Wow, she was pissed off.

I had my breakfast and shower, and rang her from home; I didn't want to go into the office and have a scene there.

'Hi, Maya, how are you? Sorry I was late last night, the traffic was horr–'

'Don't give me that shit, Lars. I have had enough, mate; I can't take any more. How much do you think I can take? Do I deserve to be treated like this? It is just not on. I have had more than enough.'

The line went silent. I could hear her crying. 'Maya – please, Maya, I understand how you feel. But what else could I do with Dad? I could not just abandon Mum when she needed me most; I am all she has, Maya, you must understand.'

I heard Maya sigh. 'But what if the worst happens and your father dies? What are you going to do about your mother then? I will tell you now, without any conscience, that she is not coming to live with us. No way, I do not want her here, understand? I have had a few sleepless nights while you have been up there, and a lot has gone through my head.' Another silence. 'I am sorry, how is your father? You must think I am a right bastard not asking, and just giving you shit, mate, sorry.'

'It's OK. Dad is in an induced coma; they operated on him, and it was not as bad as first thought. They will know better in seven to ten days.'

'Your Mum – how is she coping? Like shit I should imagine, right?

Lars, I can understand it, but I am sorry, I sound a selfish bitch, but I am not giving up all that we have worked bloody hard for. They have had their lives; I fully intend to have mine, hopefully with you by my side. I think you should know how I feel now, not when or if it happens further down the track, for it is going to happen one day. None of us is getting any younger, and there are two things certain in life, mate, and they are taxation and death. And you can't get out of either – they will both bite you in the ass one fucking day. I intend to live every day as if it is the last, for one day it sure as hell will be. I know they are old sayings, but, Lars – they are accurate as night is night. I must go – got a bit of bother on, but don't worry, I can handle it. We will talk tonight when I get home. You rest, babe; you must be shagged. Catch you later – love you, babe.'

I just stood there, numb with what was going on. I understood where Maya was coming from, but how the hell would I handle this situation? She had built up this company and gone through the bad times, first losing her mother, then her father being ill all these years, and she did not want a second dose. I understood that. I did not want to lose her, nor did I want to turn my mother away in her hour of need, so to speak. What a fucking state of affairs; I just could not think straight.

I rang Mum later, just after lunch. Mrs Kelly answered the phone. 'Oh, G'day Lars. Your mum's just having a nap. She was OK last night; I slept in the spare room, I hope you don't mind. I did not want to leave on her own, not the way things are, you know.'

'No, thank you, Mary, everyone else does.' What was I talking about? My head was in shreds.

'Sorry, Mary, yes, that's fine, whatever you think is right. I don't mind if you need to get any food or anything. Can you pay for it and save the bills? I will give you the money when I get back up next week; I think it will be, but please don't tell Mum when it will be, as I don't want her fretting, and please do not hesitate to phone me here or at work at any time. I will tell the reception desk to ensure I get all calls from you, OK?'

I gave her my home and work numbers, and asked her to write them down and keep them by the phone.

About an hour passed and I had a call from Mrs Kelly. 'Lars, the hospital just rang. Your father had a bit of a turn, but was OK.'

What she meant by 'a bit of a turn' when he was in a coma, I had no idea. I needed to ring the hospital; I knew it was not a good idea to come back to Sydney. Oh Jesus, what a state.

I rang the hospital straight away, and they told me he'd had a slight stroke but nothing major; it was to be expected. They just wanted us to know any changes as they happened. I thanked them very much and asked if it were possible to let me know first rather than worry Mum too much unless there was a significant change. It would be a lot easier on her. They agreed to carry out my wishes.

I did add that Dad would not want to finish up a vegetable if he got worse and asked not to resuscitate him. They told me they needed it in writing, but would accept it on a fax; it did not matter who was signing it, but it had to be approved by a doctor who would agree that nothing could be gained by keeping the patient alive, especially at Dad's age – he was eighty, after all.

Maya arrived home; her eyes were red and sore. She looked drained. 'Hi, babe – what kind of day you had?'

'Fucking terrible – I need a drink.'

'Stay there. I will get you one.'

Kicking off her shoes, Maya crashed on to the sofa. I handed her a glass of wine.

'Thanks, darl. I am truly rooted – what a fucking day. If one thing went wrong, everything did; will be glad to see you back.'

'I am going in tomorrow. Dad is in a stable but severe condition; he is in the ICU ward. I have told them to let me know of any changes and not to bother Mum. I have told her not to visit him. It won't make any difference; he will not know if she's there or not. I told her to have a couple of days' rest; Mary Kelly, the next-door neighbour, is keeping an eye on her.'

'That's great that someone is there, What do you think his chances are – fifty-fifty, or is it too bloody early?'

'Too early yet – we'll know better after a week or so; I told you, didn't I… or am I losing it?

'I am sorry, yes, you did tell me. It's just that my head has been all over the place since we got back. Can we get back to something like normal, Lars? I am sorry for putting even more pressure on you. We are struggling a bit at work – well, struggling might not be the right word. We need more staff, especially tradies, as the housing sector is booming. But look – let's get your mum and dad sorted first, eh?'

CHAPTER 8

LARS
Brain Surgery

Maya put her glass down and came closer to me on the sofa. She took my hand in hers and kissed my fingers, a sure sign she was horny.

'Babe, I love you so much. I don't want to argue about your parents, but you must realise it would never work if your dad did go. I could not live with your mum. I had enough of my father, if I was to be honest. I was over the moon when he met his new bride. I hate the fact that the bastard came into his life, but it saved me a lot of hassle, took the pressure off me, that is for sure.'

'What would you have done if you were still living with your dad?'

'Killed him, I think,' she laughed. 'Only joking. I don't know... my life was all work and him. I never really had a sex life or social life – then I met you, and it all changed. I'm sorry if I am a pain, babe, it will be OK. You just get your parents sorted.'

I needed to make my mind up about what came first – family or Maya. She was correct; they had had their life, and we needed to concentrate on ours before we finished up like them.

After I got a call to say they were taking Dad out of the coma the following day, I went up to Maitland, intending to stay at their house, but Mum was not in the best place. I thought she was starting to lose it. The stress was getting to her suddenly.

'Hello, Mum, how are you today? You look a bit tired, not sleeping well?'

Nothing, no reply – she just looked at me the light was on, but no one home; just a blank look.

'It's Lars, your son. Marjory, look who is here to see you,' said Mary, holding Mum's hand. Still nothing.

'How long has she been like this, Mary?'

'Only a couple of days. All of a sudden, she stopped talking and just looked at the picture of your dad on the wall.'

'Have you called the doctor? Why didn't you ring me and let me know she was like this?'

'I am sorry, Lars, I did not realise – she is worse today than yesterday; she is not even looking at the photo.'

I rang the doctor; he came round later that evening after his surgery. He examined her and said, 'She is suffering from a nasty case of depression and stress; must be all that's going on. It doesn't help that she is sixty-eight. I will give her some medication to calm her down a bit, but it's the first sign of dementia. I am sorry, Lars, but that's life; it can be so cruel. She may have been like this a while, and your father's sudden illness has hit her hard.'

Leaving Mum at home with Mary, I arrived at the hospital around 9.30am, and was asked to speak to the surgeon who carried out the operation on Dad.

'Good morning, Lars. I am Mr Stimson, the head neurosurgeon who operated on your father. I asked if you would come and see me. Your father is one of the more complicated admissions to intensive care. With the brain injury he has, an induced coma was required for more than seventy-two hours. As your father is in his eighties, it was thought that a much more extended period was needed. Now he has been stable and progressing, breathing with the support from the ventilator, we feel he will be able to come off the sedation.'

The doctor was blowing my mind with all this information, 'But what is the outcome? Just tell me in simple words, mate – I'm no doctor.'

'By minimising the drugs that have kept your father in the induced coma, he should slowly but surely commence waking up. This can take time because, just as I have explained, he was sedated with short-acting sedatives. The longer the sedative acts, the higher the likelihood that your father could get addicted to it. Therefore, getting him out of the induced coma might have some challenges, such as withdrawal symptoms, and therefore gradual weaning off the drugs might delay waking up. As a general rule of thumb, you need to be patient. Even when your dad has finally come out of the induced coma, you might experience that he is confused, agitated, tired or aggressive. And you might be shocked and maybe even embarrassed by what you see. It's OK. Know that it's nothing unusual; it happens all the time in intensive care. Also, many patients can leave the ICU while they are still confused, as long as they are stable. Most critically ill patients don't remember their time in intensive care, so don't worry too much about the confusion and agitation, if that's what your father experiences. Do I make myself clear?'

'Yes, I think so; it's all a bit much for me, but at least you have explained it in layman's language, not using too many big words. I think I get the drift.'

'OK, all in all, we think he will start waking up today as we've started the procedures I described a couple of days ago. Let us hope we are right, as in a lot of injuries and procedures, everyone is different. I will go in with Dr Lines now and see how your father is doing. I will send the nurse to let you know when you can come into the room, OK?'

I was sitting in the waiting room a good half hour, maybe a bit longer, when the nurse came in. 'Lars, you can come in now – your father is awake, but please be gentle, do not rush him, OK?'

'OK, thank you.' I followed her into the private room. The lights were dim, and there were the two doctors and another nurse around him; the tubes and other stuff had been removed. He looked pretty well, to be honest, considering what he had just been through.

The doctor was talking to him softly. 'Jon... hello... Are you OK? Are you awake? Your son is here, Jon. Want to talk to him? It's all right, Jon; take your time.'

His eyes flickered, then closed again. I moved closer, taking Mr Stimson's place, 'Hi, Dad, it's me, Lars – your son. You OK, Dad? Hello – wake up, Dad.'

His eyes flickered again, and this time they opened for a few seconds. He kind of looked like someone does when they first wake up. He then closed his eyes again, but made his first sound – a sort of grunt.

It took him a quarter of an hour to wake up, and his eyes were fully open but vacant. He still hadn't said a proper word. He looked directly at me and nearly smiled, but then he closed them again. 'Fuck me, I'm not that bad looking, am I?' I said to him, trying to crack a joke. One of the nurses giggled.

'Give him another few minutes; let's just leave him,' said Mr Stimson as he nodded towards the door. We all left, barring one of the nurses.

We walked to the coffee machine down the corridor, Mr Stimson put a key in the machine and opened it up. 'Balls to paying for it – what are you having, Lars? Same for you, Jim?'

'White, one sugar, please.'

'Yes, same for me, Mike.' It was the first time I had heard their first names.

Mr Stimson handed the coffees over and said, 'Your father should have gone to Sydney, but if they had sent him there, he would no longer be with us – the journey and time would have finished him off. He is the first patient we have carried out the operation on here at Newcastle. We are very pleased with what we have done. I know it may sound rather odd, but I have never carried out an operation like this. I have trained for it, but never actually carried out on a live patient.'

What else could I say but, 'Thank you, Mr Stimson, for all you have done, and thank you for having the bravery of using my father to be your first patient.'

'It is no problem – if we hadn't done it, he would have died, no doubt about that. I took the oath to try to save lives, no matter what. I did get into a bit of bother with higher-ups. But, hey, play what's in front of you, so to speak.'

The nurse came out and said Dad was awake – a bit tired, but seemed to be OK. We followed her into his room.

'Hello, Jon, how are you feeling?' asked Mr Stimson, taking hold of his hand to reassure him. He had an excellent bedside manner; this guy made me feel that I could trust him. He took out a small pen torch and shone it into Dad's eyes, checking pupil response. Well, I think that was what he was doing.

'Oh… Hi… What am I doing here? Where am I? What happened? Why am I in hospital – and why does my bloody head hurt like hell?' He lifted his hand to touch his head, and then felt the bandages. The nurse removed his hand gently. 'Be careful, Mr Mellows; try not to disturb the dressings, please.'

I just stood there in front of the bed, and did not say a word. I hoped Dad would recognise me, but up to now, he had not even looked at me.

'Who are all these people? What happened to me? Where am I, please?'

'Jon, it's OK, just take it easy, nice and slow now,' said Mr Stimson.

'Why do you keep calling me Jon? My name is…?' he went silent.

'Because your name is Jon – Jon Mellows,' said Mr Stimson. 'You remember Marjory and Lars?'

'What are you talking about? Who are Marjory and Lars?' He was starting to get upset, looking around at all these strange faces looking down on him in a bed in an unfamiliar environment.

Dr Lines suggested we leave, and ushered us out of the room. 'He is confused; you can understand what might be going through his head. Just give him a few minutes with Mr Stimson; he will be fine – he just needs a few soft words of encouragement.'

I was thinking about Mum right now; I needed some professional advice on how to help her. We stayed out of Dad's room for a good half hour; I rang Mum's house to see how she was getting on. Mrs Kelly answered. 'Hello, Mellows residence? Mary speaking – how can I help you, please?'

'Mary, it's Lars; how's Mum this morning, OK? She was still in bed when I left her – but you know this, as you were there when I left – sorry.'

'That's OK, Lars. I understand we are all under a bit of strain, but she is a lot brighter. She is up and in the garden right now doing a bit of weeding. She asked about you, and if you had gone to the hospital to see Jon, so her head seems OK today. The medication she's on must be working.'

'Mary, I must tell you that my father is out of the coma. He has come round and is talking, although a bit confused. Unfortunately, at this moment in time, he doesn't know what has happened to him, and doesn't know anyone – he doesn't recognise me. Even worse, he does not know who he is. I think it best we tell Mum he is still in a coma – it'll be best for all parties. Can you please tell her that for me? Tell her I have rung and will know more when I get home, OK?'

'Lars, I do not like lying to anyone; please, I would rather not.'

'I understand that, Mary, but it's just a white lie for a couple of days; it is to help Mum – please help us. I do not want to put her through any more pain than she needs to have.'

'OK, I am not happy about it, Lars, but for Marjory's sake, I will do it.'

'Thanks. I will be home as soon as I can, and thank you, Mary, for being so understanding.'

I went back to Dad's room; he talked to Mr Stimson and seemed entirely coherent as I walked in. He looked at me but never reacted; he did not have a clue who I was. It was heartbreaking; I had to keep a straight face, as I did not want to upset him. He was the primary concern, not me.

'Hello, Jon – how are you feeling, OK?'

'Not another one calling me Jon. That is not my name; where on earth did you all get that idea from? My name is…'

Then silence. He was trying to think of his name; it must have been so frustrating for him. I stayed with him for an hour or so; I could see he was getting tired. I still had not told him I was his son, having discussed it with Mr Stimson and Dr Lines. They decided it was best to leave it for a few days. It was suggested I stay away for a couple of days, then see how Mum was and bring her in. They asked me to ring the hospital first to check if Dad had made any progress, just to be safe.

CHAPTER 9

LARS

Dementia

I got back home around 4.30pm. Mum was back to her near-normal self; she even asked how Dad. It's incredible how the human brain works; how it can just turn off when it wants to. The doctor came round to the house again after his rounds to check on Mum. He took me into the kitchen to explain what the problem was.

We both sat down around the kitchen table. 'Lars, you must realise dementia is caused by damage to brain cells. This damage interferes with the ability of brain cells to communicate with each other. When brain cells cannot normally interact, thinking, behaviour and feelings can be affected.'

'But how come it has just started just like that?'

'The brain has many distinct regions, each of which is responsible for different functions, for example, memory, judgment and movement. When cells in a particular region are damaged, that region cannot normally carry out its functions.'

'But how can you tell which part of the brain has been damaged? You must understand this is all new to me – both my parents, within weeks… how can this happen?'

'Different types of dementia are associated with particular types of brain cell damage. The brain region called the hippocampus is the centre of learning and memory in the brain, and its cells are often the first to be damaged. That's why memory loss is often one of the earliest symptoms of Alzheimer's. Most changes in the brain that cause dementia are permanent and worsen over time. And depression, medication side-effects, excess alcohol, thyroid problems and vitamin deficiencies can also cause problems.'

I asked Mary to join us to see if she had noticed any changes in Mum over the past year or so. I felt as if I should have been home more; I felt guilty not knowing what was happening. I asked the doctor if any tests could be carried out to determine what was wrong with Mum.

'There is no one test to determine if someone has dementia,' he said. 'Doctors diagnose Alzheimer's and other types of dementia based on a careful medical history, a physical examination, laboratory tests, and the characteristic changes in thinking, day-to-day function, and behaviour associated with each type. We can determine that a person has dementia with a high level of certainty. But it's harder to determine the exact type of dementia because the symptoms can overlap. It may be necessary to see a specialist such as a neurologist or geropsychologist. To be quite honest, the way this has happened, I would refer your mother to Newcastle Mater, where your father is.'

'What treatment is there for it? Can it be cured, or is it irreversible?'

'Look, Lars, the treatment of dementia depends on its cause. In the case of most progressive dementias, including Alzheimer's disease, there is no cure and no treatment that slows or stops its progression.'

'Then what – you just let her wither away? No help at all – you just give up on her?'

'No, of course not. There are drug treatments that may temporarily improve symptoms. The same medications used to treat Alzheimer's are sometimes prescribed to help other dementia types. Non-drug therapies can also alleviate some symptoms of dementia; as you have seen, your mother must be at an early stage because the medication I gave her was only a minimal dose, and it has helped. Let's get her tested and then take it from there, but do try to keep her stress levels down. I know it's going to be difficult the way your father is at present. We have not received any information yet. But it will be coming through within a few days, I should think. I must add that I have never heard of two people being struck down with brain problems simultaneously. We need some help on this, and Sydney would be the best place for both of them; there are some great care homes to look after dementia patients. It may be worth your while looking into it, if not only for future reference, for the time will come when they both will need care, there is no doubt about that. I will leave you now. I will call in tomorrow, or if your mother feels up to it, bring her into the surgery. Just let us know in the morning. I will book an appointment when I get back for just after lunch, OK?'

When it rained, it pissed down, that was for sure. Wow, care homes... moving to Sydney – Maya was going to love this when I told her.

CHAPTER 10

LEIF
Could Not Believe It

'We want you to go to South America, tonight,' Jan continued. 'You are booked on a flight direct to Rio de Janeiro, and you will be met by an official of the government there and taken to the Belmond Copacabana Palace, where you are booked in under a different name. Here is your passport with that name on it; the flights are also under that name.'

I looked at the passport; the name inside said Leif Jansen. 'We made it a Norwegian and kept your first name the same to save any confusion on your part. The Brazilians like to use the first names when doing business – far less formal. You have a meeting with one of the ministers in a couple of days. He will contact you at the hotel when it is convenient to meet, so you can relax for a day or so on the beach. I hear you like swimming and the odd friendly girl.'

What did this bloke not know about me? I knew I had made a few visits to Amsterdam's windows since I had been there, but I hadn't since I had been with Connie. I'd considered it, I admit, but not ventured.

'Here you are.' He handed me a briefcase. 'This is the code for the lock. Remember the number – 270646.'

It was my birthday. How could I forget that?

I didn't believe this. He was confident I would go along with the request, and all the secrecy was based on me accepting to carry out his demand. Mind, a trip to Rio, all expenses paid, sounded good.

'Now we come to the important thing.' He opened the case.

'Fucking hell,' was all I could say. It was full of hundred-dollar notes.

'Yes, you are right to be surprised – there is $2.5 million there. Guard it with your life – along with this one.' He lifted another briefcase and placed it on the desk. 'Leif, this is a gift for the minister. You have to carry two cases; each one weighs twenty-five kilograms. It is the same amount that he received for the last contract we won, the one that was worth $500 million to us. So, you see, this –' he pointed to the case – 'is mere chicken shit, as the Americans would say. When you meet the man, you do not mention in any way about the previous transaction. For all intents and purposes it never occurred – the same as this one will not have, for we do not give bungs – another English word, I believe.'

'How do I approach the man?' I asked. 'Do you know him? Is he trustworthy?' It seemed a stupid question when he was taking a $5 million bribe, but I had no clue how to put the matter over to the man.

'He will be noncommittal – you just put the case on his desk, he will have a few words about you signing the contract on behalf of us there and then, and you shake hands on it and walk out without the case, but with the signed deal in your hand. You have another couple of days in Rio – have a good time, Leif; they tell me the girls on the beaches are stunning this time of the year.'

As I left the office, Jan handed me a suitcase; they had already packed it with brand-new designer clothes, swimwear, shoes, socks – everything down to my favourite deodorant.

I took a taxi to Schipol; my direct KLM flight was at noon. It was a hell of a long trip, but being in first class, I slept most of the way there.

Holland was five hours ahead of Brazil. As a result, we arrived at around 7pm the following day. Yes, the man from the government was there; he didn't hold up a greeting board, he just walked up, told me my name, and said, 'Come with me.'

The five-star hotel was unreal; I was glad I wasn't footing the bill. The man, who never told me his name, said, 'Everything is paid for – and I mean everything. Just sign the bill when you leave.' He gave me a card with a name on it. 'If you need anything else, just call this man. He will get you whatever you require. Do not – and I mean this – do not pick

66

up any of the street girls. They are not as beautiful inside as they are outside. Understand?' He said it with a smile, which was the first time he'd showed any flicker of being human.

I got a call to confirm that, two days after arriving, on the Wednesday, I was to meet the minister that evening at another hotel in the city. I was not given a name, but was told a car would pick me up at 8pm prompt. I had a shower and got my gear, and went down to the beach to top up my tan. I watched the girls walk by; god, they were beautiful. Not one bad body on any of them. I was getting a bit horny and had to lie on my front on the sand to hide my enjoyment. I decided I had better behave myself, thinking of Connie back home. I could not weaken and go with another woman. I was not that bad; I was engaged, for fuck's sake.

Wednesday came, and I went down to the beach again. A stunning-looking woman who looked like a film star came and asked if I minded her sitting next to me. Of all the places available to sit on this beach she wanted to sit a few yards from me. Was she on the game, I wondered? She couldn't be, surely.

I weakened. 'Yes, of course you can – it would be my pleasure.'

She sat on a towel more or less next to me; we started chatting.

'What do you do for a living?' I said.

'I am a PA for a company.'

She mentioned a name; it clicked – it was the same name on the card that the man from the ministry had given me.

'OK, that's nice.' All of a sudden, my erection was mega; god, I was aching. The sand was killing me, but looking at this girl, hoping I was going to pleasure her, was easing the pain just a little.

'I know the name of the company you work for – I suggest we go back to the hotel across the road to discuss business.'

'It would be my pleasure to help you in your quest,' she said with a smile.

We put on our clothes as you were not allowed to walk around the hotel in swimmers. There was no hiding the fact that she was with me as we walked in. The concierge said hello as we passed his plinth near the front doors.

'Is everything to your satisfaction, sir?'

'Oh yes, wonderful,' I replied.

We got to my room and as I entered I put the 'do not disturb' sign on the outside handle. I turned; she was already naked.

I can honestly say I had never been so close to happiness before I even got hard; she was everything anyone could imagine how a Brazilian woman would look. Tall, skin like milk chocolate in colour, and similar to silk when you touched it. I did not move a muscle; I was stunned, speechless.

'You don't like it?' she said.

'What? Of course I do – what is there not to like?'

I was waffling; I did not know what to say. Walking over to me, she stroked my face and undid the buttons on my beach shirt, threw it on the floor, slipped my shorts down, and then undid the string holding my swimmers up and slid them down over my thighs, bending as she did it. I was looking down at the most perfect back and bubble butt I had ever seen. She dropped to her knees. I was throbbing. You could see me jumping to my heartbeat.

It didn't take long, I can tell you. She licked her lips and got dressed. 'Shall I come back tonight and should I bring a friend?' she said.

'Yes, please – I'd love to meet your friend.'

She gave me a card with her number on it. 'Call me when you are ready. We will be waiting, OK?'

I went to the arranged meeting with the minister. My driver told me which room to go as I got out. I went up to reception, and the girl on the desk told me to go into the telephone booth, over in the corner.

I rang the number. I was asked the password given to me by Jan back in Rotterdam. I was told to take the Number Two elevator. I went over to the lifts; there were three of them, with no one around. I pressed the down arrow and, lo and behold, Number Two started to come down. It arrived, and the doors opened. A guy was standing in there with a no-ticeable lump under his arm. I got in, he patted me down, then pressed the button for the top floor.

We arrived at the room, and the man knocked on the door. I went in and was greeted by… Einar Hegdahl, of all people. I couldn't believe it.

'Hello, Leif, nice to see you again. Sorry about all the cloak and dagger routine, but I am the man you will be meeting, not some minister. That is, as you say, a load of shite. I do all the negotiating to save any embarrassment to anyone further down the line; no one knows in Amsterdam what goes on. The less they know, the better, if you know what I mean. I have been trying to get someone in with me, and after I met you and got to know you much better, I knew you were the man I needed in my organisation.'

My mind was whirring. What had I let myself into here? 'You mean this was all set up by you? I do not understand, Ein; please tell me and be honest with me. I do not know how I stand here.'

'OK, it's like this. Let's go back to the Bahamas and your position with Caporal that was never going to work. They wanted too much power. The idea was right, but the oil companies would never stand for that, taking too much away from them. Along with that, it would take a lot from me. I had set up a great business by being the middle man, and that was not going to change. I got you in at Noroil because I needed someone there to help with my little earner – for want of a better word, my little sideline. You see, I have told your company that I need to give a small sort of gift to these men of power, ministers and government officials around the world. How you think me and Borg can afford such a luxurious life? We don't always have to use the silver palm or whatever it is called. However, while they are willing to pay one, I still ensure they pay it. The last man I had inside got too nervous and resigned a few months ago, and luckily there were no meetings set up until now. I needed someone I could trust. Hence you are now my man – interested?'

'How on earth did you come up with this idea? Surely someone will find out sooner or later; you will never get away with it.'

'But I have up to now, and no one is any the wiser. If it had not been for the last man not being able to take the pressure, he would have been a multi-millionaire, as you can be if you want to come on the journey with me.'

'OK, Ein, tell me more. Yes, I am interested; this trust thing goes both ways, you understand. Now, please explain how I can be a multi-millionaire?'

'The deal is the same amount – always $5 million. We split it $2.5 million each, or if the man does get a present, or there could possibly be two men, then we cut it again – understand? I will tell you which contracts to go for when a certain country is ready to put them out for tender. They come to me, put the project in front of me, and ask for recommendations on who I think could handle the job. I keep a check on all the projects, both ongoing and future, for the whole world. I know who is doing what, where and when. This information collecting is something I have always done with all oil-producing countries worldwide. It was a bit like the Caporal idea, but I made sure that never got off the ground; don't forget I was in as a consultant before a lot of these companies were born.

'It is common knowledge that there are times when contracts are put out to tender the contractors have too much work on that they don't even want to bid; they put silly prices in to enable them to be considered for future inquiries, and vice versa. Then there are times when they have no work on the drawing board and are desperate to win a contract, but then they try to rip off the client with extras to make up for the low price they have given in the hope of winning it. The governments have learned the hard way; that's where I came in. They now trust me, and what I say goes, ninety-nine per cent of the time. I have helped them with estimating. They now know roughly what each project will cost. I can tell them who to send the enquiry to, which means I can tell the contractor roughly how much to bid. I have a man inside of most of the big contractors like Noroil; I know when they have enough work on and what they should bid for, and when they do, they get it; I get my bit, and so will you if you join me.'

'Sounds too good to be true, Ein, and you know the old saying – if it sounds too good to be true, it most likely is no good.'

'Yes, but I know the result before the race. I have set up a system based on oil production barrels per day from the installation. This number is always known before the cost of the relevant platform or land installation is designed. It is still the same process, don't forget, Leif. I have been in this game for many a long year; no one knows more than Einar Hegdahl. I am the king. Noroil, on average, bids for three or four projects per year around the world; it knows full well it won't get every one. But if the relevant information is passed on to them to target the most profitable and, they know full well they will get it with my help, then we all make a few dollars, and everyone is happy.'

'Can I ask you, does each and every contractor bidding for the job give you a bung?'

'No. They would soon get sick of bidding for jobs, and word would spread. I don't like that word, Leif; a gift is more like it. They only give a gift when they are invited to come for the final interview, to sign the contract. I did try to implement a system where the three invited to tender – is nearly always three companies – each included a million for the other two losing companies, to be paid to each of them after the contract had been awarded, as a subsidy against the estimating cost. Still, it got frowned on and never got off the ground.'

'Fuck me, Einar, you are on a fucking gold mine.'

'Yes, I know some of the countries do not use me in the final negotiations as they only ask me to submit the recommendations of who to submit bids to, and that's where I finish. They pay well for the service, but that's as far as it goes. The bigger jobs, I get my bonuses, if that is the right word. So, are you in? I know you would be a perfect partner. When you get back with your money after this trip with a contract in your bag, just enquire how many deals they have won since they started up and how many have they lost. The one you are coming to see tomorrow does not take anything. I look after him out of my share. He gets the odd girl and hotel trip, a mere pittance, but he is happy. He gets to fuck a beautiful girl he could only dream of, and we get the millions. Now, are you with me or not?'

'Yes, count me in. What do we do now?'

'You get to meet the man who signs the contract, but do not mention money. If he asks questions, just play along with him, OK? Leave the talking to me, understand?'

The following morning we met. Einar carried one briefcase, and I took the other.

We had been sent to another hotel on arrival, and we were met by bodyguards in the reception who frisked us down. Einar had said this was a formality, and they would not ask to look in the cases – he was right; they didn't. We went up in the lift. When the doors opened, there were another two bodyguards. One, who was about 6ft 8in and built like the proverbial, frisked us again.

We went to the meeting room door and were told to wait. One of the guards went in, leaving the giant with us.

'The guard came back, and said, 'OK, que você pode ir em.' I looked at Einar, and he nodded. 'He said, "OK, you can go in," in Portuguese.'

There was no messing – it was straight on with the contract signing after discussing some minor points, and I was given a copy with specific clauses highlighted. The minister said, 'Shall we just go through these items as I would like some clarification there – about six of them. It will not take too long, is that OK?'

It was going well. Jan had informed me that there were some minor clauses on the exclusions that might be questioned. I had been given the authority to make any changes as required. I had a separate sheet of paper with them signed off by him in my other case.

I removed it and handed the folder to the minister. He took his time reading the document, then smiled and nodded.

Einar looked at the sheet. He said something to the minster in Portuguese, which I did not understand; it worked, whatever it was.

'OK, excellent, no problem. Shall we sign the contracts now?'

He opened up two folders encased in a posh leather cover with the country's emblem on them. He invited me round to his side of the desk, and we duly signed the contracts.

We shook hands on the deal, he asked me if I would like a drink, we sat and had a friendly chat, and that was it. He said he had other business to complete, and more or less told us to fuck off.

I picked up my briefcase and left; the car was waiting to take me back to my hotel.

I was thinking about how lucky I had been to be able to open a bank account in the Isle of Man, as I was now a self-employed contractor. It was a way of rifling away a few quid off the taxman. All I needed to do was take a trip over to Douglas the following weekend when I was due to go home and put the money in the bank. As I walked to the car with Ein, I was made for life, even with just this one $2.5 million. I would have no more money worries; I could do whatever I want. Nothing could be traced back to me. Jan would deny any fraud, and the man in Brazil would deny ever taking a bung. Why would any questions be asked, as nothing illegal had taken place?

I got back to the hotel and asked them to put the case in the safe behind the reception as it had essential documents in it – all two and a half million of them.

I rang the office and told Jan that everything was signed, sealed and delivered. I never mentioned the 'bung' as it seemed better not to. The only thing that bothered me was why there had been all this cloak and dagger routine with 'The Man', Einar – or did Jan not know his name? This was still confusing me. But the so-called 'bung' had been handed over to the man, and the third party was irrelevant. He didn't take this one. I fucking did.

I went up to my room. I was buzzing, and could not stop smiling, I was like a dog with two dicks, I needed to celebrate. What to do? Go out to a club and get blathered… or make a phone call and have a private all-night party in your room with only three guests.

I got the card the woman had given me. Then I realised that I had shagged her and did not even know her name – but did it matter? Oh, it was on the card. Branca – it sounded as good as she looked.

I rang the number and a voice answered in Portuguese at first, but as soon as I said hello, she spoke in English. 'Looks like you had a great day and you want some fun again? Or you would not have contacted me. You would like my friend Lani to join us?'

'OK, but first of all, one question – can I ask where does that name come from, Branca?'

'It is a beautiful name which represents hope. It means bringer of peace, and is also popular in the Hawaiian language, where it means sky.'

'It certainly brought me peace. I look forward to seeing you later. Bye, babe.'

I had a shower, and half an hour later there was a knock on the door. I had ordered two bottles of champagne and three glasses. The waiter gave me an odd look when he brought the tray up and could see I was alone.

There was another knock ten minutes later – and the girls arrived. Wow… how could I describe them? Remarkable. What a pair of beauties. Of course, Branca I already knew, but the other girl was equally as gorgeous. This was just too good to be true.

We started just chatting and drinking. Branca asked if there was anything that I found erotic. Now, that covered many scenarios, but one thing that had always turned me on ever since my Amsterdam days was watching two girls have sex with each other, or a lesbian show. I had seen a fantastic set in a sex club only a few weeks before. But I could not afford the cost of two girls together.

With that, they started kissing and playing, touching, stroking, undressing each other in the middle of the room as I sat in a chair watching them perform, stroking.

They did everything I had hoped to see, and now it was my turn. Now we were all naked in the bed. It was good job it was the American-style super-king.

First, Branca had me with Lani lying next to us, watching, and playing with herself as we fucked. I was lying on my back at one point with Branca facing away from me, riding me, when Lani started licking and biting my nipples and kissing me, sucking my tongue. Now that had always turned me on, and made me rock hard.

Then she sat on my face. Fuck, it was so good; she was kissing and licking Branca, not that I could see as my face was covered with her arse. I could hear the two of them moaning as they reached climax time after time.

Lani got off me and said, 'Please, Branca, my turn. I want him now.'

They swapped places, and didn't take long for a happy ending, but they wanted more.

Branca went over to her bag and pulled out the most giant double-ended dildo I had ever seen. They continued on the bed sharing this monster. Now I am decent when it comes to cocks, but this was King Dong.

We were at it most of the night, eventually falling asleep, cuddled up together. It was a night to remember. I woke up first between the two girls. Branca's head was on my shoulder, and Lani was lying between my legs with her head on my thigh.

I ordered a room-service breakfast for three – the full bifter, including champagne. Money was no object, as I wasn't paying. I was king of the world.

The girls went and had a shower; it was not quite big enough for the three of us, so I abstained.

There was a knock on the door. A voice shouted, 'Servico de quarto!' Room service, in English. So Lani went to let him in, wearing one of the hotel robes that just about covered every bit, with just enough left over for the boy to perv on.

Branca was sitting with a bath towel around her; I was in a pair of tight-fitting shorts, my old man bulging. The boy's eyes were going from one to another, then back to me. It seemed he preferred men to girls as he looked at my groin more than the girls' tits and bodies, but who was I to judge.

I was forty years old, and my working life was now over, or so I hoped. I could buy Mum the house she had always dreamed of owning. I knew then I had better things to do with my life than to work for someone else, but I also knew I had to be restrained in my lifestyle for a few months, maybe a year, before I started scattering the cash.

Everything was tied up, and I did not meet with Einar again as was arranged. I left Brazil on the Thursday early evening flight. There was only a three-hour time difference going back the other way. I arrived at 10pm and went straight back to my hotel to get my head down. I was well and truly fucked in more ways than one.

The only downside was that I knew I had cheated on Connie. I had been a good boy for quite a while, but I could just not knock back the opportunity laid out for me back in Brazil. I told myself that what she didn't know wouldn't hurt her, but for the first time in my life, I felt guilty. I promised myself it would not happen again.

I went into work the next day. I had slept on a few ideas; it was my long weekend coming up. I still had the briefcase with the money in it; I was worried sick. I had asked my hotel if they could put it in its safe as there was some jewellery in it I had purchased for my fiancée, and they agreed, which was a relief.

CHAPTER 11

LEIF

How Did You Manage That?

First thing in the morning I had a meeting with Jan and went through all that happened in Brazil. There were a few awkward questions, but I got through it. At the end of the session, Jan said, 'Thank you, Leif, for your fine efforts in Rio. In next month's salary, there will be a bonus of £5,000 tax-free.'

'Wow, thanks, Jan, that's great. I was only doing my job, but I very much appreciate it.'

I did not go home that weekend. I stayed in Holland and just relaxed. I rang Connie and gave her an excuse, saying they'd wanted me to stay and provide a rundown on what had gone on in Brazil. She was not happy – she was still going on about why I had suddenly shot off to South America without warning, but accepted it when I told her I had a present for her.

I got into the office first thing on Monday morning. Aart was not in; he was away on business. He had asked me to look at a new enquiry that had come in from another client.

The following morning, Aart called me into his office and asked me several questions about my Brazil visit. 'Seeing as you did such a good job, I think you deserve a couple of days off. You should go home on tonight's ferry instead of Thursday.'

'Thanks, Aart, I appreciate that. I will have to leave a bit earlier as I need to go back and pick up a few things.' I did not mention the $2.5 million that I needed to take home.

'No problem, leave when you are ready. I am out for the rest of the day. See you on Monday.'

I arrived back in Hull early on the Wednesday and drove straight to Leeds Bradford Airport to catch a flight to the Isle of Man. I went to the bank and, with no questions asked, I opened a new account that paid a much better interest rate for more considerable sums of money, even in cash. This was not your typical bank; it was a multinational organisation and, being such, you could bank monies from any currency in the world. I had been getting paid in US dollars for quite a while, and at the time it was the strongest currency. If you carried out any transactions into any other currency, it was no problem, and it was converted at a higher rate than most banks would charge. But they worked in denominations of large amounts, and I mean massive. As they used to finance some of the world's biggest companies, this is why you got better interest rates; it was a bit riskier but gave good results most of the time.

I left on a later flight with the chequebook and new card to follow within a few days, and I asked them to post it to my Amsterdam address.

I arrived back in Leeds, having told Connie I had come home earlier than expected because I had to nip over to Manchester to meet a client.

When I got back to Hull, I went to see Mum and Connie. I had to keep my good fortune to myself. I did not tell them what was going on as Einar had made it quite clear that this must not get out to anyone. He told me only to take out a few thousand now and again, but under no circumstances start spending money like it was going out of fashion.

I knew Einar was getting on, but I still didn't appreciate how much he knew about the oil game. I decided to do some homework on the subject. I felt it would be a good idea to quote dates and places when conversing with these overseas dignitaries. It would appear like I knew what I was talking about.

I was aware that Einar's ancestors had moved to the States, but I wasn't sure when. It must have been in the mid-1880s. I needed to get him alone and pick his brains on what I had found out.

He rang me a few days later to ask how everything was going, giving me the chance to ask him. 'Einar, I have been thinking. Have you got a bit of spare time? You know we discussed me being a bit more convincing when we are having discussions with these ministers and the like. Well, I have been doing a bit of digging – excuse the pun – and some of the things seem mind-boggling to me. I never knew that many of the earliest offshore oil wells were drilled from piers around 1896 – is that is right?'

'Oh, yes, I recall there was this innovative businessman called Henry L Williams. He and his associates had the idea to build a pier from the beach 300ft out into the Pacific – and place a standard cable-tool rig on it. My Grandfather Johan was working in California at the time and managed to get a job in the new oil industry, in 1911. I know that was the year because it was the year my father was born. Later, the Gulf Refining Company stopped using piers. It drilled Ferry Lake No. 1 on Caddo Lake, Louisiana, using a fleet of tugboats, barges and floating pile drivers. When the well came in at 450 barrels per day, Gulf placed platforms every 600ft on each ten-acre lakebed site; the boom times were on their way.'

He was on a roll now; I wished I had never asked.

'There were several innovative ideas bearing fruit. Rowland of Greenpoint, New York, patented a submarine drilling machine on May 4, 1869. Rowland's design included a fixed working platform for drilling offshore to a depth of almost 50ft. The anchored four-legged tower – with telescopic legs, resembles modern offshore platforms. My father Kare was working alongside his father when in 1938, the so-called Gulf of Mexico Technologies came in. The Pure Oil and Superior Oil Company built a free-standing drilling platform in the Gulf, despite everyone thinking it was impossible due to various difficulties in logistics, engineering and communication. They then brought in one of the big names; you will recognise the name now in the new UK oil industry – Houston-based Brown and Root Marine Operators. My father worked for them; he was part of the crew who built a free-standing wooden platform in about a mile offshore near Creole, Louisiana. It was designed to withstand winds of 150mph. He always said it was a hell of a job. They installed 300 treated yellow pine wooden piles by driving them five metres into the sandy bottom. Unfortunately, the platform was wiped off its pilings by a hurricane in 1940; it was quickly rebuilt and put back into production pumping in the four million barrel field. Back then, It was assumed that the Gulf of Mexico was a potential source of salt-dome oil; it was considered more cost-effective to explore these waters. Did they exist? That was a question for the future to answer.

Kerr-McGee, whom I worked for later when I got into the industry, dramatically answered the salt dome question in 1947 with an experimental offshore rig. It was a precarious business, as not much equipment specifically designed for offshore drilling existed, and exploration remained for the most part a speculative and risky business venture. An offshore dry hole could easily consume the enormous capital costs sunk into constructing a large, permanent rig platform. Nevertheless, Dean McGee of Kerr-McGee Oil Industries partnered with Phillips Petroleum and Stanolind Oil & Gas Co to secure leases for exploratory wells in the Gulf of Mexico. They hired Brown & Root to build a freestanding platform ten miles out to sea. They decided to explore the areas where the potential prolific production might be in salt domes.'

'Einar, you keep talking about salt domes; what are they?'

'Oh, sorry – a salt dome is a dome-shaped structure in sedimentary rocks, formed where a large mass of salt has been forced upwards. Such structures often include traps for oil or natural gas. They decided that the good ones on land were gone. Still, they could move out in the shallow water and, in effect, get into a virgin area where they could find the natural class-one type salt dome. Supply vessels were needed to provide supplies, equipment and crew quarters for the drilling site, forty-three miles southwest of Morgan City, Louisiana. It was found that the gradually sloping Gulf of Mexico reached only about 18ft deep at the drilling site. It was decided a second platform would be built about eight miles from the first at Ship Shoal Block 28. Sixteen 24in pilings were sunk 104ft into the ocean floor to secure a 2,700 sq ft wooden deck. The Kermac No. 16 well stood in almost twenty feet of water, ten miles at sea. Disaster struck again, this time in 1947. The biggest hurricane of the season arrived a week later, with winds of 140mph. Kerr-McGee had $450,000 invested in the project. Both platforms were evacuated during the hurricane, but the damage was minimal. Drilling promptly resumed. On November 14, the Kermac No. 16 well came in at forty barrels per hour. This was great news; it was speculated that a possible 100-million barrel field, ten miles at sea, would produce 1.4 million barrels of oil and 307 million cubic feet of natural gas by 1984.'

I now knew where Einar had done his work experience, where he started, and how he had got into the position, having worked for some of the big hitters – and not only him, but his father and grandfather, for quite a few of the things I had read he had mentioned.

'How has the transportation of men to these locations changed? Have you seen much difference over the years? You must have?'

'Yes, greatly. Transport to and from these offshore platforms was carried out using supply-type boats, then Bell Helicopter became the first company to provide transport to offshore platforms in 1954. A flat area on an LST made from Second World War landing ship tanks was anchored next to Humble Rig 28 and it served as a landing pad for one of the first helicopters to be flown offshore. Helicopters are now a common way of getting crews to and from offshore platforms. It is now commonplace, as you know, that platforms are now constructed on land; as components of an offshore rig are completed, they are shipped to the drilling location. Sometimes assembly takes place as the rig is being transported to its intended destination.

'One thing you must remember – if questions are ever asked about the North Sea, you always mention how it all started, to give them a brief history of the UK North Sea oil and gas industry, how it was initially dismissed by many as a potential source of oil or gas. But they were wrong, those doubters, as the North Sea has, over the past four decades, become the centre of one of the world's most productive energy industries. Remind them that gas was first found in quantity in the Groningen area of the Netherlands in 1959, followed by the first British discovery of gas in the West Sole field, off the coast of East Anglia, by the BP jack-up drilling rig Sea Gem, late in 1965. I don't need to go any further back – you know the rest yourself, surely? How the excitement of the first British North Sea gas was overshadowed almost immediately when, only days later, on Boxing Day, the Sea Gem capsized with the loss of thirteen lives. This was an early reminder of the danger of the North Sea as an environment to work in. The British industry in the southern North Sea snowballed in the early years. The UK's deepening economic crisis meant enormous pressure on the industry to get gas, with oil flowing later. For the oil and gas producers, there were great profits to be made. British self-sufficiency in oil and gas, hitherto an impossible dream, was becoming a possibility.

'Indeed, as exploration and investment moved further north, it became clear that there was oil to be found in great quantities. I recall that it was not until 1975 that a small entrepreneurial American company, Hamilton Brothers, working in the Argyle field, brought the first British oil ashore, to be followed very soon after by BP in the massive Forties field. Discoveries of oil grew in number as more companies, British, European and American, took leases on the North Sea sectors. By the mid-1980s, there were more than 100 installations. As you well know, two of the industry's critical centres have been the Great Yarmouth/ Lowestoft area, the centre of operations for the southern North Sea gas industry, and subsequently, Aberdeen, now regarded as the oil capital of Europe. Concerns that safety was not a high enough priority in the race for oil and gas was confirmed by the Piper Alpha disaster.'

Einar had talked to me for well over an hour and I was getting a bit bored. 'I think you have told me enough,' I butted in. 'With some of the research I have done, I am now convinced I can bluff my way through any conference and question thrown at me. We should draw up a kind of script before each meeting. I think we have a great thing going – I am the blue-eyed boy back at Noroil in Holland, and we should all make a lot of money.'

CHAPTER 12

LARS

Breaking Point – Two Years Later

Time had flown; it was now 1990. I had been keeping in touch with Christine back in Hull ever since we left to come home in October 1988. It had been so hard talking to her when we left so suddenly, but we just had to go back; there was no option.

But with one thing and another, I just never seemed to have enough time to do everything. We were up to our ears in work; it was just endless, and the pressure was getting to me big-time.

I think everything just caught up with me. I had not realised, but my brain was utterly broken to the point where I was screaming at my team for absolutely no reason and even drove on the wrong side of the road at one point without even realising.

When I eventually took two weeks off, things just got worse. The time to rest only made my mind and body give up entirely. I could not carry out simple tasks, take phone calls, get dressed, or get showered. I had not been to the doctor; I refused to go.

I lived with it for more than twelve months until it had got so bad that in 1991 I had a minor nervous breakdown. I was in the office, and suddenly I felt claustrophobic; I just had to get out. I got into my car without saying a word to anyone and just drove out to Watsons Bay, parked up and walked to the ocean side of the peninsula. I sat on the beach, and just broke down in tears. I could not believe it was happening to me, but it was, and I could not stop.

My mobile phone kept ringing, but I ignored it. I never even looked to see who was calling. At about the sixth time, I looked at it. Maya had tried to get in touch. I could not talk to her; I just needed to be alone.

I just knew I had a bad case of burnout. Eventually, I answered the phone. It was Maya again.

'Where the fuck are you? What's going on? Lars, talk to me. Where are you, baby? Lars, answer me, please.'

'Hello… I need to be alone, sorry,' I said, and turned the phone off. I did not even give second thoughts about her; I was fucked.

I was sitting there for what must have been three hours, just watching nothing, staring into space. I turned the phone on – thirty missed calls and messages, all from Maya. As quickly as the feelings had come on, they disappeared. I rang Maya. I could tell by the sound of her voice she had been crying.

'Where are you, Lars? Please, baby, what's wrong?'

'I'm OK. I don't know what's come over me. I just could not go on. I'm sorry, Maya, I will come back.'

I eventually went to the doctor and was diagnosed with depression in 1992. I had lived with it; a silent killer is what it was called, and by fuck, it nearly was.

CHAPTER 13

LEIF

The Time Had Come – Three Years Later, 1991

I had been to Brazil, and twice to Venezuela; I could not believe my luck. There was a new minister in Brazil who was as green as grass and hadn't a clue what he was doing or was even supposed to do; Einar had him eating out of his hand. We made a killing with him and won two of the four jobs we had quoted for. We did not want the others, as we could not have done them if we had won them.

In Venezuela, they were as bent as corkscrews; everything was a bung, but Einar sorted it. The money had gone up because of corruption, but so had the quotes; we were still coming out with our $2.5 million each; excellent work if you could get it.

It was now May 1991, and I had amassed about £12 million in around three years, with the past twelve months the most profitable, from visiting four of the South American countries. It was time I exited before the shit hit the fan. Also, Connie was nagging me about getting married. I'd had been putting it off for quite a long time – too long. She had the patience of Job, that girl. I was now forty-five, and it was about time I settled down. Mum was sixty-two and had hardly seen her son, and Billy was not in the best of health. I wanted to treat them before they got too old to enjoy life.

I hung around for just over a year after giving in my notice, and they did not want me to leave; they even offered me more money to stay. I eventually worked my month's notice and went.

I had called Einar and told him the script; he said he was pleased as he was also looking for a way out and looking at retiring anyway. Even he had enough. He had made a fortune over the years, and wanted to enjoy it, for Borg wasn't getting any younger and had been ill for a few months; he wanted to take her on one last holiday – somewhere expensive, somewhere money could not buy, and he asked me if I wanted to come along. He could get me any woman I fancied; money was no object.

'She will be the most ravishing, sexual woman you have ever made love to – insatiable,' were his words. It sounded tempting, but no, I was going home to my Connie to marry her after all these years, and buy her a new house, settle down, maybe buy a pub, or even go into politics.

I had done some research; I'd always had an interest, but needed more time to look into it, for Labour had been in power in Hull for years. I always believed the place had been held back; the city fathers did not want any big companies coming in. They would have to up their wage rates to keep the staff they had; no way they wanted that. I and my family had consistently voted Labour, but it was about time we had a change.

One thing that had always bothered me was the state of Hull's fishing industry; it had been decimated over the years, ever since the Cod Wars, and the price that the fishing industry had paid over the years with the loss of so many men. The first one I could remember was in 1953, when the Norman ran aground in thick fog on the Skerries east of Cape Farewell, South Greenland, with only one of the twenty-one crew saved. I was seven at the time, but these things always were in my memory bank. The second one I could remember was when I was about nine, in 1955 – the first Double tragedy with the loss of the Lorella and Roderigo in Norway's horrendous weather conditions, with forty Hull trawlermen lost. I remember Mum coming in as we had no television or radio back then, so the first we heard was when she said she had listened to the Hull Daily Mail newspaper boy shouting that the Lorella was missing. The two boats sank on the weekend of January 25-26, falling off Iceland's infamous North Cape. You could see women, whose own husbands were away at sea on other ships, down the street with friends and neighbours asking if there was anything they could do. Everyone was trying to help.

Things went on as near to normal as possible despite the news; kids went to school the next day as there was nothing else they could do for those involved; their mothers tried to protect them from the distressing news. But it was about two days later the news came through that all hope was gone, and what made it even worse was the Roderigo had gone as well. It was devastating for everyone to hear all hope of finding the crew alive was gone.

Someone had to stand up for the city. Our MPs had had it too easy for too long every election; they just sat back and waited for the people to vote for them automatically. Talk about taking it for granted.

I got back home after saying all my farewells to friends and acquaintances in Holland, and had a great welcome from my best mate and partner, Connie. She had been making her wedding plans for months now, and it was all going to happen on July 25, 1991. I was finally going to get married, settle down, and enjoy life with my new bride Mrs Connie Askenes.

It was not a big affair – only Mum, Billy, Martin, Hans Jnr, his mother Angela – who was now OK and a brisk sixty-six – a few lads from the King Edward I had known for years, and that was about it. Martin was my best man. Something I will never forget is how he cried when I asked him to do it; I was so proud to call him my son.

We had a civil ceremony at Hull Registry Office and a reception at my favourite restaurant, The Lantern, where I had booked the whole place for the entire night – only me, my family and close friends. Everything was on me, and what a night it turned out to be, as usual; the food was fantastic, the wine flowed, and we all had an evening to remember.

I was now officially married and unemployed, two things that I had never voluntarily done before. I needed to do something with my life, apart from making my new bride the happiest woman in the world.

We honeymooned in Amsterdam; she always wanted to visit me there but never got round to it. I had often talked about the place but never taken Connie. Well, all that changed.

We stayed at the best hotel in the city, The Grand; it boasted a rich history, from a fifteenth-century convent to royal lodgings to Dutch Admiralty headquarters to Amsterdam's City Hall. The hotel was one of the best, and I wanted Connie to have the best money could buy – for it was no object. She worried about what we were spending as I had never told her of the money I had saved over the years. This would be the surprise to end all surprises when she found out.

The hotel was bang in the centre of the city, Oudezijds Voorburgwal 197. I wanted Connie to see everything, from the finest restaurants, art galleries, and even a tour of what was my playground for quite a few years in the red light district.

I recalled finding that magazine in which Connie had written comments about sex toys and the like, for I knew she had no idea what you could obtain. She had never bought that strap-on that she wanted, and I was most definitely not wanting. No, thank you; leave that to the boys who like it, but I wanted her to have one because she could.

One thing she had put in her magazine was the fact she'd wished I was circumcised. Connie thought it was more hygienic, but she had never complained to me, and had never told me to my face. Did I wonder if she ever would? I wasn't sure.

We had booked into a suite for a whole week – and what a place. Connie had never seen anything like it; she was speechless. There was a walk-in shower room with two showerheads, one each to the double bath where three people could get in, never mind two. She started to cry. 'Hey babe,' I said. 'Come on, you deserve the best, and you are going to get the best – now stop your crying.'

'But, Leif, we can't afford to stay here; this will have cost a fortune. Just think what we could do with that money. The house needs decorating for a start, and we need new curtains for the living room, and the bath taps are leaking.'

I smiled at her and gave her a hug. 'Connie, you don't have to worry about them, just enjoy the night. Now, come here, Mrs Askenes. I want to make love to a married woman.'

Holding her close, we kissed as we undressed each other very slowly, one item at a time, savouring the moment until we stood looking at each other soaking in the view, stroking, and touching. She shuddered as I touched her sweet spot; picking her up, I carried her to the gigantic bed, laying her down, then standing back. I was hard as a rock; she put her hand out and took hold of me – it felt so nice.

'Leif, I love you so much. Come fuck me, please, I want to feel you inside me. Please, make love to me, make me scream with pleasure… you are so good, baby. Now, come on, I am your wife – I demand fucking.'

She had to stop reading these women's stories; they were going to her head.

'I started to caress her body, not rushing into it. I was close already; I'd got as far as Dewsbury Crown Flat, but I wanted this session to be the best sex we had ever had.

We did everything that a man and a woman could dream of doing. I could not believe it; she was insatiable. I had bites all over my body; she was an animal. Talk about letting herself go on her wedding night; it was not as if we had never made love before. But this was so special, for we were lovers as well as best mates. I would die for this woman; I had found my life partner, that was for sure.

We had a great time in Holland; the week just flew by. We did everything two people in love do on their honeymoon and more.

Still, it had to end; we were travelling home on the Saturday night ferry. Since we had arrived, Connie had been saying that she wanted to go around the windows. I had kept her away from it. I don't know why; I just did not want her to see the sleaze, if that is the right word. I just did not want her to go. You might think I am stupid after all the antics I had got up to during my life up to now, but she was my wife, and I don't know; it just did not seem right. OK, I had taken Lynn to sex shows and bought her sex toys, the works, but Connie had talked me into it.

Now I knew the different areas of the windows, and where the higher class of girl worked, along with the better clubs, but I'd only been to them with a group of men, not a woman. Connie was going on about how wrong it was that these poor women should be used for sex.

'Just look at her. Fucking hell, the state of her – just look, Leif.'

'Where?' I turned around.

'No, not there – over there in that window, the one with the pink curtains.'

'I can't see any pink curtains.'

'Her over there, look at her – tits like cold dumpling mix with a cherry stuck in the middle; she should be ashamed of herself.'

I told her quite a lot of them were married, and it was a job to them. They had no feelings for the guy they were fucking; it was just another shag to them. We were walking past one window, and I knew the girl. I had been with her at one of the 'social occasions' one of the companies had put on about a year ago.

I was kind of nervous, hoping she did not recognise me with my clothes on. She had only ever seen me in my birthday suit. As we got closer, I saw the look in the girl's eyes and could tell she had recognised me. Oh, fuck, it would not have been so bad – but then she got down from her chair and came to the door. 'Hello, Leif – it's been a long time… how are you,' she said in Dutch. I made out I did not understand her, but she then said in English, 'My, you are looking well – did you get home OK from the party? Wow – it was a great night, that thing we did on the stage, I loved it. It's not often I do what we did, but I loved it. Anyway – must go… got a customer coming round soon, one of my regulars. I just had to say hello. Have a nice night.' She blew me a kiss as she went back inside.

The look on Connie's face was like thunder. 'Don't say a fucking word. I do not want to know. Just get me back to the hotel, Leif. I have seen enough.'

'Connie, I don't know what to say; it was a long time ago.'

'Shut the fuck up, Leif; I do not want to know. It can't have been that long ago – she remembered you and your name, and whatever you did "on the stage". Now get me back.'

We walked in silence all the way back to our hotel room. Then all hell broke loose.

'You fucking no-good bastard! There's me at home like a good faithful woman, and you are travelling the world fucking who knows what, taking the chance of catching any fucking disease, coming back and telling me you have not played away. I am fucking disgusted with you. I don't care what you did before we got engaged, but after more than four years, I have waited for this week to be the most memorable time of my life – a week that will live with me until the day I die. For what reason? To find out my husband is a liar and a cheat! We are finished, Leif. I can never trust you again. Now, get out of my life.'

She took off the rings and threw them at me; she then broke down in tears, dropping to the floor in a heap. I had never heard a noise like it. I tried to lift her, but she just told me to 'Fuck off and leave me alone.'

Eventually, she stopped crying and got up, and went into the bedroom, slamming the door. I could hear her crying again; the sobbing sounded terrible. I felt like shit, like my world had ended as quickly as it had started. What a fucking useless bastard I was. Why did I take Connie round the windows? I should never have brought her to Amsterdam. I must be mad. Why could I not keep my dick in my trousers? Why oh why?

I lay on the sofa and must have nodded off. As I woke up, I looked at my watch; it was 1.30am. I could not sleep. There was no sound coming from the bedroom; she must have cried herself to sleep. Oh, fuck, what was I going to do? How the fuck could I put this right? By 4.30am I had eventually got to sleep but woke up suddenly. Connie was standing near the sofa, looking down at me. 'You OK, Connie? Talk to me. I am truly sorry, babe; it was just one of those things – it was in the heat of the moment.'

'Leif, do not try and explain; I am sorry I overreacted. I have been thinking. I could not sleep. We must talk, OK? I don't want it to end.' She bent down and kissed me. 'Come back to bed; please forgive me.'

We went back and cuddled up; holding her close was so good. I thought this was never going to happen again. I needed to talk to her – not now, but first thing in the morning.

We both woke up around 9am. She was still lying in my arms, her head on my chest, her hair spread across my belly. 'Morning, babe, you OK? Sleep well?' I sounds stupid when I think of it now, but I could not think of much more to say.

'Mmm, yes, suppose so… let's put that episode behind us, babe. A new start, OK?'

I could not believe what I'd heard after last night.

'I know you had a better sex life than I'd ever had – a lot more experienced than little old me. I often wished I had been more of a free spirit, but that is the way I am. I have learnt so much from you about making love. I can see why you are like you are, for good sex like we do now is better than whatever I had done in the past. I was thinking last night when I realised I was wrong. Will you take me to one of those sex shows you talked to that girl about? You know the party you went to – was that at a sex show?'

'You want to know the full details?' I could not believe the change of attitude. 'I don't mind telling you, but don't go off on one again, OK?'

'No, I want to know the truth. I don't want any secrets between us; you have never discussed your previous life and how you learnt to do the things you do to me, how good it makes me feel. Please, can we?'

We spent the day going to a couple of museums and had lunch at a small Italian restaurant on the Grand Canal. Then we hired a couple of pushbikes on a bit of a tour.

It was just getting dark when we took the bikes back and returned to the hotel. 'I am going to take a quick shower, OK?' I said to Connie.

'No, hang on, wait for me – we can do it together; won't be a second.'

She disappeared into the bedroom, then came out naked. She grabbed my hand. 'Come on, then; you can wash my back, to start with.'

We finished drying each other after consummating the shower. I got dressed – only casual for me, a pair of jeans and a T-shirt, nothing over the top – but Connie had put on a new pair of leather trousers, a low-cut top and lots of makeup; well, more than usual. I had wondered why she had taken so long to get changed.

'Wow, you scrub up well, lass,' I said. 'But why all the fuss? We are only going out for a meal, not the Grand Opera?'

'You promised you would take me to one of those posh sex shows. I want to see how the other half live, Leif; you promised – you are not going back on your word, now are you?' Her pet lip dropped.

CHAPTER 14

LEIF

Never Mention It Again

'No, OK, if that is what you want. Do you want to eat first or after the show?'

A big smile came back on her face as she clapped her hands together. 'I am not that hungry right now. What about after? We can go to an Indonesian for a rice table, which you always mentioned.'

'It is rijsttafel – you pronounce it "rice tarfel", not rice table.'

'Rice tarfel – is that it?'

'Yes, near enough. We can go there; we passed a good one yesterday. Come on, then, let's go.'

We set off to walk to the red light district and the street where most of the sex shows were. I knew of one that was a bit 'exclusive'. I had decided I would take her there; it cost a bit more to get in, and the drinks were a bit more expensive, but I knew there was a better class of perverts there. It was called Onverzadigbaar, or Insatiable; I had been there once before, and the clientele was not seedy – there were often lots of couples, and they put on a good show – sometimes the audience joined in.

'Here we are – now you sure you want to go in, Connie? No chickening out now.'

'No, come on – and to be quite honest, I am looking forward to it. I've never even seen a porn film, never mind one in real life. Wow, I can't believe I am doing it – but come on.'

After dropping the head waiter a few guilders, we were given a table near the front to make sure we got the best attention.

The lights went down, and the music started; the curtains opened to a girl on a bed, clad in basque, thong and stockings. She was stunning; she started her routine stripping to the music and then took a vibrator and started to get pleasure from the plastic dick, much to the audience's enjoyment. She climaxed about three times – or was she an outstanding actress? She finished off licking the vibrator and her fingers before leaving the stage to a round of applause.

There was the same again the next time – a gorgeous black girl, more or less the same routine. Halfway through, Connie whispered to me, 'When will we see some cock, Leif? I have seen enough fanny.'

'Shhh, just wait, it won't be long; you getting a bit horny?'

'Mmmm, yes, it's good, but I am not into women; not that I have tried, I might even like it?' She smiled and blushed at the same time.

The next act was two girls. Most of these sex shows ran along the same lines as the majority of the clientele were men; at these higher-class ones you got a bit of a mixture – couples, tourists, the odd girl on her own, but I think those were more on the lesbian side than straight. The girls gave on an excellent performance; they were definitely lesbian and not acting. They finished up with an extra-long snogging 69 to rousing applause; all the crowd were on their feet, and you could tell the guys had enjoyed it, for as the lights came up, most were standing with bulges in their trousers, me included.

I looked at Connie; she was licking her lips – she was enjoying the girls after all.

There was an interlude for a few minutes, and the main attraction was to come on stage. The MC came out to introduce the actors and informed us that there could be audience participation if anyone wanted to volunteer. They had placed a heart-shaped disc on each table – one side green if you wanted to take part, the other side red if you didn't. I had forgotten about the disc; it was showing green.

'Don't you fucking dare' said Connie. 'Not while I am here you don't, OK?'

I nodded in agreement. The show commenced, the lights went down, the sultry music began, then the curtains opened. I was watching Connie's face as the two artists walked on the set.

The man was black, about 6ft 3in with a body like a bodybuilder; he looked like he was made out of polished onyx. His member was slack as he walked on – it must have been ten inches long – and having been covered in oil he glistened under the lights.

His partner was also very tall. I would say about 5ft 10in; she had on a white toga. They did a short dance routine and finished up kissing. As they were dancing, a big round bed rolled on to the stage by itself. They glided over to it and lay down; they started off stroking each other, kissing, working on each other's bodies. I was looking at Connie; she was spellbound, staring at the scene in front of her. I was rock hard; we had turned our chairs, so she was sitting in front of me and to the side, resting her hand on top of my thigh, stroking my leg as she watched the show develop.

The guy was now erect. Jesus, what a cock. The girl was giving him head as he stood there; he had not entered her yet. He had been down on her. While all this was going on, there was a big screen behind the set, showing close-ups. I don't know where the cameras were situated because there was no other person on stage; it was all very well produced.

The man then started walking around the edge of the stage, which was at the same height as the audience, looking for volunteers. He walked up to our table, and held his hand out to Connie. She looked like she was going to die. Her nails went into my thigh, and she was staring down at his member. Now I'm not too bad for size, but he was gigantic and uncut; it was an interesting reaction from Connie. This must have been the biggest she had ever seen. She was trembling as he pulled her out of her seat to stand up with him. She turned and looked at me, smiled, and went with him. He walked her to the stage area; she sat on the edge of the bed, and the girl got up and came to join them.

She took hold of Connie's hand and placed it on the guy's erect penis. Connie started stroking him; her eyes were wide open, and she looked like a bush baby. She was licking her lips, and gently she wrapped her tiny fingers around him and started to massage him. No inhibitions no nervousness now – she was using both hands. My Connie was in a sex show and being filmed.

I couldn't believe what I was seeing. They were undressing her, and she let them. She stepped out of her trousers, stripped down to her in bra and panties, and the crowd applauded. She enjoyed this, and then kissed the girl – not a peck but a full-blown tongue snog.

I was watching this scene with amazement. Connie began kissing the girl's nipples, then stroked her mound. She just smiled as if she was drugged, not knowing what she was doing. She'd only drunk the same as me – or was there something in her drink?

As the guy put on a condom, Connie went down on the girl, lapping away like a cat on a bowl of milk, and then the girl returned the favour. Connie was just lying there absorbing every minute.

The two of them lay Connie on the end of the bed; he stood in front. The top camera came on, and then the girl put some lube on her. The guy entered her; about an inch went in. I heard Connie say, 'Oh fucking hell, yes.' It had to be her. It was a Hull accent.

I wanted to get up and stop it, but I was engrossed in the scene. He threw his head back. He wasn't fucking acting – he was fucking my wife, and I was letting him.

Connie was now kissing the girl as this black mountain was shagging the arse off her. I was up on my feet now. The girl got off the bed and came over to me. 'It's OK – you want to join us? Come on.'

She took my hand, and we go to bed. I undressed. I couldn't take my eyes off Connie; she had gone. She was on cloud nine as the girl went down on me. I was lying next to Connie; she turned her head and looked at me. I was at Warrington now – about to explode. I heard the guy grunting; he was just about there. We both reached Wigan together – but he didn't know where Central Park was.

'Oh fuck!' I yelled.

He shouted something in Dutch.

'Oh, fucking hell!' screamed Connie.

Only the girl didn't say anything. She'd clearly always been told not to speak with her mouth full.

The audience were on their feet, shouting and clapping. I looked at Connie. 'We are even now, darling,' she said. 'I love you so much – sorry.'

They took us back stage and thanked us for helping put on an excellent performance. The manager asked us if we fancied a job at his sex show clubs, which we declined; we both said it was a one-off.

I asked about the filming, and he said it was just closed-circuit TV and not to worry; I asked him if I could have that in writing, and he said he would give us a certificate signed by him and us. It stated that we had voluntarily taken part in a sex act on stage and that no filming took place; it was all legal and above board.

They took us to a dressing room where we showered and got back into our clothes, all done without speaking. I looked at Connie; she was crying. 'What's wrong, babe? It is OK, don't cry; that is one off the bucket list, OK?

'I am so sorry, Leif. I do not know for the life of me what came over me, then. It went too far, but I was enjoying myself. I now know why you did what you did with that girl; I forgive you, babe. Let us just promise we will never do it again.'

We just hugged and kissed. The manager came back and gave us two vouchers for a meal at his Indonesian restaurant – everything on the house.

After the meal, we walked back to the hotel, not mentioning what had gone on earlier. Connie was still very quiet. I went into the bathroom to brush my teeth; when I returned, she was lying on the bed, naked. I didn't need to ask. That night we had, without any shadow of a doubt, the best sex either of us had ever had.

We got home from our honeymoon refreshed, and certainly a lot wiser about each other – and we vowed never to mention the sex club again.

CHAPTER 15

LEIF

Can't Stand Secrets

It was a Monday morning and Connie and I were alone having a cup of tea. She had not gone back to work. Martin, now nineteen, had got himself a girlfriend. He was also employed full-time, as I had called in another favour and got him an apprenticeship with Peter Cager.

'Connie, I have something I must talk to you about; it's about our finances. Now we are married, we have never discussed what we have between us. We spoke of selling both of our houses and pooling the money into somewhere more extensive with a bigger garden, some-where outside of Hull; what do you think?'

'Outside of Hull – away from Hessle Road? But why? All my friends are here; why would I want to live anywhere else?'

'I can understand that. Mum lives in Gipsyville, but I feel we need somewhere bigger. It's beautiful down here in Graham Avenue, but still, it's an old house. OK, it was modern when they were built in the 1930s, but we need – no, deserve – somewhere better, maybe Kirk Ella or Swanland, up that way.'

'How the hell can we afford a house in Swanland or Kirk Ella? Only money people live up there, not working class like us.'

'What do you mean working class? We are not on the bones of our arse. Connie, give me a bit of credit for what I have achieved in my working life. I have been contracting for most of it, working for myself – OK, on a payroll most of the time, but I've always had good-paying jobs.'

'Yes, but you have still worked for someone else, so you are working-class no matter how you try to butter up it, Leif. You are working class – sorry, but that is a fact.'

I was beginning to get annoyed now. I was not a snob, but I worked on staff for a long time for various significant concerns high up on the payroll.

'Listen, Connie – now you are my wife, it's about time you know all about me and what I have been doing these past few years.'

Her eyes narrowed. 'What secrets have you been keeping from me? You were bad enough in Holland. Leif Askenes, if you are lying to me again, I will –'

'Now, just listen. It is like this. We can afford a house in Kirk Ella – anywhere in Hull; you name it, we can buy it. We have over £12 million in the bank.'

She covered her mouth with her hands. 'What? Fuck off!'

'It is true. Twelve million pounds, and the way the interest is mounting up, it is going to be a lot more. I haven't looked at my account. But I know that is what has gone in the bank over the past four years.'

'But how? Where did you get it? Come on, you are taking the piss, Leif. Truly? Twelve million, really? I don't believe you. Twelve million?'

'Yes – but you can't tell anyone about it. It's not for public knowledge. You must swear on Martin's life that you will never tell a soul about it – promise me, babe.'

'But, Leif – how come? Why you did not tell me before? We are supposed to be partners – no secrets.' She started to cry.

After she'd calmed down a bit, I said, 'Look, we need to discuss this rationally; no crying, for fuck's sake. I could not tell you – there are only three people in the world who know what I have been doing over the past four to five years, and two of them are in this room. We can have a much better life if you accept what I am about to say, Connie. I told you twelve million. That is a very rough estimate. I have never discussed money matters with you at all, but now we are married, we must be open about our assets, don't you agree?'

'I suppose you are right, Leif; it's just that I can't stand secrets. OK, where do you want to start? What I have got saved is not a lot; I have never had money, you see. I've more or less lived from day to day what with bringing up Martin and everything. I have struggled most of my life.'

I put my arm around her shoulder. 'Connie, forget it – you will never have to struggle again. You will never have to work again. You can re-tire. We will have more than enough to keep us for the rest of our lives, you understand?'

'But I like work. I like doing what I do; I would miss all of my friends. What would I do with my time all day? Where would I go? I can't drive. I would be stuck in Kirk Ella or Swanland. There are only buses, and god knows how often they run. I would be bored out of my head.'

'We would be away on holidays more, travelling the world, seeing places you have only dreamed of – the world is your oyster and all that bullshit.'

'But what about Martin? What would he do? He can't look after him-self. I could not leave him for weeks at a time; he would starve to death. He can't open a tin of beans. Come on, be reasonable, Leif, you must understand.'

'Must fucking understand? I can't believe what I am hearing. Let's just sit back and think about what I am saying. I am giving you the op-portunity of being free from the shackles of working forty-eight weeks a year. You'd never have to get up every morning at 6.30am, catch the bus, or walk in the pissing rain to get to the office for 9am to work for someone else. Now, you had a go at me about being working-class – you'd never have to bow down to a boss who thinks he owns you. Be free, and give your notice in. How many weeks would you have to give him?'

'Three months – I have been there at Jacksons for over twelve years.'

'Three fucking months? Tell him to shove it. Walk out, tell him you have finished today.'

'I can't do that; what would he do? No one else can do what I do; I do the ordering, the wages, the contracts.'

'Hold it there, Connie. I am not getting through to you, am I? You do not have to do anything. You will be free; you will not have enough time in the day to spend everything.'

I gave up; in the end, I just could not get through to her. I decided I needed to go to the Isle of Man to sort out my bank and find out how much I did have in my accounts. I had never kept a check, as splashing the cash would have raised questions. I just left it gaining interest, so I needed to take a trip and see for myself.

I landed at Ronaldsway Airport at 11.30am and caught a taxi to get me to the bank for my 1pm appointment. I had rung in to book a meeting with the manager and was told it I'd have to wait two weeks before meeting him.

'OK, fair enough,' I'd replied. 'I would like to close my accounts and to transfer the funds to my Swiss account.' I was bluffing – fuck knows what I would have done if she had said, 'OK, give me the sort code and account number.' The girl asked for my details and told me to hang on a second. She returned with, 'When would you like the meeting for?'

'ASAP,' was my answer.

'Can you come back at one o'clock, please?'

Time to play top dog here. 'Yes, but don't make it any later. I have a flight to catch, OK?' The girl nodded, not looking at me.

At 1pm I went to meet the manager.

'Good morning, Mr Askenes. So good to see you; you have been well, I hope?'

'Cut the bullshit out, mate, you don't need to waffle to me; I'm fine, thanks, and how are you? OK, I take it? I have come over personally because I have not been keeping track of my accounts for quite a few years. The business deals have kept me too busy, but I would like to know how much I have accrued with interest to date. Is it easy to find out by year what the rates have been, just to satisfy my mind that I am banking with the right people?'

'Yes, no problem with that – just a second. I have your file here now. Let me see. Er, right... Please take a seat.'

He pulled out a paper and lay it on the desk in front of me; it read £17,480,774.99 as of that day.

'That can't be right, can it? Have I put that much in since I opened the account? There must be some mistake?'

'No, that is correct. Look, here are all your statements, which you asked us not to send you, but we still kept them in your file for reference.'

He was right. I had requested no correspondence from them until I asked for it. I did not want any evidence of what I earned other than the payments into my UK bank.

I looked at all the paperwork; it was spot on from first opening the account in 1987. I had been putting my income into this bank, then when I started with Noroil and was being paid two cheques a month, it had mounted up. The manager gave me a slip of paper that showed the interest I had been earning on the funds:

1987: £329,503.00
1988: £811,599.00
1989: £1,192,56.00
1990: £1,259,058.00
1991: £1,066,901.00

The interest rates had been around 12.85 per cent, 14.87 per cent, 13.50 per cent and 10.00 per cent, down to 6.50 per cent.

This was on top of my salary of £164,230 a year tax-free for five years, including the 20 per cent bonuses I had been earning. I had been taking £10,000 a year out, and also paid £26,850 in tax and stoppages. It had left me a wealthy man, with £17.5 million and still growing. I left the bank a delighted man. At forty-six years old, I was set for the rest of my life.

I arrived back in Leeds at 8.30pm, picked my car up, and set off for home; I had rung Connie to tell her the good news, that we were far richer than we believed by a long way.

She did not seem happy; I just could not understand her logic. I knew money did not mean a lot to her, and she was worried about the future. I was sure she would come round to my way of thinking – or would she?

Connie was in bed when I got home; Martin was still up.

'Hi, mate, how was your day, OK?'

'Hi, Leif, yes, fine – good trip? Mum told me you had gone to the Isle of Man. Why there? You said you had retired from working – wish I could.'

He looked a bit pissed off; he must have had a crap day at the office. 'Why, what's up with work? You have only just started, mate; there's a long way to go yet. Are you having a rough time of it? Can I help?'

'Nah, just one of the guys is giving me a hard time, that's all. He keeps having a go at me because you got me the job; he thinks I am a gaffer's man, keeps saying things like, "Don't say too much around Martin, or it will go straight back to the gaffer," or "Loose lips sink ships," that sort of thing.'

'Who and what is he? What does he do? Give me a name, Martin. I will have a word. It is bad enough having to go to work without that sort of shit going on.'

'No, please don't. I will sort it myself; please don't say anything to Mr Cager – that would make it worse if it got out that you had been round.'

I told him I wouldn't, but I wanted to see Peter anyway. I had been thinking about my plans and wanted to discuss with him a possible expansion.

*

I called in at the office the following day and asked his secretary, Gwen, if Peter was in.

'Hello, Leif. Yes, he is – just a moment. I will tell him you are here.' She picked up the phone and smiled at me while she was waiting; why do people do that? 'Mr Cager – Leif Askenes is here; OK, I will send him in. Please go in; he will see you now.'

Peter was sitting with his feet up on his desk, reading some documents. 'Hello, Leif – nice to see you again; been a while. Now then, what can I do for you?'

'Well, I was thinking – I have finished working away and was wondering if you would like to go into business with me. You do not specialise in pipework in oil and gas, or petrochem industry or any sort of industrial piping contracts, do you? It might be an added string to your organisation?'

'Well, that was short and sweet – what makes you think I would be interested? It is something I have given consideration to in the past, but it's a lot to take on. More importantly, we do not have the expertise on board to handle that sort of work, plus it would take a lot of money to set up – at least half a million. I don't have that ready cash to invest, and I'm not prepared to go to the banks for capital.'

'That is where I can help – you would not have to. I can fund it. I have had a few good years and saved a few quid. I am sick of working for someone else and making them wealthy – I believe it is about time I did it for myself and my family.'

'Oh, yes, you are married now. Sorry I could not get to the wedding. Thanks for the invite, but I had a previous appointment in Manchester that weekend.'

'You mean you were away shagging, Peter, don't give me that shit. I have heard it all before; don't forget we go back a long way.'

'OK, I will hold my hands up – you are right; you are always right. Don't you ever get fed up with being so fucking perfect?'

'No, and that is why I think we can make a go of this idea. What do you think? Look, I have drawn up a business plan.' I handed him the folder. 'It shows all the requirements and their costs, including a forecast for year one, two and three. That is taking into account we get the work. But with your contacts in the refineries and chemical plants around the UK and Europe, I am sure we would get the chance to get on the bidding lists as you are already a preferred contractor with ISO accreditation; you just need the expertise to make it work. I am willing to fund myself for the first year but would want twenty per cent of your company. I do know you have had a bit of a cash flow problem of late, and this I could help with. What do you think?'

Peter was rubbing his chin. 'Hmm, let me mull over it, Leif. This does look good, and yes, you are right; we did and still are suffering a bit with getting money in. We were looking at expanding the business, but we have put it on hold due to a lack of funds. What were you thinking of putting into this endeavour, moneywise?'

'Including a cash injection into your existing company, a million, for a start. After the first year, I become a joint partner with you in Cager Engineering with a twenty per cent stake. Of the piping division, I get the eighty per cent; you get twenty per cent. How does that sound? The million is an interest-free loan, paid back to me over twenty years, which would give me a nice pension pot when I am sixty-six.'

'Fuck me, mate, you have gone into this. I will need my accountant to run these numbers – you understand that, don't you? It may take a week or so to look at it and draw up the documentation with my solicitor, but yes, at first glance I am interested.' He put out his hand, and we shook on it. 'I have always liked you, Leif, and I trust you – let's hope it happens.'

'Great – look forward to hearing from you; just give me a bell if you need anything else. My funds are in my account offshore and would be available for inspection should you require it, but I could give you a cheque or bank transfer today if required. That is how safe the money is. Bye for now.'

As I left Peter's office, Gwen said, 'Hope to see you again soon, Leif.'

'So do I, Gwen, so do I.'

I had been thinking, as I was listening to Peter when he said he could trust me. He had no idea how devious I could be when required and how I had got the funds I was offering him. After buying new houses for Mum and us, it still left me £16 million after putting my money into the business. I had not mentioned Martin's little problem he was having; best leave it for a while and let him sort it out himself – he needed to learn what a bastard life could be.

All I needed to do was convince Connie it was a good idea. Maybe I could groom Martin to take over from me in the company and she could continue working, but for me as office manager.

I never mentioned the deal to Connie until I heard back from Peter. I was not that bothered about seeing my solicitor as I had read enough legal documents in my time to look over the contracts, if indeed there was one to look through.

We had a couple of phone conversations, and Peter agreed in principle to go ahead with the deal, saying there were just one or two minor things to sort out.

It was another two weeks until we arranged a meeting with him and Mike Barrick, his accountant, and Ken Minster, his solicitor, along with Gwen, to take notes.

Mike Barrick, like all accountants, was as quick as a flash to spot any ways of saving money while making a profit. He was a great asset to the team; he could save us a fortune in tax matters in the long run.

Ken Minster was an excellent solicitor, with a mind like a machine; his mental awareness in company law was beyond belief. If you gave him a problem, you could rely on him sorting it for you, without any doubts.

We went through the contract, page by page, and everything was in order and laid out in great detail. Ken had done an excellent job of putting it together. However, Mike was not that happy about the split of eighty-twenty that I had suggested. Still, Peter insisted that it was fair, considering the sum I was putting forward, and the payment terms were agreed to be paid back into a new account I had set up at my Isle of Man bank.

We agreed that my salary was to be £10,000 a year plus expenses and a dividend to be taken out of profits. I was to get a team together to run the new piping division, and I had sole control of all affairs of the company, with only two directors, Peter and me. At the end of the meeting, we all shook hands – it was a done deal.

Mike and Ken left the room. 'Well, what do you think?' said Peter. 'I reckon we should be able to do well. I believe it will be a good partnership. I did not realise what a fucking legal brain you had on you – where did you learn all that?'

'Just experience, Peter. I didn't need to go to some posh university; when you have worked with some of the people I have worked with within the oil game, you have to be thick not to pick up some of their knowledge. I always kept notes of any meetings I had and made a dossier up in simple language that I could understand; it has never failed me yet. Hence that is where I earned the few quid I have saved up.'

'You certainly impressed them two, that is for sure. When you went for a piss, they both passed excellent compliments about you. Even Mike said I had found a gem.

'Peter, I did not go for a piss. I left the room to give you all chance to pick the bones out of it without me there. I knew they would want to speak to you alone, or it would have meant another meeting being set up, and I wanted it settled today.'

'You crafty bastard, but thanks anyway. I am pleased with the outcome. All we have to do now is make some money.'

Martin was already home, and in his room. Connie got back from work at around 6.30pm. I had prepared a meal for the three of us – once again, some very expensive fillet steak, with fat chips, an excellent red wine, flowers on the table, the full bifter.

'Hi, babe, had a good day? Got some great news for you.'

'What is going on, Leif? Something has happened. You don't usually go to this extreme if you haven't done something wrong?'

'Now, that is not very nice, dear.' I hugged her, 'Why do I need to have done something wrong to make you a nice meal? I will tell you when Martin comes down, OK?'

'All right, I can wait. I will just go and have a quick wash if I have time. Oh, there are times when I wish we had a shower instead of a bath; that thing we bought that fits on to the taps is no bloody good; it keeps falling off. Next time we have a bit of extra cash, we will get a proper shower fitted; what do you think?'

'Yes, OK, dear. Now, hurry up the chips are about cooked – and give Martin a kick up the arse and tell him to get down pronto.'

CHAPTER 16

LEIF

Got Some Great News

I just could not weigh Connie up at all; I had been trying to convince her about buying a new house. She could have what the hell she liked – a walk-in shower, sauna, anything she desired. Why worry about a poxy shower and a few extra quid?

'Hi, Leif, I am starving,' said Martin. 'Is it ready yet? Why the flowers and stuff? What have you done now? Bet you dropped a bollock with Mum. She's never happy lately – I think she is going through the change, whatever that is. Guys at work are always moaning about their wives and the menopause or something like that.'

'No, nothing, just got some great news – well, I think it is anyhow. OK, here she comes – take a seat; I will start to dish up.'

'Ah, that's better. I am famished, love; what we got?'

'Steak and fat chips, with grilled tomatoes and garden peas, ma'am, is that to your satisfaction?'

We started eating; Martin was like a vacuum cleaner. 'Slow down, Martin – no one's going to pinch it off you.'

'He has always been the same,' said Connie. 'Ever since he was a baby he used to scream and shout, even when he went on to solids. When he was still on the bottle I used to have to make a bigger hole in the teat as it would not go through quickly enough for him. Martin, slow down.'

'OK, you two, now listen. I have some news that I need to share with you as it is a big step forward. Right – don't interrupt until I have finished. We can then debate it. I don't want a load of questions until

109

you know the full story. Connie, I took note of your comments about me, and that we have always been working-class and always will be because we work for someone else. Point taken. Well, I have listened to your comment and have now done something about it. Ever since that statement, which hurt me a little, Connie, I must say, I have been having conversations with Peter Cager at Cager Engineering. No – not yet, Martin – and he has agreed for me to go into partnership with him to start a new division of his company called Cager Piping Services Ltd. It will be based in a building he owns just around the corner from his main works. It will be a standalone company, but we would be tendering for turnkey projects using all the expertise of his structural and fabrication engineering facility. We would be sharing the welders as and when we needed them – but those details you don't need to know about. Alongside this, I would have a twenty per cent share of Peter's existing business as he would own twenty per cent of my new company. The other thing, and most of all, that I want to discuss with you, Connie, is that I want you to come and work for me, running our business as office manager, looking after the running of the day-to-day office needs.

'Martin, I want you to complete your apprenticeship with Peter's company. When you are twenty-one, you will transfer to our company; coming under my wing to learn what is needed to take over from me when I retire. You would then run the company. Right, OK – you have both gone quiet; any questions? Connie, what have you got to say about it? Come on; you must have something to say. OK, what about you, Martin? Give me your thoughts. Come on, say something, or do you both need time to digest what I have just put forward to you?'

Connie was the first to speak. 'You want me to leave Jacksons, where I have been for twelve years? We've had this discussion before. I will not leave him in the shit, you understand? Have you no loyalty in your body, Leif? Would you like it if in, say, twelve years, I had been working for you, and I walk in and say sorry, Leif, I am leaving on Friday, take a week's notice? No, you wouldn't, would you?'

She was correct; I would not. I did not have an answer to that. 'So I take it you do not want the job I am offering you – is that correct?'

'No, thank you, Leif, not until I discuss it with Roger at work, is that OK? It may well make his mind up; I know he was thinking of retiring and this might just make his mind up for him, for I just about run the business myself.'

Now, this set me thinking. I knew it was a small company and, to be honest, I did not know that much about it. Maybe I could incorporate it into my new setup. I decided to give this Roger a call tomorrow after Connie had spoken to him.

'OK, Connie, have a word with him in the morning and see what he says. If he talks about wrapping it in, ring me here, and I will call and see him. Maybe we can do some business. What is it they do at Jacksons? I know they are engineering, but what field are they in?'

'Electrical and instrumentation contractors, design and installation work; we work all over the UK on petrochemical work and the like.'

'Why did you not ever tell me this before?'

'Because you never asked me, that's why – what difference does that make?'

'Because we would be subcontracting the E&I scope of work out, but if we had them in-house, we could manage that part of the work ourselves, using our project manager to oversee the full scope; it may well kill two birds with one stone. Do you have anyone in the office who could take over from you if, heaven forbid, you dropped dead?'

'Yes, Jennifer, she is my assistant; she has only been there seven years, but she does know the job inside out.'

'Then why are you so worried about leaving them? If they would have your position covered and you did join us as general office manager, could she work under you running the E&I part of the group?'

'Yes, I suppose she could, but that's not the problem, is it? I am loyal to Roger.'

I nearly said fuck Roger, but kept my mouth shut; I'd ring him the next day. Martin had not said a word, then the master's voice spoke up.

'I am overwhelmed with your generosity, Leif, and would look forward to working with you when I reach twenty-one. I am not like Mum. I want to get on in life; no disrespect, Mum. Let me get my City and Guilds in design engineering – will I be able to take my ONC and HNC after I come out of my time?'

'No problem; if it means you even going to university, we can look into that when the time comes – and thank you for your backing, mate.'

That was that settled. I had one on board. Maybe I would be able to work on Connie nearer the time once we got the company up and running, for it would be a while before she would be needed, and anyway if I could get Roger Jackson in on the act it was not going to be a big ask.

*

The next morning, as Connie was leaving for work, I said, 'Now, don't forget what we said last night about asking Roger about his retirement. If you left, you might just add that I would be interested in buying him out and would like to talk with him. If he would be so kind as to give me a few minutes of his time. OK, you know how to put it to him; I will bow down to your more considerable judgment, my dear.'

'Fuck off,' she said as she walked out of the front door. I took that as a yes.

At 11 am I was just going through a few figures; since computers had become cheaper to buy, it had made things ever so easy to work in offices. The one programme that I loved more than anything was Excel, and being able to use spreadsheets was like magic.

The phone rang. 'Hello, Leif here? How can I help you?'

'Stop putting your telephone voice on; it is me. I have had a word with Roger, and he wants to see you. Can you come round today, as he is away tomorrow until next week?

'Er, yes, no problem; what time suits him?'

'As early as you can; he is going out but will be back by 12.30pm. Say 1pm, OK?'

I arrived at Roger's office at 1pm prompt.

'Hello, Leif,' he said. 'So nice to meet you at last. I feel as if I have known you all my life as Connie never stops talking about you; she never stops telling me about your adventures overseas. By the way, you are one lucky guy snaring that one – she is a gem, I hope you don't mind me saying?'

'No, thank you, Roger. Yes, I agree with your sentiments exactly. I do not know what Connie said to you this morning. Can you enlighten me, please, as to why you wanted to speak with me?'

'Well, it seems that you are looking to take her away from me to start your enterprise; you would be taking my right arm, you do know that, don't you? She also mentioned that you were looking at setting up an E&I division in your group, and if I would be interested in selling my company to you or integrating it as a subcontractor, but working entirely for you, is that correct?'

I could not have put it better myself. 'Yes, you are correct. One thing that I don't think she would have mentioned was something that crossed my mind this morning after she had left home. Would you be willing to come with the package and work maybe three to four days a week while the transition takes place, or even longer if you so wish? To manage the division, office-based, we would be putting the project manager and management team on all projects we win. You, in turn, will still have your contacts that you work for, but instead of Jackson Engineering, it would be Cager Electrical & Instrumentation Engineering Services, part of the Cager Group. We would all be under the same banner, so to speak, and then could offer a complete service from structural, piping and E&I.'

'Leif, you will not believe this, but I have been thinking of selling up for quite a few years now as I have no children to pass the company over to, and my wife has not been that well either. There have been times when I was just going to wrap it up. I have a loyal workforce who have been with me, some of them well over twenty-five years. I did not just want to close the doors and say sorry, but you are all out of work. What you have just offered me is a godsend. Having said that, I am a businessman, and you want to buy my company and all the goodwill that comes with it. How much is that worth to you? Now, don't insult me by offering me a sum of money and then trying to barter with me, for I do not work like that. If I give a price for a job, that is my price. If it is too high, then, sorry, I will not come down. I would rather sit at my desk with my feet up then try to do the job cheaply, for no one wins – you understand me, don't you?'

'In answer to your last statement, I could not put a price on the table. I do not know what it is worth. All I can ask you is what you would be willing to ask for your business. I would add the same to you – do not come up with a high price and think I will barter you down. I ask you, as you seem an honourable man, to put a price on the table and, if I can see mileage in the deal, also tell me what you would want as a fee to run the company for say twelve months. I would take all of your staff on the same deals as they are now, for, as you say, they have been with you quite a long time – they must be a good workforce, and good tradesmen are few and far between in this day and age. They would keep their same benefits, as the only thing that is changing is the name of the company, for you will still be subcontracting as the same company, but would be looking for maybe larger contracts than you did before, along with your current clients. This only leaves now the two costs – one to buy you out, and your day rate charge for managing the company. I will leave you now; if you can give me an answer within seven days, I would appreciate it. Thank you for your time, Roger. I hope we can agree on a sum for both items.'

'No, thank you, Leif, the answer is yes – you have sold the deal to me, and I will work some figures out and be back to you within the seven days. Thank you so much.'

I went straight round to sound out Peter on the deal I had put forward to Roger Jackson for his company, but not knowing how much it was worth. Roger had given me an idea of his workforce and the size of the company, which I gave to Peter to give to his legal team and accountants to see if they could advise us. He asked for a couple of days, and he was sure they could come up with a cost. Roger's day rate fee was not a deal-breaker as we would pay him the going day rate for a two-discipline engineer, about £350 a day. All was left was the company's price, for which I would be paying out of my funds.

Five days had passed. I had a call from Roger – could I go round and speak with him about the takeover? He had come up with some numbers.

'Hello, Leif, and thank you for coming round. I will not beat about the bush; these are my figures.'

He handed me a piece of paper with just two numbers on it.

£350,000 and £0 – and one sentence, 'Lock, stock and barrel.'

He had included the building, the works and offices, including all equipment vans and stock – everything. I could not believe it. He had also built in his day rate of £300 a day for three days a week for forty-six weeks – that was worth £41,400. It meant I was getting the rest, including the building, for just over £300,000. That was a bargain – for Peter's men had come up with that number for just the company and goodwill alone.

Part of the agreement was that we took on all of Roger's men and all that came with them – their pension schemes, all the benefits they were used to; nothing must change. I had to make a phone call with Ken Minster to confirm this was in order. He told me he would have to have a word with accounts but could not see any problems. He phoned me back twenty minutes after and gave the thumbs up. For the amount we were paying for the company, it did not matter.

After shaking on the deal, I left Roger's office saying we would get our legal teams to draw up the paperwork. I was now the owner of two new companies within a week.

Connie had a change of heart; not long after I had purchased Jacksons, she did a bit of a handover to her assistant while I was getting the piping division up and running. I had brought in my team of QC engineers that I had worked with in the local area. Keith Green was an expert in quality assurance. He put me on to a couple of ex-welders who had gone into inspection – Dave O'Neill and Garry Thompson, both Hull lads. I set on a new fabrication shop foreman, Peter Moon, who had worked with me at Paratec; he was a great organiser. We brought in a couple of excellent experienced pipe welders who were self-employed travelling limited company lads, but were getting a bit sick of roaming the world looking for work and wanted to be at home for a bit. John 'The Hollywood Welder' Dixon, whose favourite saying was, 'I could weld a broken heart' was brought in as welding foreman. With these on board and the welders Peter had, we would be able to take on any type of contract in most scenarios.

We ran a complete set of welding procedures that we knew would cover most requirements. It had cost a fortune, but was a necessary expense if we were to be up there with the top contractors. We set up the fabrication shop with all-new welding equipment, laid it on with welding booths complete with air extractors, and a new store with brand-new modern tooling, and a guy to run it, Billy Mathews.

I would be the project manager and estimator until we got up and running. I intended to bring in contract staff to cover everything else once we got some orders on the books. All we needed now was some work.

I was out on the road visiting potential clients and meeting others I had been involved with over the years, when, out of the blue, a guy contacted me. He had been given my name by a guy who was in a very high position with one of the biggest oil producers in the country, if not the world. They were looking at an extension to an existing plant and wanted a company that could handle the full scope from civils up to E&I. Were we interested in meeting up with him, and he would be in Hull in just over a week.

Peter, myself, Roger Jackson, Keith Green and Peter's legal and accounts teams met the guy at the Station Hotel. We discussed everything that could be addressed without going into too much detail and came away thinking we had done OK. And we had – for the following week we received an invitation to tender for the job that 'The Man' had mentioned in his original telephone conversation.

They asked for the quote to be submitted in one month; this worked out brilliantly as we had the three divisions working on it flat out for a month. Peter had gone to one of his civils contractors, one he used all the time. I did the piping using the estimating schedule I had invented using Excel; Roger took the E&I scope.

The quote was submitted by courier to their head office, three copies all in A4 folders as requested. All we had to do now was wait.

Two weeks later, we were asked to go to another meeting to clarify one or two points; just Peter, Roger and myself went to that one.

One week later, we received a letter of intent. This was followed by the official order a week later for the full scope of work with a total value of £3.5 million.

CHAPTER 17

LARS

Came Good – Two Years Later

It had been a hell of a year with my illness, but I had done the right thing in seeing a doctor, who thankfully got me right. I was a fool to leave it too long. With the proper medication and talking about it instead of bottling it up, I came good. I must admit, but without Maya, it would never have happened; she was my strength, my shoulder to cry on. As the old saying goes, no one is as blind as those that cannot see – or don't want to see.

It was 1992, and Mum Christine (I was now referring to each mother by Mum, followed by her name, to save any confusion), told me that Leif had just married a wonderful girl called Connie. She had one boy, Martin, who was a teenager. He had been on honeymoon to Holland, and was busy starting his own business. After been working all over, especially in South America, he had done ever so well.

I told her all about Mum and Dad here in Australia. It seemed so odd, talking about two mums and dads. I kept them up to date on how they were doing as we had been staying in contact. She wrote me a letter every few months, and I rang her now and again when the timing was right and I remembered to do the calling. Work, and running backwards and forwards to Maitland, was taking up a lot of my time.

I had promised we would come back one day, and we had not got married yet. That had been put on the backburner for a while.

We'd had a tough time in the past few years, what with my breakdown and my parents, but I'm pleased to say Dad eventually got his senses back. He recognised both me and Mum after about seven months of treatment. I remember the day he nearly got back to normal; we had gone up to Newcastle and walked into the nursing home/hospital.

'Hi, Dad, how are you today, OK? You have been out in the sun; you look a bit tanned?'

'Yes, he has,' his carer butted in. 'Jon was out there most of yesterday, he is going OK. Mind, he doesn't say much, do you, Jon?' Dad did not respond. 'He was asking me only yesterday if he knew someone called Lars. Of course, I told him he did – he is your son, and he will be here tomorrow.'

With that, Dad turned and looked straight at me.

'Hey, Lars – you are Lars? Where have you been? Since yesterday, I haven't seen you. Why did you not come this morning? I was waiting for you to take me to the pub?'

Now, I had never been to the pub with my father; this was a surreal conversation.

'I know – I got caught up in traffic; it is terrible on the highway today. Three crashes between Hornsby and Gosford, and one looked really bad. We were in traffic for over an hour. Sorry, Dad.'

'Where's your mother? She went out for some bread from the deli and has not been back. I am hungry.'

'You want a sandwich, Jon? I can get you one; it's not long since you had lunch.'

'No, Marjory will be bringing me something; why is she not back?'

I could see he was getting irritated, but that was the first time my father had mentioned my mother's name for months; I could not believe my ears.

'She won't be long, Dad, have a bit of patience. Wanna play dominoes?', Now, he loved his dominoes, but last time we played, he just put any number next to any; he hadn't a clue how to play the game.

'Yes, OK. I beat you last time, didn't I? It's a wonder you want to play me again; you always sulked when you got beat.' He laughed – another first for a long time.

He was right. I hated losing at anything. When I was growing up,

Dad taught me how to play dominoes and all the old games from back home in the UK. He loved Fives and Threes.

'Remember when we used to go with Mum down the club and play Fives and Threes, eh, Dad?'

'Oh yes, we should play now. Do you want to play, Katie?'

She turned to me, looking bemused..

'What's Fives and Threes?' she whispered.

'Oh, you never played dominoes, then? It is a very skilful version of dominoes played in pairs or fours. The aim is to be the first player to exactly reach a set number of points in a round, often sixty-one. Each player has a hand of dominoes and play proceeds as standard dominoes matching an open end. The total number of pips at the open ends, with doubles counting twice, are used to decide if a player scores points. It is a very complicated game; it takes a bit of an explanation.'

'I don't think I will bother,' she said. 'Thanks all the same, Lars, but I don't think somehow your father is up to that right now, do you, to be honest?'

'No, maybe you are right. He used to play it a lot when he was back home in England. It was a very popular game in those days – no TV and not much radio.'

*

It was a long haul running backwards and forwards to Newcastle. It was starting to get to me and Maya; the strain was beginning to tell, and we nearly split up a couple of times, but we pulled through.

While Dad recovered from the blood clot in his brain, he gradually went downhill along with Mum. She was diagnosed with senile dementia, but later on, it was found she had vascular dementia, where changes in thinking skills sometimes occur suddenly after a stroke, which blocks major blood vessels in the brain. The doctor explained that in time it would gradually worsen, so they eventually moved into a home in Sydney to be closer to us. We sold their house to help pay for the home, and we funded the rest.

CHAPTER 18

LARS

Only Lasted a Year

It only lasted a year until, sadly, my father passed away in April 1992, aged eighty-four. He had a decent run, as we did not think he would have lasted that long but, being the stubborn bastard he was, he refused to give in and fought it until the end.

His funeral was a quiet affair; not many people turned up, but they did not know that many people. There was Mary, and the other next-door neighbour, Bluey Clawson; I think I'd only ever spoken to him once in my life, so it was nice of him to come. Two ladies from the bank turned up, but no one from the head office bothered to show. All the years he put in moving from town to town, and no recognition; so sad.

My father loved Maitland and had often said that when he died he wanted to be buried there, so his wish was granted. He was buried in the town at the Rutherford General Cemetery. It was a very old burial ground, first opened in 1874. Considering the first fleet with Captain Cook only landed in 1788, Australia was not even a hundred years old by then. I noticed that there were many unmarked graves, and some with no headstones or damaged headstones.

The ceremony did not last long. We stood by the graveside as the vicar said the final words, and Mum kept asking where Jon was, and why hadn't he come. God, I hope I don't finish up like this, I couldn't stop thinking. Maya was holding my hand. I had an arm around Mum. Thinking about it, she should not have come, what with the journey north, but Dad deserved all his family around him at the end.

I didn't know where my life was heading. Mum was still plodding on but was totally out of it; she did not know us, and just lived in her private dream world. To be honest, we expected her to go before Dad, but she was still there – barely alive, just existing. She lasted another two years, then passed away peacefully, in her sleep, aged seventy-four. We got a phone call one night around 2.30am saying they had found her just lying there with no sign anything was wrong. Then, realising she was not breathing, they tried to bring her back, but she'd likely had been dead a couple of hours or sol the death certificate was dated April 17, 1994.

It was back to Rutherford again for the funeral and the same ritual. Only Mary turned up this time, for Bluey had passed away. It was a short service. Life can be so cruel sometimes. Both of them had a good innings, I suppose, but there again, seventy-four is not that old. I was hoping I would live past that, but not knowing who my natural birth mother or father was, I had no idea what was in my genes. That was yet to come; well, I hoped it would.

Maya had been a tower of strength throughout all this apart from the odd occasion; as I said earlier, my parents' passing was a relief, to be honest. Neither had much of a life over the past few years. I hope I do not finish up like them; I would rather die earlier than go through the torment of dementia and illness.

I remember we had one massive bust-up. I had been back up to Maitland, and the trip lasted a bit longer than a couple of days, so I rang Maya. She had organised a meeting with one of our major clients for the following day.

'Hello, Maya – some bad news… won't be back until Thursday, OK?'

'What do you mean, Thursday? We have a meeting with Mr Svenson from Direct Build tomorrow at 9.30am You better be back, or we are in the shit, mate. You leave everything to me! Now get your butt back here tomorrow – no fucking excuses.'

'But I can't. Mum's not in a good place.'

'I don't give a flying fuck what fucking place she is in; you better be back.'

'Maya, I can't; it's impossible. The doctor is coming in the morning to assess her again.'

'Listen to me, Lars, and listen well; why have we become fucking enemies? What did you do before you met me? You were a fucking bricky! I have made you. What would you be without me? Fucking nothing! Now get back tomorrow, or we are finished – you hear me? Fucking finished.'

She slammed the phone down on me. I gave her a few minutes and rang her back; no answer. I left it another half an hour, then rang again.

'What? Have you made your mind up? What comes first, our relationship and our business, or your mother? I can't go on like this. It is just not fair. I am up to my ears in work, and you are running up and down to your mother; it just can't go on.'

In the end, she rescheduled the meeting for the following Monday, and everything turned out OK, but I never forgot what she said to me. It hit home. But we had been together for far too long to let it fall apart. It may have sounded very selfish of her to ask me to put her and everything else before my parents, but she was right; they were at the end of their innings. We had our future in front of us.

CHAPTER 19

LARS
Relief

Life went on after my parents had gone. Maya and I settled back into the routine of running what was now a very profitable concern. We had branches in NSW and Queensland, and whatever we touched turned to gold. We not only manufactured and hired out tower cranes, we had bought out a mobile crane company in Newcastle and opened a branch in Sydney.

We took a punt on purchasing the bigger end of the mobile units, not freely available in Australia, from Laufkran in Hamburg, Germany. They manufactured what were widely regarded as the biggest and best cranes in the world.

There were cheaper models available, but the Laufkran units were far more reliable, and that was what was needed as long as they were well maintained; they never broke down. For when you were on a project, the last thing you needed was downtime due to a malfunction on the plant, for it not only lost you money but often there was a back charge for loss of production by the client.

I had been in touch with Mum back in Hull; she told me she had been to the doctor as she had not been feeling too well. They had found a couple of lumps. They sent her for X-rays, and it was discovered she had cancer in one of her breasts.

Oh, not another one. Was I a fucking Jonah or something? She told me she was going to start treatment and not to worry, that everything was OK; it was hoped that she would not need a mastectomy and they would be able to get rid of the tumour.

Mum had not told anyone about it. I knew she was good at keeping secrets, as Leif still did not think he had a brother alive in Australia; she would speak to him next time we planned to go back and get married.

We were sitting watching TV one Saturday afternoon, and Maya came in from the sun deck.

'Jeez, it's bloody hot out there today, darl, I need a drink.'

'OK, what will it be? Beer, wine, iced tea? Your wish is my command, babe – anything for you, my sweet thing?'

'Give over – what you after, a root? You are always the same Saturday arvo; you get horny – why?'

I just laughed as I came back with two glasses of white wine. 'Maybe it's because I used to extend all that energy playing footy. I miss the challenge of the fight, and a root at my age I can do. Go and play footy, no chance.'

'Anyway, I have been thinking,' said Maya. 'You are not having me again until you tell me when you are eventually going to make an honest woman of me and put a ring on this finger. Well, when is it going to happen?'

A Year Later

Nearly another year had passed, and we still had not decided when we were going back to the UK. My short spell of not getting any sex lasted about two weeks, of which one was down to Maya straining her back at work giving one of the guys a hand with a truck repair.

There had been good news on the cancer front, with doctors saying they had caught it early enough and Mum Christine didn't lose her breast, but she had to keep going back for a check-up every six months. At least that was a relief.

Halfway through the year, we had great results from the business's crane hire side; it was booming. We could not keep up with the demand, and needed to import more units but were struggling to get the correct prices. The agents were screwing the clients, and prices kept going up and up. It was decided we would take a trip overseas again in the hope we could meet face to face with the manufacturers in Europe, to bargain the prices down. Apart from that, it was a good excuse for another holiday.

*

Six months had passed; we were sitting having a beer. 'Lars, what do you think about making that trip? It seems to have settled down a bit. It would be a hell of an outlay if we were to expand the group. It may be best to hang fire for a while and if we are in the same frame of mind then do it, but I think we should wait. I know I may be shooting myself in the foot here, babe, but what's another year or two before I can root a married man again? But I can wait if you can.'

'You sure, Maya? When did you come up with this idea? I thought you were dead set on going back to the UK and getting wed.'

'I am, but the business comes before my wants, always has done. You must realise that by now, babe; we have been together now for too long. I know we have had some rocky times, but that's behind us now. It's the future we should be looking at together.'

'Fine by me. Everything is going smoothly apart from having problems getting the right people on board to operate and run the crane hire. We can live with what we have now if we cover some of the admin and train our own people up, take on some younger blood and bring them through. What do you reckon?'

'I know all you want to do is fill the offices with young bimbos who might not be able to type, but have a nice ass and big tits. It won't matter to you, Lars. I know what you have in mind; I can read you like a book, mate, like a book.'

'Life being a boss has its rewards, Maya. I hadn't thought of it like that, to be truly honest but that does sound like a good idea. Hmm, some young girls about twenty-one with brains and good bodies... sounds perfect to me! It'd save money on redecorating the office, that's for sure.'

CHAPTER 20

LEIF

First Project – A Year Later

Fantastic – our first project was from one of the big hitters. We could not believe our luck. Mind, we had worked bloody hard to get the estimate out on time. For one, I worked through the night on a few occasions over the month; I know the other teams had done the same, but it had all been well worth the effort.

We had included for a10 per cent profit margin, so all being well we would come out, after all costs, with a profit of £350,000 – not bad for just over eighteen months' work, including shop fabrication.

We needed a workforce of twenty men, all trades plus supervision; we were over the moon. Having been awarded this contract meant it would also put us out in the marketplace to other big companies looking for turnkey projects.

I was sitting in my office a couple of weeks after receiving the order when my mobile phone rang and an unknown number flashed up on the display. I was just about to disregard it when I changed my mind. You never knew. 'Hello, Leif Askenes. How can I help you?'

'Hello, and congratulations on winning the job, my son; you thoroughly deserve it.'

'Sorry, I am afraid I do not know you, do I? Forgive me, but who is it, please?'

'What do you mean, you do not recognise the voice? I will give you one chance, and then I am gone.'

'Einar, you bastard, now I know the voice. How the hell are you, my friend? How did you know about us getting the job? In fact, how did you know I had started my own company?'

Then it dawned on me that he knew everything that is going on, for he was the man.

'Don't be so stupid, Leif. Of course, I know everything. Now how do you think you won that order? New company, no track record other than in the structural game? Peter Cager has a good reputation, and I had heard you had gone in with him and Roger... er... Jackson, isn't it? You should know better than to ask questions like how did I know. That is your free one. Now any more you win, I want my cut, OK? It is business from now on.'

*

I was back on my quest to become a city councillor as 1993 arrived. A couple of guys I had known quite a while suggested I put my name forward to the local Labour party. I did not want to join Labour, for in my eyes, they had never done anything to help Hull. All they seemed to do was feather their nests.

I didn't have a clue about how to go about it. I was thinking of standing as an independent candidate. I was told I could contact the council's electoral services department. I needed to become aware of our local area's issues, what the council was doing about these them, and how my opinion differed from the political parties.

Once I had decided to stand as an independent candidate, I had to make sure that I was officially nominated as the election date drew nearer. It required getting ten people to sign my nomination papers, and the signatories had to be registered electors in the ward where I chose to stand. It all seemed relatively straightforward, so I started making further inquiries with a view to standing in the next local election, which was due that May. I had set up a group of friends to help me get my name out in the west Hull area, and had a load of leaflets printed with my ideas on what was needed.

More affordable housing
Better schools
Selling the city more to the rest of the world

More jobs, and bringing in more prominent multi-national companies
Better transport links
Get better fishing rights back from the EU

These were my significant aims, but the fishing one was the main bone of contention in my eyes.

I laid on the fact that I was a self-made millionaire local lad who had made good and wanted to put something back into the community.

The city council election took place in May 1993, and twenty wards were up for re-election. There was controversy in the election run-up as the national Labour party suspended the local party over claims of intimidation, nepotism and membership rigging. This made the Liberal Democrats confident of making gains in the election, which they did, as Labour lost four seats on the council.

I was one of the independent candidates chosen. I aimed to make a name for myself and become an MP.

*

We had completed our first contract on time and under budget; we became one of the UK's wanted contractors. We had proved we could do it, and nothing fazed us.

Einar was keeping in touch, giving us leads on where and what projects were coming up. We had won a couple at the right price; he had had his two per cent, which could have been twenty per cent because it was added to our cost once we had come up with a valuation.

I rang Einar one afternoon just to touch base. 'I was under the impression you were retiring when we split on the partnership we had previously with Noroil,' I said.

'I did. Borghild and I travelled the world on a cruise – let some else steer the fucking ship, so to speak. We stopped off for a few weeks in each port then caught a ship up. Not always the same ship and not always the same cruise company, but I have an excellent travel agent I have used for years. We just tell her to work out a holiday for us, and just go. There are times we don't even know where we are going; she has never let us down. There are quite a few now sailing the seven seas – you can plan great fly-cruise-type holidays. Fuck sailing long voyages – it's much easier, especially when flying first class. There are always seats available, and staterooms on ships are often accessible – nothing less than Promenade Deck, anyway. Borg being the way she is, she just buys new clothes in whatever city we are in, then just gives them away to the maid or someone in the hotels we stay at. She does not believe in dragging a load of luggage about with her; you know her, she prefers to be naked anyway.'

'By the way, how is my favourite lady? Still well? Still playing up for you, Ein?'

'She is fine now. Had a bit of a rough time but she's now back to her best. She still talks fondly of you, my boy; she still reckons you were the best fuck she ever had. Mind you, having said that, you nearly lost your crown last year in New Zealand. We met this young boy; he was only twenty, a backpacker from Austria – a fucking giant of a man, built like the proverbial, 6ft 6in with a dick to match. We were in Christchurch, a beautiful city; you ever been there? You must go, it's superb. Anyway, I digress. We were in this bar, and this adonis walked in; Borg almost climaxed when she spotted him. The place was packed, but fortune had it, we had a spare seat on our table. To cut the story short, we took him with us for a couple of weeks touring the South Island, got down to Queenstown, and when we parted, he had serviced Borg every night; he was well and truly fucked when he left. I think Borg had worn him out. She still just loves fucking younger men, and she still screams my name every time she reaches the climax. I don't mind; it keeps her happy. I still love her to bits. She would have left me years ago if I had objected. It is not her fault I can't get an erection; I still love listening to her enjoying herself, and I still come when she does, but just can't get the old boy up for it.

'I had decided I was not cut out for retirement, so I went back to work, but I don't do as much as I used to. The odd contract here and there keeps me busy. Plus, I still keep my eye on the construction world – that is a full-time job, and it's how I found out about you again, my boy. I'm so pleased for you. You know me – I always look after my friends. You will do well. Don't you worry about that; old Einar Hegdahl will ensure you do. I must go now – will be in touch.'

'Thank you, Einar, give my love to Borg. Will you tell her I was asking about her?'

'Yes, I will; the old vibe will come out when I mention your name,' he laughed. 'Bye, son – oh, while I think on, we may be in the UK next year. We'd love to meet Connie – she sounds like a lovely girl… maybe we can get together?'

'No fucking chance, Ein, you would have more chance of having a gangbang with the Queen than getting Connie into a swap session or threesomes; sorry, mate, no chance.'

'Never mind, just a thought from a dirty old man. Bye, son, you take care.'

The inquiries were coming in; we had got an estimator and engineers on permanent staff with three other large projects on the table, and things were looking rosy for us.

Martin had been put with the estimator as his assistant, for I knew it was hard to keep them; they were a rare commodity, like rocking horse shit. I decided it best we produced our own, and if nothing else, Martin was a whizzkid on Excel; he just loved spreadsheets. The new guy, Gary Bagley, could pass on all his knowledge to him and I knew we would have a good estimator for a while. It was working well. Martin was working on his own projects from estimating to completion, with Gary working on other jobs. We were also training up two engineers on estimating; they were still hard to find. We had a lot of work coming in and needed the extra bodies.

CHAPTER 21

LARS

Expanding

We advertised for a plant manager, accounts manager, and two trainees to learn from the new guys and us, and had quite a few good responses. Daniel Masters was a Pom from Manchester and had been a plant manager with a prominent civil contractor. And the accounts guy, Hugo Vogel, from Germany, had been in several industries, manufacturing components for the motor industry, valve manufacturers, offshore drilling components, and one or two others. He had emigrated to Australia in 1962. Both came with lots of experience, and excellent references; it seemed that we had dropped lucky. We wanted to be in on the final say as we would be working with them, not the personnel department.

We gave them both interviews after personnel had done all the basics. We had left it to them to find the candidates and narrow it down to the ones they believed we would be able to work with; Maya and I would pick the wheat from the chaff, so to speak. I had brought this system in to save us having to interview every applicant, and up to now, it had worked well.

We interviewed Daniel first; he was a decent, very well-educated guy of thirty-eight, married with two boys, and had been in Australia just over two years. He had been working in the south Sydney area he was moving house. As his wife's mother was coming out to live with them, they moved out towards Cronulla. They were hoping to find work nearer to his new place.

Everything looked good. He'd been out here long enough and there was no chance of him leaving to go home because both his parents were dead. We hired him on the spot, as he talked well and was very confident using Excel, which all our office information was based on. There was no doubt about it – he would fit the bill.

Hugo came in next. We gave the usual greetings, and introduced ourselves. After a few minutes, I sat back, and Hugo kept looking at me in a strange way.

As the interview neared its end, I asked, 'Do you have any questions you would like to add, Hugo?'

'Yes, I am quite happy with what you have told me, but, on a personal note, but have we met before somewhere, Lars? I feel we were on a survival course together in Holland a few years ago. I must admit I'm not 100 per cent, sure, but your face just rings a bell.'

'No, I haven't. I have never been to Holland, so you must have got the wrong guy. I am sorry, but it could not have been me.'

With that, Maya chipped in to save any further probing. 'Well, if that is all the questions, can you leave us for a few minutes? Hugo, just give us time for us to have a chat, please.'

'Yes, thank you.'

He got up and left the room.

'Well, what do you think? He has all the right credentials, ticks all the boxes; I think we should hire him?'

'Yes, I agree,' I said, but I was still wondering about his final question. It seemed he had met Leif and had mistaken me for him. No one else in the company knew about my long-lost brother as we did not want endless questions about it. But it seemed this was too good an opportunity to miss. We were getting what seemed to be the right candidate, and I was possibly getting someone who could enlighten me on my brother.

'Yes, you are right; he is our man – let's bring him back in.'

We also took on two graduates from Sydney University; Debbie Harriman, who had a degree in accountancy and Jake Menses, who had studied engineering. These two completed our recruitment drive for the time being.

Debbie was a great-looking girl, with brains as well as beauty. I reckoned if you were going to employ someone you might as well go along with the cute chick. It made it much better when you arrived at work – better than a potted plant, that was for sure.

Jake was the studious type, an absolute perfectionist for detail; he was a master of Excel and spreadsheets. His first job was to bring us up to spec with the latest computer programmes available.

The good news from home – UK home, that is – was that Mum was OK, but just had to keep going for checks, so we kept our fingers crossed.

CHAPTER 22

LARS

Talked to Mum

We never made the trip, but we had some bad news – Mum's cancer had returned, but this time in the other breast and in a more severe way, and she would have to undergo a mastectomy.

I rang her. 'Hi Mum, it's Lars; how're things, OK?' I just did not know what to say; I seemed so helpless. 'What have they said? Are you having radiation treatment as well now?'

'Yes, the cancer had spread and travelled into my body, but by removing my breast that should have got it all. They put me on a course of radiation and chemo to make sure that it all cleared up, and all being well, it has. I am glad you rang. I wanted to ask you if you and Maya had given any more thought about getting wed. Now, don't start at me; it's just that me and Billy want to tie the knot before it's too late. We have been together now for forty years, and it might seem stupid to you that two old fogies like us want to get wed, but we feel we must – what do you think? On top of that, we were hoping you would come and get married the same day with us in Hull. I know it is a lot to ask, but it would be wonderful, and what a surprise it would be for Leif to meet his brother for the first time. I do not know how I have kept it a secret so long; he has no idea. I even got on to the lads in King Edward after you had gone home in 1988.'

God, was it that long, I thought – nine bloody years; this had to happen now.

'I know Billy's mother, and she had made him promise never to men-

139

tion he had ever met you. It cost me a few pints, I can tell you.'

What could I say? 'All right, let me and Maya discuss it as it will take some organising this end, but I think we can do it. It would be great – it would be an honour to get married same day as my mother. Now, that's something to tell the grandkids, if ever that happens. I will get back to you. Bye, Mum – love you.'

'Love you too, baby – give my love to Maya.'

I rang her back a week later and told her that we would come over, no problem, but it would have to be in February or March 1995.

'That will be great. I will organise the dates to get all the paperwork done for you; at this end, all you will need to do is get in touch with the British Embassy in Sydney again and organise the special visa thing, OK?'

'Fine, Mum. I will get the flights booked and whatever, once you give me a date.'

Mum rang back a week later. 'Lars, great news. I am clear – the latest scans and X-rays show negative results for cancer. I will live to get married – isn't that wonderful?'

I was in tears. 'Oh, Mum, that's more than wonderful – it will be perfect. Have you any dates yet?'

'I changed my mind about a registry wedding and went to see a church vicar. He wasn't worried about us not being in his parish as it's mostly factories and not many houses surrounding it. He was quite happy; the money will be a bonus to him. He said he would get back to me after I had explained the situation. He came back and agreed to marry us all and gave me Wednesday, March 8, at 3pm. But I'll confirm the dates in a couple of days; is that OK? I asked about what you needed, regarding paperwork, and he said just get a marriage visa again from the embassy in Sydney.'

'Yes, fine. I will get on to it straight away and look to book flights to get us home the weekend before. We can stay outside Hull until the wedding day and turn up at church. Think about how we are going to plan this, so Leif only sees me at the ceremony. I will leave that to you and the vicar; they will have some idea how to do it. I will have to think in between. We can then compare notes, OK? I assume that Leif now knows about your illness; you can't have kept that a secret from him – not having a breast off, surely?'

'No, he knows now, I have told him. He took it really badly, but he has had a few weeks now to get used to the idea that his mum is poorly, for we are getting on, and we can't live forever.'

'OK – have a think about how we are going to surprise him and or-ganise a double wedding, without him realising it is me getting married alongside you.'

'It will be the wedding to end all weddings; what I have in mind has never been done before – well, I have never heard of one. The vic-ar I have been to see loves doing things out of the ordinary. I went to a christening once; some friends of ours are Red and Whites. But that doesn't make them bad people; they've been Rovers supporters for years, which is odd, coming off Hessle road, but it but takes all kinds. The service was amazing – and they sang, 'When the red, red, robin comes bob-bob-bobbing along,' and the vicar marched in carrying a Rovers flag. It was like a party. Anyway, he has agreed to do it my way. Just you wait and see what I have in mind.'

CHAPTER 23

LEIF

Things Were Going Great – Two Years Later

It was 1994, things were going great, and I was starting to take a bit of a back seat. Why have a dog and bark yourself? I had convinced Connie to cut back on her hours, so she was working three days a week, Tuesday to Thursday.

I had also managed to convince her into moving; we found a big old house up Ferriby Road in Hessle; it was a massive five-bedroom detached place on its own grounds. We got it for under £200,000, including two garages and a huge conservatory on the back. It was love at sight. We had it wholly redecorated, new furniture, the works.

We were standing outside just before I carried her over the threshold.

'Leif, never in a million years would I have ever envisaged me in a place like this,' she said to me with tears in her eyes. 'The times I have walked down this road from Little Switzerland as a girl and looked at this house, green with envy; pretending I was a princess walking down this drive – and now it is mine, and you have given me a life to go with it. I suppose that makes you my prince charming. Thank you, baby – oh, thank you.' Once again, the tears flowed. Still, they were tears of joy. God, I loved this woman so much.

We had taken a few more holidays; we had enough managers and staff to look after the job. A few months previously, Roger sadly passed away. It was a shame, as he had worked bloody hard all his life. His wife, Mary, was still alive, although very frail, and was in a nursing home.

Roger's neighbour, Fred, had found him lying on a sunbed in the

143

garden with a book on his chest, and was under the impression he was asleep. He had sunglasses on. Fred had said good morning to him, but there was no response. Returning an hour or so later, Roger was still in the same position. He called out to him again; still no response. He went round to the back gate, which was locked, and he shouted again, but there was still no answer. Being an older chap, Fred could not climb over the fence. After calling the police, who luckily had a car in the vicinity, they climbed over and found Roger dead. With Mary in the care home and no other relations to contact, they got in touch with me; they had seen my name in his diary when they were trying to find a friend or member of his family.

I had been in close contact with Einar on numerous occasions, and, taking a leaf out of his book, we were planning a trip around the world. I wanted to take Connie to Australia and New Zealand before we got too old to enjoy it. I was now forty-eight. Mum was still going strong, now aged sixty-four, and Billy, who had given up work three years earlier, was seventy. He'd always had a bad chest, and the cold weather in England didn't help. It must have been all those cold early mornings down the dock, working in all temperatures with no cover.

I was still looking at getting into politics as I was sick to death of the government. The fat cats were getting fatter, while the working class was becoming even more worse off. I believed I could make a change, but I wanted to get a holiday out of the way first, mainly for Connie. She had earned one.

We left Manchester on July 3, 1994, on a Singapore Airlines flight, business class, bound for Sydney via Singapore for a two-day stopover, with the same in Bangkok on the return journey. Why Thailand? Connie wanted to see it.

I was aware that I had to be careful not to let her see too much, mind, for she would not want to go to the places I had been. I hoped.

First stop, Singapore. I had booked the Marina Mandarin Hotel on Raffles Boulevard – a brilliant hotel, though a little expensive, but hey, why worry? We were on holiday. It took about half an hour in a taxi to get to the hotel, and after a long flight, I was ready for bed.

It was early when I opened my eyes. Connie was reading the usual paraphernalia hotels leave out for guests. I was still suffering from the flight, but she was as bright as a button,

'Come on, hurry up. I want to get out and see the place, do some shopping.'

I got dressed to go down for breakfast. We left the room, and all we could hear was the sound of birds twittering; I had not noticed that caged birds were hanging from the ceiling around the inner walkway – I had never seen anything like it.

They said the malls there were out of this world – they were, and so were the prices; all the leading retail names on the planet were in Singapore. Good job I wasn't skint. After six hours of walking from shop to shop, we managed to get back and have a cold beer; even this was over the top at £7 a pint.

We left on the evening flight to Sydney, another eight to ten-hour flight; if you didn't get on one with the right timing, you had to fly to Melbourne and hang around there in the airport building as Sydney was closed for evening flights. They had stopped night flights to curb complaints about aircraft noise.

As we were only going to be away for a month in total, we had only booked to stay in Sydney for three days as we were going on to Auckland for just over two weeks to tour the South Island. Connie had always wanted to visit New Zealand rather than Australia, but I thought while we were in the southern hemisphere, we had to see Sydney at least.

We did all the tourist things in the capital of NSW. There was so much to see and do. I have always said that if Sydney's harbour is not the most magnificent in the world, I would like to know it is.

The flight to Auckland was OK, but we could only fly economy and pay extra for our luggage. I told Connie not to do too much bloody shopping but she would not have it. There was not enough legroom for me, but I managed to get near the exit doors, which made it a bit better. God knows how big people fly economy all the time. It must be awful.

We stopped two nights before moving on to Wellington, and hired a car to take us down to where we were getting the ferry across to Picton. We stopped halfway at Lake Taupo for a night to break the journey, and pulled in to a small motel as all we needed was a bed for the night. A decent meal and breakfast were both supplied by Guy and his lovely wife Hahana, which means radiance, shine or brilliance, in Maori.

The following day, bright and early, we were off on the final three-hour drive; we had booked in for one night at the C Hotel not far from the ferry port. The Interisland ferry took about three and a half hours to cross the Cook Strait, arriving at midday. We had to swap cars as rental cars could not go on the ferries; don't ask me why.

Waiting for our hire car took a hell of a long time. I was at least an hour in the queue. Then once on the road, it was unreal; every turn, there was something new.

We headed for Kaikoura, an old whaling town on the east coast; we spent three nights there. One thing we found was that the fish and chips, which is supposed to be a specialty in New Zealand, seemed no different from that served up in any fish shop in Hull, apart from the types of fish caught.

The area was famous for its earthquakes; mind you, most of New Zealand suffers from some sort of tremor nearly every day somewhere, and some you do not notice.

From Kaikoura, we headed for Christchurch, which is a beautiful city and one I would visit again. We had a great time there in our three-day visit.

Our final destination for a week was Queenstown. This was our longest journey to date at 300 miles, about six hours' driving, and we had booked for eight nights in the Crown Plaza Hotel bang in the middle of town.

Whatever you wanted out of a holiday destination, it was in Queenstown, from a helicopter ride to the glacier or Milford Sound. We took a light plane, which was more expensive than the chopper. We also took a jet boat ride up the Shotover river – another one to cross off the bucket list.

All in all, we had a fantastic time. We flew back to the UK via Sydney and Bangkok – now it was time to worry. I knew it had been a while since my last visit to Thailand, but the sex industry had not changed much since the Vietnam war when the US troops used to go there for their R&R.

We had booked in the Sheraton Grande on Sukhumvit Road – a fantastic hotel which even had direct access to the Skytrain station. Not far from this hotel was what one might call the hotspots of Bangkok – Soi Cowboy, Nana Plaza and Pat Pong.

Soi Cowboy was just across the road. I took Connie down there during the daytime, and it looked like any ordinary Thai street with tea shops and a few traders selling street food. But just after sundown, it attracted a thriving crowd of people with only one mindset – to have a good time.

We did not visit the Nana Plaza or Pat Pong. I did not want to show Connie too much, as it was also known for having a great selection of 'ladyboy' bars. There were also beer bars on the ground floor and even short-time hotels where the girls or boys could take their punters for a happy ending.

We did visit the night market there. Connie kept saying how unusual it was to see so many older European men with young Thai girls walking along happily holding hands and obviously in love. 'Hmm, yes, dear,' I replied on numerous occasions.

I could not get out of there quickly enough; it just took me back to my last visit. How things change when you are married, especially when her indoors is with you.

But sadness and my girl Intera came to mind when I watched the European guys with the young girls. I often wondered how things might have been different, but life goes on. I had Connie now.

Our beautiful holiday over, we landed at Manchester on September 1, a Thursday. We drove straight back to Hull, and what was to become an entirely new venture in my life – one that I never thought would happen.

CHAPTER 24

LEIF

Finding Rita

It was October, and I had been back at work around a month or so. I felt like a spare dick at a wedding; things were running smoothly, but they just did not need me on a day-to-day basis.

Talking about weddings, Mum told me she was thinking of getting married after all. She must have been with Billy forty years; I wondered whether there was more to it than just getting married, as she had been looking a bit off lately, but never complained.

I was still thinking about entering politics, but how would I get into it? I did not want anything to do with the three major parties, either. They had, in my opinion, done nothing to improve Hull. OK, they had built the Humber Bridge, but that was a road to nowhere and had only been a vote catcher for the Labour Party and Barbara Castle in 1966.

Hull had been Labour-run for far too long. The fishing industry had been decimated, and the city council did not want any large companies coming into Hull. There had been rumours for years about Ford wanting to build a new car factory up at Saltend, but that would bring higher wages. That was the last thing the city fathers wanted because it would mean they would have to put up their salaries if they wanted to keep their employees.

I was going ahead making enquiries into how I could become a member of parliament as an independent at first, with the hope of starting my own party to attack the big three. I knew the unions put people through education to get in as members; even John Prescott from Hull got in and made a bloody good living after being a ship's steward.

I started looking into politics and its history, especially in Hull, so I headed to the Central Library. I was walking around the shelves, and to be honest I didn't have a clue what I was looking for. Then this lady came up to me – now, she could not have been anything but a librarian, early forties, I supposed, and quite attractive in a way. It was hard to tell what she would look like without her blouse, cardigan and long skirt, but my mind was trying hard to imagine it.

'Hello, sir, can I help you? You appear a little bit lost?'

'Oh, hello, yes. I am looking into the history of politics, mainly in Hull, and, well, in general, I suppose.'

'That leaves a lot to work on. Is there anything particular? It is a vast subject, one that I studied at university. Can I ask why the interest? No offence, but you do not look like you're a student.'

'Do I look that old?'

'No, sorry – I didn't mean it that way, it is usually the younger people who are studying that are interested in politics, not people of your age – and you must be fortyish, aren't you? Whoops, sorry, I should not have said that.' She blushed.

'Well, thank you for the compliment. I am nearer fifty, thank you. May I ask your name?'

'Rita. Miss Rita Bradshaw – and you are?'

'Leif Askenes. Pleased to meet you, Rita. Do I need to enrol or join the library, or can I come and go as I please?'

'You only need to join if you want to borrow any books, otherwise it is no problem – just come in and use whatever reference books you require. We would rather you do enrol; it's just a formality. We do like to know who is in the establishment at any one time; you do understand, I hope?'

'No problem, Rita; where do I join?'

'Just come with me. I will get the relevant forms; it will only take a few minutes, then you are free to browse if you like. I can help you look in the right direction; it was my favourite subject, and I like to think I know quite a bit.'

I followed Rita to the reception desk and duly filled in the forms. She looked very attractive with her half-rimmed spectacles on the end of her nose. The way she looked over the top of them as we were talking was, in a way, quite sexy.

'There you go.' She handed me my library card. 'That's sorted now; where do you want to start?'

'Can we start on Hull to give me a feel of it?' I said. 'Feel' might not have been the right word.

'Well, that is easy. Using its proper name, Kingston upon Hull is a parliamentary constituency in Yorkshire, which started off electing two members of parliament from 1305 until 1885. It has had numerous well-known MPs, including the anti-slavery campaigner William Wilberforce, the poet Andrew Marvell and of course John Prescott.'

'I know Labour have been representing the city for quite a few years. Has it always been a Labour stronghold?'

'Not always, but I think you should realise it has not always been the three main parties as we know them today. There have been numerous parties with names that no one would recognise nowadays, going back to the first parliamentarians, or better known as Roundheads. You have no doubt heard of Oliver Cromwell, the Roundheads leader during the English Civil War of 1641-1652. They fought against King Charles I of England and his supporters, known as the Cavaliers or Royalists, who claimed rule by absolute monarchy and the principle of the divine right of kings. The Roundheads' goal was to give Parliament supreme control over executive administration of the country or kingdom.'

'You certainly know your stuff, Rita. You just rattled that off without even looking at a book.'

'It is all in here,' she said, tapping her head and smiling. 'The next party that I doubt you know anything about were the Radicals. They were a loose parliamentary political grouping in Britain and Ireland in the early to the mid-19th century who drew on earlier ideas of radicalism and helped to transform the Whigs into the Liberal Party. This party is still in existence in one form or another, changing the name on quite a few occasions – in 1987, the Liberal Democrats, then back to the Liberal Party in 1989. They had been the main rivals to the Conservatives until around 1920 when Labour got stronger.'

'I never knew that. I always thought Labour had always been top or thereabouts.'

'No, see, you are learning already. Did you not cover this at school?'

'Suppose so – but I never took a lot of notice in those days. I was more interested in other things.'

She looked at me over her glasses again. 'Yes, I suppose you would have,' she said, smiling.

'Right – shall I go on?'

'Please.'

'OK, another party who you may or may not have heard of were the Peelites. They were characterised by their commitment to free trade and a managerial, almost technocratic, approach to government. Though they sought to maintain the Conservative Party's principles, but they disagreed with the upper wing, the landed interest, on trade issues, particularly whether agricultural prices should be artificially kept high by tariffs. The Peelites were often called the Liberal Conservatives in contrast to Protectionist Conservatives. Are you following me, Leif? Not boring you yet, I hope?'

'No, not at all; I am amazed how you know it all. I feel quite humble being in your presence,' I said, laughing.

'Please don't – you will make my head swell. It is just implanted in my brain. There's not much more – I am just giving you a brief rundown, so to speak. Anyway, the Whigs slowly evolved during the 18th century. They supported the great aristocratic families, the Protestant Hanoverian succession and toleration for nonconformist Protestants, the dissenters, such as Presbyterians. Now we come to the two main parties that have been at the forefront of the political scene here in the UK for quite some years. The Conservative Party is the heir to the old Tory Party, whose members began forming "conservative associations" after Britain's Reform Bill of 1832 extended electoral rights to the middle class. Finally, we come to the Labour Party, whose historic links with trade unions led it to promote an active role for the state in creating economic prosperity and providing social services. They have been the dominant party in Hull for several years now, but I assume you already know that?'

'Yes, I have looked up a bit about what you might call modern times, but you have enriched my brain, Rita, with what you had just told me. I am very grateful for your time and effort; I will look for you when I come in again, is that OK?'

'Yes, Leif, please do. I have enjoyed your company. It will be a pleasure to help you. Can I ask why you are taking such an interest, or is it none of my business?'

'No, I don't mind telling you. I am on the town council, but haven't been on it long, and I am considering standing to represent the city as a member of parliament.'

'Wow, very good – it is a hard line and quite expensive to do. Are you with any particular party at present, or are you hoping to be an independent?'

'I am considering standing as a Labour member as I am an independent councillor, although I do not agree with quite a lot of their manifesto or ideology. That is all I can say on the matter, you understand?'

*

Having done a lot of research, I was only scratching the surface. Did I want to be tied into any of these organisations? I needed more time to look further into my future.

A few weeks had passed, and I had been in and out of the library, often managing to pick the brains of Rita whenever I could. I was sitting looking at some historical references on Hull when I felt a hand on my shoulder.

'Hello – back again, then, I see; how is your research doing?'

'I am struggling, to be honest with you, Rita; I learnt more from you on that first visit than I have since. There is just that much to sift through; I just seem to get bogged down.'

'Yes, I can understand that; listen, I have a day off tomorrow – how would you like to come to my place, out of the way of all these books? We can go through the notes I have on my PC, and maybe – just maybe – you will find what you are looking for.'

'Wow, that would be great. You sure you don't mind?'

'No, it would be a pleasure. I just love local history, and there are not that many people who take the same interest as you are showing. I would be more than willing to help; I wasn't planning on anything, and if you fancy it, then great.'

'Then I would love to come. What time suits you, and where do you live?'

'Let's say ten, OK? Just hang on. I will get you my card; it has all the details on it. I used to do private tutoring, but I got fed up with snotty-nosed kids who weren't that interested anyway.'

Rita went away. I thought, was there more to this woman than just helping me in my research? I was not looking at getting her into bed. I was a happily married man – or was I just reading between the lines?

She came back half an hour later.

'Sorry, I got caught up with another customer. There you are – that is my address on there, OK? I have to go. See you in the morning around ten, then?'

Rita Bradshaw, 22 Hinderwell Street, Princes Avenue, Hull. Princes Ave was a big student area, not far from the university, with good nightlife; she'd picked a decent spot to live. Maybe she had been in this place for a while? My mind was running away again. You are a married man, Leif, get a grip, I told myself.

I found number 22, which was at the bottom of the street, and knocked on the door.

'Oh, you found it OK, Leif. Come in –give me your coat.'

'Yes, you are well tucked away down here, Rita. Lived here long?'

'About three years now, I suppose.' She closed her eyes and twisted her mouth, biting inside of her cheek as she thought about it. 'Yes, just over three years. Fancy a coffee or tea? Nothing stronger, I am afraid.'

'Yes, coffee would be fine – white, one sugar, please.'

'OK, coffee it is. I will just put the kettle on. Sit down and make yourself comfy – I won't be long.'

I was a nice little place, well furnished, with a lot of G-plan stuff.

There was an excellent rack hi-fi system, just the right size for a single person.

'There you go, one coffee.'

'Thank you. Nice place you have. Are you a Hull girl? You don't seem to have an accent of any sort.'

'No, I am from down south – well, Hereford to be exact; I came up here to uni when I was twenty-two, loved the place, and stayed. My father was in the Army; we moved around a fair bit but finished up there when he got a promotion. They are still there. I visit now and again, not that often, but that's another story. Anyway, what about your research? We need to look at that.'

'Yes. Nice coffee, by the way – it is not instant, right?'

'No, I always prefer percolated. Have a pot on the go keeps me going. It is Brazilian – best coffee in the world; in my opinion, anyway.'

'Thought so – I spent quite a bit of time in South America, but as you say, that's another story.'

There was more to her than met the eye. She was a fascinating woman – and a different person in her 'civvy' clothes. She was dressed in jeans with a low-cut blouse, tight-fitting, which showed off a lovely body, and was barefoot along with painted toes to match her nails. She was sitting in a big chair with her legs tucked under her, holding her cup in both hands as we talked. Unlike the frumpy librarian I had met, I must say I liked the new look very much.

'I want to know as much as I can about the history of Hull and the political scene,' I said. 'I just want to look like I know what I am talking about, so it appears that I have had a better education.'

'That sounds a good idea to me; I told you history was my subject at uni, didn't I?'

'You did not mention any specific subject. You just said history; I think that is what you said.'

'Yes, that is correct; well, to put the right title to it was politics and English history that I got my masters in, without sounding big-headed.' She smiled and kind of blushed when she said it.

'Then my statement about better education was right – a lot better.'

'Now, I told you about all the different variations of political parties over the years, didn't I? What more do you need to know?'

'I just want a brief outline to give me a feel of what I am getting myself into, or trying to get into, if you get my drift?'

'OK, well, let me see. Let us go back and look at Hull, and its past.' She sat there for a few minutes, then got up and said, 'Come with me into my office. It is upstairs. I had my spare bedroom done out with shelves for all my books and documentation.'

We entered the room and what a place – every wall had shelves on it. I'd never seen so many volumes. Each shelf was numbered from the top down and had labels marked with letters.

'Very impressive, Rita; when did you put this lot together? Do you know what is in here? How can you ever know what to look for?'

'Leif, it is my job to know what to look for. I am a librarian, don't forget,' she said, smiling, turning on her PC.

Her screen lit up, and she put in her password. A picture of a German shepherd appeared on the screen saver. 'Oh, that is Mac, my dog. Well, I say he is mine, but not really. We had just got him as a pup when I left to come here. He is twelve now, and does well, considering his hips have not been so good for a while. He is still at home with my parents. I miss him so much. But anyway, on with why we are here.'

That made her around thirty-six; she looked well for her age. I wondered if she went to a gym or swam. I tried to concentrate on the history lesson.

'I have each book and document itemised on my computer, which also has a backup on a floppy disc, just in case my PC goes tits up... I mean, breaks down.'

CHAPTER 25

LEIF

What a Memory

'Anyway, how far do you think I need to go back? I want to quote days and old names to show that I have put some work into finding out about the background of Hull's political scene. I am not just doing it for what I can get out of it. I have a deep, personal connection to the fishing industry and the way the trawlermen of Hull and their families have been treated over the years.'

'Oh, I know a little about Big Lil and her friends, the headscarf ladies, and how she fought back in the 1960s; I read about that. Yes, you are correct – they were "Shit on from a great height." Now, that is a Hull saying, I believe?'

I was getting to like this Rita; she had won me, for sure, the longer we talked.

'OK, I think we should go back no further than say 1332, when William de la Pole was a member for Hull, until around the late 1500s when there were numerous changes in members and parties – far too many names for you to try to remember. Then there was the civil war when no Parliament convened.'

She talked at length about the various colourful periods in Britain's political history, including William Wilberforce, who was a Hull MP and one of the leading lights in the abolition of the slave trade.

'Jesus, look at the time,' she said eventually. 'It is almost lunch – fancy a break and a sandwich? I am starving.'

'Yes, you are right; my belly thinks my throat's been cut. How on earth do you know all this information, Rita? You are unbelievable – I bow my head in tribute.'

'Give over – it is just a gift, I suppose; some people have those types of brains, I understand. My father is the same; he can remember anything about his life, and just needs a trigger, some word that brings back a recollection. That's how he got on so well in the Army – that, along with being super fit. Well, you have to be to join the SAS. He was a professional soldier who joined up as a young man. He never wanted to do anything else. First of all, he joined the Royal Marines and thought about joining the Royal Navy or the Army, but could not make up his mind. So he decided on the Marines – best of both worlds, or so he thought. He got transferred to the SAS when he was twenty-four, I think it was; he does not tell us much about it. It was all highly secretive; I am not sure if I should be telling you about it, to be honest. He met my mother in the forces – she was in the Navy as a Wren, serving in Malta, or Gibraltar. My father was being transported out on some mission somewhere. She was serving on the ship carrying them out, they met and fell in love. Yet another long story. Anyway, come on – what do you want in your sandwich?'

We went down into the kitchen. Once again, it had all mod cons. She was not broke, that was for sure. Librarians must be on a fair wage, was all I could think.

'Right – ham or beef? I have both. Your choice – but I have some great homemade horseradish mustard. I prefer it on the beef. Would you like celery and spring onions on the side?'

'Beef with the extras, please, Rita. You are spoiling me, you know that?'

'Give over – I bet Mrs Askenes treats you like a king; you don't look as if you have ever starved in your life, that is a certainty.' She softly punched me in the stomach. I still had a bit of a six-pack, which I think impressed her, going by the look in her eyes.

'No, we do OK. We've got our own business – we both work there, along with her son Martin. I should say, our son; I am his stepfather and always refer to him as her son – just a habit.'

We talked for a while about our past and what we were looking for in the future. The conversation got round to her and what she had done with her life.

'No men in your life, Rita? Good-looking women like you must have one or two banging on the door?'

'No. I have had a few boyfriends over the years, and nearly got engaged once, but that fell through. I caught him cheating on me. It shook me up, I can tell you.'

'Oh – he was seeing another girl at the same time he was with you?'

'No. I could have understood it if he was, as I had always said I would save myself for the right man, be a virgin, you know, all that stuff some girls dream of. No, it did not bother him, for he blew me out for a younger model – a male model. No wonder it did not bother him us not making love; he did not want it unless it meant going in the back way, if you know what I mean. Must say, he never attempted it; heavy petting was me giving him a hand job. Just shows you never can tell.'

'No – and that's something I have never been able to get my head around, two guys making love.' I wanted to say 'fucking', but did not want to upset Rita; I had not sworn in front of her yet.

'Oh, you mean two men fucking? Me neither – I just can't understand it. Now, two girls, I don't mind watching; that is sexy.'

I could not believe Rita was coming out with such a statement.

'Hey, look at the time. Am I keeping you from doing something else? Do you want me to go, maybe reconvene some other time?'

'No, it is OK with me. I am happy to have the company; a good-looking man in my home does not happen much, so please stay as long as you wish. Come on, let's go back upstairs.'

I did not think she would say that, and I did not want to take it the wrong way.

'Right, where were we? I won't go on about all the history,' she said. 'What area of Hull would you like to represent? They have changed the electoral boundaries quite often over the years.'

'West Hull, I think – that is where I was brought up, and the fishing industry interests me. I would love to get the fishermen their rights back.'

'Right – West Hull it is, listening to you all points to this constituency.'

'OK, that sounds good to me.' I had been busy making notes as she was talking, not in shorthand but good enough for me to rewrite at a later date when I got back to the office.

'Have you got a recorder, Leif? We could record future meetings – if you want to, that is; save you writing notes. You can then listen to my dulcet tones away from here.' She smiled and blushed again.

'Good idea. I have one at the office, though I never use the bloody thing. Yes, I would love to meet again – the more I can learn from you, the better. Thank you, Rita,' I said, touching her hand.

She looked over the top of her glasses again and bit her bottom lip. 'Well… oh yes… Sorry, I lost track for a moment then. In 1885, Charles Wilson, a Liberal, won Hull West and held it until 1907 when another Wilson – Guy, another Liberal – won the seat. He also kept it until in 1915, Labour man Alfred Gould won the election. In 1918, the constituency was abolished and then reinstated in 1955, when Mark Hewitson won the seat for Labour, holding the seat until 1960 when it was won again by Labour, but this time it was James Johnson until 1983. Then Stuart Randall took over once again for Labour, and he is still there. I think that will do for now, don't you? Look – it is nearly four. I need to do some shopping. When are you free to meet again? Next Tuesday, I have another day off, and we could go through a bit more history and facts about long-lost members of the House of Commons. Also, you need to know how the House works, some of the stupid archaic laws, and how the Speaker comes into it. I will turn you into an MP if it kills me, Mr, Askenes, member for Hull West!' She laughed out loud and touched me again on the arm. I responded by holding her hand, and she looked up at me and stared, just for a second, but something clicked between us. 'Well, yes. As I was saying… we must carry on next time. Off you go. I will look forward to our next session.'

'OK, yes, I must be off; you are right.' I had suddenly got nervous about what just happened. Was I falling for Rita? I hoped not, but she was certainly getting to me.

I was back home. Connie asked me how my meeting had gone with Rita. She had no idea, and what she did not know would not hurt her. What was I thinking about, saying that to myself?

'She is a walking book of knowledge, Connie, being a librarian – well, she was cut out for the job. Her mind is like a computer – her memory... well, I can't explain how Rita does it. She just churns out the information. She was a lucky find, for sure.'

'Sounds like she has made an impression on you. Just don't get too friendly, that's all.'

'What are you talking about, too friendly? Don't start getting ideas; it's a working relationship, that's all.'

'Oh, now it's a relationship, is it? Sounds very nice and cosy. So when is the next edition of this saga? When do you meet again, as old Vera Lynn would say?'

'Next Tuesday at her place – she has all the information on her PC, or floppy disc.'

'I hope that is not the only thing that stays floppy, Leif, OK?'

'Give over, Connie; I do believe you are getting jealous.'

'What would I be getting jealous of? What is going on that would or should make me jealous?'

I thought I had better shut up. I was digging myself a hole.

Tuesday arrived and so did the same time, the same place. It was a lovely day; the sun was shining but it was a bit cold for October. I parked outside number 22 and knocked on the door.

'Hi, Leif, come in – how are you, OK? Done any more research yourself? It's just that I haven't seen you in the library. I thought you had gone off me. I hope not – I enjoyed last week, and it was nice to have a bit of male one-to-one company. Did you bring your recorder this time? Or have you a secretary at your work who could type up your notes for you?'

'Yes, I brought it along. I;d never thought of that – that's a good idea; I will look into that when I go in tomorrow.'

'Oh – no work today? You must have a decent boss.'

'Yes, that's me. I am the boss, so I can do as I like.'

'Sounds good. Come on upstairs; we need to get down to it.'

If only, I couldn't help thinking.

'Right then, sir, we had better begin. I have been giving some thought as to what you want or might need. You have had a brief history of Hull's past parliament members and the lowdown on all the previous parties. What we did not cover were hidden nuggets of information that not a lot of people are aware of. It will show you had taken an interest in the House before you applied to join the crowd; what do you think, good idea or not?'

CHAPTER 26

LEIF

Chosen by the House

'Yes, sounds good to me. What I do need to know is how it runs, like how does the Speaker get his position? How can they have so much power? For I believe they are only elected members who have been put forward and then chosen by the House?'

'Yes, partly right, but we will come to that later, but let us look at what I was talking about. I think I must add two interesting points about British politics. Over the years, it had its ups and downs. In 1918, for instance, women over thirty who owned property were given the vote along with men over twenty-one, but they did not have to own any property. In 1928, women were given equal status, and all were given the vote.'

'Yes, I like that. I did not know that – never heard of it. I see what you are getting at, so what other points of interest can you come up with?'

'OK, then, let's see… things that are good talking points, that will make you look interesting – not that you aren't in your own right, sorry Leif.' She shrugged her shoulders and kind of smiled downward when she realised what she had said. I could see her mind working overtime.

'Now, yes, I have it – just a second. I have a file on my PC with the relevant information I gathered together when doing a thesis.'

Her fingers danced across the keys like a ballerina, not like my one-finger prodding.

'Ah, there it is. I won't print it all off; we can just pick out the odd points of interest. You got your recorder on? I always think it is better when one reads it out. Showing is much better than telling – that is one

163

of the rules of being a good writer or author. Show, don't tell, is what my tutor Brian used to tell me.'

'You write books as well? Is there anything you do not do?'

'Now that would be telling, Mr Askenes,' she said with a glint in her eye. 'Right – where shall we start? Oh yes, the oldest in years, now, he was a chap called Stephen Owen Davies, Labour member for Merthyr Tydfil; he was ninety-two when he died in 1972.'

'God, he had a good run, and was still working at that age? It just shows you it can't be that hard a job sitting in the House doing fuck all; whoops, sorry about swearing.'

She gave me that look again, peering over the top of her spectacles and shaking her head.

'Next we have the longest-serving – that was a Navy man, Admiral Francis Knollys; he was a member of Parliament for seventy-three years for Oxford and Reading. He served with Sir Francis Drake and was involved in piracy in the Caribbean, returning in 1586; he died in 1648, aged ninety. Coming to the shortest-serving – and there are a one or two of those – let me see… ah, yes, Edward Legge 1710-47, was elected unopposed MP for Portsmouth in December 1747 – four days before the news came from the West Indies that he had died eighty-seven days before. Then there were was Henry Compton. He was elected on December 6, 1905 with a majority of 199 votes. However, the Conservative government had collapsed the previous day, and the new prime minister Campbell-Bannerman would soon call a general election. As Parliament was not sitting at the time, Compton was unable to take his seat. That will do for that subject – just imagine when you are making your speeches during your election campaign, throwing in these little anecdotes will serve you well, and make you look a very learned gentleman,' she smiled.

'Now then, a woman in Parliament is always a good topic,' she added. 'Women love men who take an interest in them, other than as sexual objects and for breeding purposes. ' She looked over her spectacles again. 'The first-ever woman MP was Constance Markievicz, elected as member for Dublin St Patrick's in 1918, but refused to take her seat as she was a member of Sinn Fein. The first woman ever to take her seat was in 1919 when American-born Conservative MP Nancy Astor later became Viscountess Astor; she served from 1919 until 1945. Fancy a coffee, Leif? I am dry as a bone.'

'Yes, please, white one sugar'

'Well, go on then, you know where the machine is. The mugs are in the cupboard above; mine has got my name on it – but don't look for Rita. It says Sexy. Now hurry, there is a good boy – oh, and just a dash of milk.'

'Here you are, sexy, love the name – it suits you. Is there enough milk in there, or do you want more?'

'No, that's fine, thank you. While you were away, I thought this was interesting. Did you know that Shirley Summerskill, Labour MP for Halifax, is the daughter of Edith Summerskill, who was Labour MP for Fulham West and also Warrington from 1938 to 1961?'

'No, as a matter of fact, I had never heard of either of them.'

'You must be joking – especially Edith; she became a baroness in later life. She was a physician, feminist and writer – don't tell me you've never heard of her?

'Here, this is interesting; how many sets of twins do you think there have been in parliament over the years? OK, I will tell you – James and Richard Grenville sat together for Buckingham from 1774 until 1780. Then from 1837 to 1841, Edward John Stanley was MP for North Cheshire, while his brother William represented Anglesey. I feel you must try and cover most eventualities – you must try to get at people's consciences and why their fathers voted for Labour, or whatever party you decide on.'

'What do you mean, consciences? Why would that come into it? They should be voting for who is going to work for them. Not what happened in the past, surely?'

'Yes, but in real life it just does not happen; most people follow their parents. It has been the same for years; you have said yourself that you feel Labour has, in your words, "shit on" the Hull people. Why? Because they knew damn well they would be voted in.'

She went on to teach me about the grisly fates of MPs who had been killed in action, died accidentally, were murdered, or took their own lives.

'Quite a few have committed suicide over the years,' she said. 'The first one was John Darras, an English soldier, a politician for Shropshire in 1393. In the Hundred Years War, he had served against the Glyndwr Rising, the Welsh's last uprising before incorporating into the Union in 1542. He hanged himself at Neenton in 1408 for what reason I could not find out. The last one was in 1989 when John Heddle, who had been MP for Gateshead West, Lichfield and Tamworth, and Mid Staffordshire between 1974 and 1983, committed suicide due to his property business collapse. There are about a hundred MPs who have sadly taken their own lives – which makes you wonder if you are looking at the right profession, Leif?'

'I am sure, Rita – I've never been more sure in my life. I have always wanted to make things right for Hull, and the only way I believe that this can be done is to get to where the power starts at the top in London and Westminster, so let us get on. I need as much help as I can muster. You don't know how good you are for me.'

I put my hand on her shoulder and looked into those brown eyes; a shiver went down my spine as she touched my hand. 'It will be my pleasure to help you, Leif. Anything you want, I will give you. I can see in your eyes that you are deadly serious,' She squeezed my hand again, holding and stroking it, still looking into my face.

'Well, we must get on if we are going to turn you into an MP. I suggest we look at those that disappeared, and there are eight on record. The last one most will remember was John Stonehouse, Labour MP for Walsall North. He held the post of Postmaster General from 1968 to 1969, and in 1974 he faked his own death. In Miami, Florida, he left a pile of clothes on the beach, making it look like he had gone swimming. In reality, he was en route to Australia to set up a new life with his mistress and secretary. I could go on, but at the end of the day, he survived after being released from prison and becoming something of a star, doing television interviews and writing three novels. He suffered ill health and died of a massive heart attack in 1988. I must read his books; he had another one published posthumously in 1989. It's some story,

Leif; you see, crime does not pay, for eventually you will get found out.'

'What are you trying to say? I have no intentions of committing any crimes.'

Did I look like a criminal, I wondered? Was this woman psychic? All I had done was taken a few bungs in the past, and there was nothing wrong with that – or was there?

'God, just look at the time – we must adjourn this session and meet again; what do you think, OK?'

'Yes, for sure, I am hooked on this investigation stuff. You should have been a lecturer or teacher in schools, with history as your subject. You are brilliant – thank you so much for your help.'

Rita saw me to the door, and just as I was leaving, she kissed me on the cheek.

'Thank you for coming too, Leif. I do so look forward to our meetings; it's great fun. I love your company – it gets a bit lonely, being here alone.'

I put my arm around her waist, pulling her close to me. She looked up, and our lips met – a soft, sweet kiss – and then I pulled away. 'Sorry, I should not have done that. I'm so sorry, Rita.'

With that, I left. What was I doing? What about Connie? Don't throw it all away, I told myself Your playing days are over. You could have fucked for England if it had been an Olympic sport, but that is in the past… or was it?

The following week I didn't meet up with Rita, and wondered whether I should ring her. Connie said to me on the Wednesday, 'You not meeting Miss Rita this week, then? She blew you out or what?'

'No, she did not have a day off this week – next week, hopefully. I have learnt so much from her. I will ask her to help me when I try to get in as an MP in the next General Election. You must meet her, Connie. We must invite her for a meal one night. Is that OK with you – to thank her for helping me?'

'Wow, you are keen. Well, I suppose it won't hurt – at least it shows you are not trying to get into her knickers, or you would not ask her to meet your wife. Thank you for that.' She kissed me and added, 'Yes, OK – next time you meet, set it up. Any night is OK with me.'

CHAPTER 27

LEIF
Do You Still Work Out?

I rang Rita the following week.

'Hello, Rita Bradshaw? how can I help?'

'Hi, it's me, Leif.'

'Oh, hello – I was thinking about you only this morning; I thought you had got frightened off at our last meet. Did you not enjoy our embrace?'

'I am sorry about that – I should never have kissed you; I was out of order.'

'No, you weren't. I was as much to blame. It won't happen again; when are we meeting? I am off tomorrow if you can make it?'

'Ten, same as usual?'

'Yes, fine. See you at ten – looking forward to it.'

I arrived on the dot; it was pissing down. I could not park in my usual place; I was further back down the street. I sat in the car for a while until it eased off a bit, and then set off to walk – but the heavens opened, and the rain was bouncing off the floor; the proverbial stair rods.

I was soaked just getting to the front door, I had only just knocked, and it opened.

'Hi, Leif, thanks for coming. Come in – you look wet through; get that coat off.'

'Here,' she handed me a towel. 'That coat wasn't much good – your shirt is even wet. Look at you. Come on, take it off – you will get your death of cold. Don't be shy; I have seen a naked body before.'

'Thanks, Rita. I should have stayed in the car, but all of a sudden, it poured down.'

I took off my shirt and handed it to her; she was staring at me and biting her cheek inside.

'You OK, Rita?' I broke her concentration.

'Oh, yes, sorry… yes. I was miles away; you are fit for your age, Leif. Do you still work out? You look great.'

'No, haven't for years; I try to eat the right stuff, and do not drink as I used to. I try my best, I suppose.'

'Well, you look good to me. Hang on, I will get you one of Dad's old shirts; he leaves some stuff here, but hasn't been for years, though it might be a bit tight. I will put yours on the radiator to dry.'

As she'd said, it was a bit tight, but not too bad; he must have been a big guy, her old man.

'Leif, before we start, I would like to ask you something, OK?'

'That sounds ominous. What is it – not too serious, I hope?'

'No, nothing that you won't like, or I hope not. I have been thinking – I would like to offer my services as your assistant and be part of your team, which I believe you will need when you go forward in your attempt to become an MP. I realise I have not done anything like this, but it excites me. I believe we could be a good partnership; I am willing to do the groundwork for you, I have lots of contacts in London, who I believe would assist me and you. I have one or two favours to call in, so what do you reckon, or do you want to think about it?'

'Well, that is a surprise – but I don't think I need any time to think. What I have seen from you is a very, very thorough, clever woman whose brain far exceeds mine, and I think we would make a good pair. Thank you – and it is a yes. While we are on the subject of pairs, we would like you to come to our place for an evening meal, do you fancy that? I would love you to meet Connie, my other half; if we are to be working together, I think it best you two meet, OK?'

'Oh, yes, please – I would love to, any night. Just let me know, and I will be there.'

'Fine, I will organise it with her indoors and give you a call. This joint

170

venture we will undertake – how do you want me to reimburse you for your time? As you used to be a tutor, what was your hourly charge? You aren't going to do it for free; I am sure of that. I am quite happy to pay you, and please do not refuse as I won't hear of it. I can afford to pay you, Rita; now, how much do you want?'

'Let us discuss that later. See how we get on. Let us finish what we started by looking at the MP information and bringing you up to date on the whys and wherefores of the House of Commons. There is so much to learn, Leif; we can always discuss terms later. But I am not leaving the library. It would only be part-time, is that understood?'

'Yes, OK, I understand.'

'Right then – by the way, that shirt suits you; it reminds me of Dad.' She rubbed her hand on my chest, with a sad look in her eye. Had there been some conflict between them that needed healing, or was I overthinking again?

'Now we are up to executions; now, there is a subject to savour,' said Rita.

'We can't list them all, but I think you should always start way back; it shows you know the history of Parliament. A chap called Sir Andrew Harclay, who was the MP for Cumberland, was hanged, drawn and quartered in 1323, for high treason in making a treaty with Scotland. One very famous one, Sir Thomas More, was beheaded in 1535 for committing high treason. He was MP for Middlesex and Speaker of the House of Commons in 1523, among other high ranking positions. He was beheaded on the order of Henry VIII, and the Catholic Church later made him a saint.'

'He got rid of quite a few, old Henry; I thought most of them were his wives, though. That's one way of ending an unhappy marriage.'

'Yes, they all went, but also quite a few of his government followed them. Francis Bigod was another hanged, drawn and quartered in 1537. John Hussey, around the same time, was beheaded not far away in Lincoln. Thomas Cromwell, chief minister for Henry, was beheaded for high treason and heresy.'

'I have heard the term before, but what is it?'

'Well, now, let me think – oh yes, it is any form of belief or theory that is strongly at odds with established beliefs or customs, in particular of a church or religious organisation. A heretic is a supporter of such claims or beliefs – understood?'

'OK, if you say so.'

'One local guy we should mention was John Wharton Wigg, MP for Beverley, who died in Fleet Prison in London for being a debtor; they were hard times back in those days. I think that is enough – do you agree? There is enough there for you to include in any number of speeches during your campaign.'

'I know I keep saying it, but watching you going down that list and then adding the story behind the name is nothing but amazing.'

'Give over, I just love it; doing this, I mean,' blushing as she said it. 'Now, let's look at what an MP does, shall we, before my head bursts.'

'What do MPs do in Parliament?'

'Well, you would generally spend your time working in the House of Commons, which can include raising issues affecting your constituents, attending debates, and voting on new laws. Most MPs are also members of committees, which look at issues in detail, from government policy and new laws to wider topics like human rights. The next thing we should look at is what do MPs do in their constituency. Quite often, sometimes every month or so, MPs hold a "surgery" in their office, where local people can come along to discuss any matters that concern them. You would also attend functions, visit schools and businesses, and generally try to meet as many people as possible. Will give you further insight and context into issues they may discuss when you return to Westminster. It is all about offering a service to your constituents, for, after all, they put you in there, and it is they who can vote you out just as easily. Never forget that. It seems that once an MP has become, shall we say, settled in office a few terms, which is usually four years, they often get blasé about it, and take it for granted that they have made it. Remember – you are only as good as your last term; a bit like a rugby player is only as good as his last game. For once you get a bad name, you are out on your ear.'

'Tell me, you say you would like to be my personal assistant to help me win an election, but how can you do that? Would that mean you'd become my agent?'

'Agent is a big commitment, and as I said, I would not be willing to leave my position at the library. I can show you what an agent is required to carry out, and you will see that it may be a too big a job for me. You may well need to employ an experienced professional, but we will see. Now, if you were to stand for what you might call one of the bigger parties, Labour or the Tories, heaven forbid. They would have the responsibility. You see, political parties represented in Parliament employ party agents, mostly based at party headquarters, usually in capital cities. Opportunities are advertised in political party magazines, by careers services, in national newspapers, and relevant publications and on websites. There are not that many required when you think there are only 650 seats in the House of Commons, including the four nations. Therefore, the competition for jobs is intense, so while there are no set qualifications for becoming a political party agent, employment is usually reliant on you having a reasonable degree. A degree in any discipline is OK, but preferred subjects include politics, government, public/social administration, social policy, law, history, business studies, and economics. Also, a postgraduate qualification may be beneficial, particularly for graduates without relevant undergraduate degrees. It is also normally essential to hold substantial relevant experience – this can be gained via paid or voluntary employment with the appropriate party, through campaign work or a European Commission placement. When looking to employ an agent, you would be looking for someone who show initiative – someone who can work without any real supervision. They would need to be very diplomatic and can be able to be very discreet at times. They must have good research, analytical, interpersonal and communication skills, along with IT and leadership skills.'

'Seems like they have to be superwoman or man.'

'You would also require an office as MPs are individual employers who staff their offices much as any small business does. I must add I do not know if there is a single model for organising an MP's office or offices, if you do manage to get in. I am sure there are ways of finding out.'

CHAPTER 28

LEIF

Did Not Realise

'I did not realise that each MP had to employ his staff and what was involved.'

'MPs employ their staff directly on agreed pay scales that are set in stone. Practice varies widely among MPs on whether they employ their staff full-time or part-time, and whether their staff is based at Westminster or constituency.'

'Does each MP get a private office to himself and his aides?'

'Some MPs have no office at Westminster, and some have no constituency office. You will often find caseworkers and other employees in the constituency office responsible for local events or local media. In the Westminster office, you are more likely to find staff directly involved in assisting the MP with parliamentary work. Mind-blowing, isn't it? Are you still intent on going into politics, Leif, or am I frightening you off?'

I was numb. I had no idea what was involved. I supposed the common man in the street did not appreciate what went in down in London. All we would see were these people sitting in a chamber waving pieces of paper or asleep, as others waffled on, like children at a bun fight.

'No, not yet, but you have certainly opened my eyes. I may have to change my mind about standing as an independent, that is for sure. I need to take a closer look at that.'

'You could always join one of the parties, get elected using the relevant party for a couple of years to get your feet under the table, then leave and go on your own. Many have done it before, and I suppose there will be others who do it again – worth thinking about? Let us have a break; I need a coffee. Let's sit in the lounge and have a decent rest away from politics.'

I took the sofa, and Rita came and sat next to me. That was a first – she usually sat on the other side of the room, not that I minded being so close. I could smell her perfume, and almost feel the heat coming from her. She curled her legs under her as she usually did, but at the same time rested her hand on my thigh. We chatted for a while, not about any specific subject, but she never moved her hand off my thigh. I was not too sure what move I should make. Was this a come-on or just being friendly? Rita made the next move and made my mind up for me.

'Well, we had better get back to it, I suppose. We need to look at the protocol and what is expected from you if you do win the election. I do not want to appear negative – it is a big ask you are looking for, but you have to be in it to win it, as the saying goes. Come on.'

Settled back at the PC, she continued. 'We said we would discuss the Speaker, but first of all, you should know the House's rules and customs. You must understand that much of the parliamentary procedure has developed through continued use over the centuries and is not written in the standing orders.'

She went on to explain that there were rules on how and where MPs sat and spoke. 'You must remember that if you are talking about another member, you call him by the Right Honourable member for, say, Fulham, for example – never his name. You must also never say they are lying or not telling the truth. Everything is honourable – no slagging – and everything must go through the Speaker. One point I must add is when a new Speaker of the Commons is elected, the successful candidate is physically dragged to the chair by other MPs. This tradition has its roots in the Speaker's function to communicate the Commons' opinions to the King or Queen. Historically, suppose the monarch didn't agree with the message being communicated. In that case, the early death of the Speaker could follow, so, as you can imagine, previous Speakers required some gentle persuasion to accept the post.'

'I will repeat it – you must be sick of hearing me say it – but how the hell do you know all this?'

She put her finger on my mouth and carried on. 'To participate in a debate in the House of Commons or at Question Time, MPs have to be called by the Speaker. MPs usually rise or half-rise from their seats in a bid to get the Speaker's attention – this is known as catching the Speaker's eye. The role of the Speaker is multi-faceted; part-chair, part-referee, part symbolic representative of the Commons as a whole. There's not much more, Leif. I know you must be getting bored with me rabbiting on, but while I am in full flow, I would rather just carry on.'

'That is quite all right. I must admit I am having doubts about doing this, but it may be just trying to absorb all this information about the rules.'

Rita continued, explaining even more about the Speaker's role, how MPs and Lords vote, and even the dress code in Parliament.

'It's changed since the early days, of course. Members' dress now is generally that which might ordinarily be worn for a fairly formal business transaction. The Speaker has, on several occasions, taken exception to informal clothing, including the non-wearing of jackets and ties by men, so no jeans and T-shirts – understand? As you can see, the Speaker is the main man or woman, and nowadays is politically impartial. To ensure this, the Speaker is expected to resign from their party on appointment and does not campaign in general elections – usually standing unopposed by the major political parties. However, they are still a serving MP and undertake constituency work.'

'How does he or she decide on who can speak, or do they have favourites?'

'No – there is usually a standard practice of calling the official spokesperson from both the government and the opposition to end the debate. Or it could be that the MP has a direct link with his constituency or has expertise on the subject. There are other reasons they will be asked to speak – for instance, their seniority, or whether they have had a previous opportunity to speak and would like to add more of an input. Sometimes, they are running out of time, and they do not have enough left to give anyone a chance to speak.'

'What if there any amendments to a bill? Surely they don't make it through unless it is cast in stone and all parties agree with it – now, that must be very rare, from what I have seen?'

'Yes, the Speaker has the power to decide whether, and which, amendments to bills or motions can be debated and voted on. Doing this risks putting the Speaker in a bit of a dodgy position. He or she has to judge which amendments are worthy of debate. However, several principles guide the Speakers' decisions and seek to ensure impartiality.'

'What if there is a stalemate after a vote? What happens then? Is there a recount, like in general elections?'

'No – one of the most important, albeit very rarely used, powers the Speaker has is to exercise the casting vote in the event of a draw. The use of this power is governed by a long-standing principle aimed at maintaining the Speaker's impartiality, namely that they should not vote against the overall majority. The Speaker should vote in favour of allowing further discussion and avoid making final decisions.'

'The Speaker certainly has a lot of power, but can they ever question his input or decisions he has made?'

'Yes, without doubt. MPs can criticise the Speaker by putting down a motion for debate, which the Government can provide time for it to be debated on the floor of the House. Only three such motions have been debated since the Second World War, so it is improbable, but never say never. If MPs do vote to criticise or "censure" the Speaker's behaviour, the Speaker would come under pressure to resign, but is not automatically ousted from the post. At the end of the day, the UK public – us – elects MPs to represent our interests and concerns in the House of Commons. MPs consider and can propose new laws and raise issues that matter to them in the House. These include asking government ministers questions about current issues including those that affect our constituents. Well, I think we have covered everything you need to know. I realise there is a lot of information to take in, but you have taped this conversation, and if you get it typed up, it will give you something to read over and over again. It will also give you some good quotes when making your bid to get in the club. I will give you all the help I can – all you have to do is ask, Leif, you know that.'

CHAPTER 29

LEIF

Personal Question

'Thanks, Rita. God, look at the time – I must be getting off. I will get this put into some sort of format and let you have a copy. I don't know why – it is all in your head. I still can't believe you can hold so much in there – you are amazing; thanks again.'

We were sitting closer than we had ever been since we met.

'Can I ask you a personal question, Leif?'

Now, that was my line again; I was hoping it would not be my second verse.

'Yes, of course, what is it?'

'Well, since we have been meeting, I have grown very attached to you, and I was wondering… if we do finish up working together, it might lead to things neither of us wants to happen. Does that make sense to you? It does in my head; I'm not sure if it came out right.'

That was not what I expected to hear. Was Rita afraid we might become lovers or just bed partners for fun? I didn't think she'd had much of a sex life; listening to what she had said previously, maybe I was getting into waters I had never been. I knew I had to play this canny.

'I am not sure what you are getting at, Rita. What do you think it might lead to – or are you hoping it might lead to, considering I am a happily married man and would never do anything to hurt Connie.'

Rita put her mug on the table. She turned to look at me, and put her hand on my thigh again.

'Leif, please listen to me. I do not know how to say this, for it has

179

been a very long time since I had a man in my life. I did not think I would ever fall for someone, but I have. I want you. I want you to make love to me. You are honest with me and say you do not want to hurt Connie. Well, neither do I. I can't remember the last time I felt like this. I realise I am being selfish, but does your wife need to know? Could we not just have an affair purely for sex? I do not want to marry you, but I almost climaxed when you came in and took your shirt off. When we have been close upstairs talking, being enclosed in that small room, I have wanted to hold you close, and feel your body touching mine. You do not know how hard it is for me to talk like this, for I have never done anything like this before; it has always been the man that has tried to get me in bed, but I feel that, unless I make a move, I will never know if you would have me. OK, if you say no, then that's it, no problem – we can just forget this conversation ever happened. It will be hard. I realise that, but…'

'Do not say any more.' I took hold of her hand. Our faces were so close. I could smell her breath, the coffee aroma mixed with her perfume. I stroked her hair; she always wore it up in a bun, and one of the locks had fallen. I brushed it away from her face, touching her cheek as I did it. She took my hand, and it had to happen – we kissed – and, oh my, what a kiss. I pulled away – I had to.

'Rita, I do not know what to say; this is new territory for me. I am truly flattered that you have been so honest with me. Yes, I fancy you – any man would; you are a beautiful woman. I am torn now. I do not want to cheat on Connie. I have before, but we were not married then. It was when I worked away. I love women – I could not get enough; the thrill of the chase, the fun of meeting new women, different cultures, colours and nationalities – and the sex. Yes, the sex I just adore, pleasing a woman, hearing her moaning as we make love – feeling her body tremble as she climaxes. For it is not just me who needs pleasing, it is the woman; it took me a while to realise that the woman needs more. One happy ending for the guy is not enough, for we just want to roll over and fall asleep. A woman needs more. Over time I developed a technique, if that is the right word, where I thought more about her than me. But I must say no. I want you – oh yes, I want you; but I must say no. Can we still meet? It may sound selfish after what you have just asked of me, but will you still help me in my efforts to be an MP?'

She sat looking towards the floor, as if she was going to burst into tears. How could I refuse such a plea? But I just had to.

She smiled, turned, and looked at me. 'Of course I will. I believe in you, Leif Askenes; you have proved me right – you are a true and honest man. You will make a good Member of Parliament. You have just passed the test.'

'You mean that was a test of me? If I had said, "Yes, let's go to bed," that would have been it – you would have walked away?'

'Yes – good, wasn't I? If I'm going to throw my hat in the ring with you, then I need to trust you. Part of what I said was correct, but which part is my secret. Now it is time for you to go. I do not think there is much more to cover.'

'Oh, I almost forgot. Do you remember when I asked about coming over for dinner? How about Friday, say, seven – is that OK? Is there anything you don't like, any allergies or anything?'

'Yes, great – love to. I will eat anything. I just can't wait to meet Connie. Thank you.'

*

Friday came, and sure enough, right on time, the doorbell rang.

'Hi, Rita, do come in – my, you look beautiful; I would not have recognised you,' I said. I nearly added, 'with your clothes on' – but held that back, just in case Connie could hear me.

'Thank you, kind sir; good evening.'

And god, did Rita look different. Her hair was no longer in a bun. It was down her back, almost below her shoulder blades; she also wore what looked like a silk skirt down to her ankles; when I took her coat, revealing a black backless top, and no bra – well, no fastenings anyway – she looked stunning.

'Wow, you scrub up well, Rita – not the frumpy librarian; you should do it more often; you look beautiful.'

Just as the words left my mouth, Connie came into the hallway.

'Well, hello, so glad you could come, Rita. I am Connie. So pleased to meet you at last. Leif has talked so much about you I feel as if we have been friends for years.' She turned her head and gave me the kind of look only a woman can provide.

'Thank you, Connie – thanks for inviting me; what a beautiful house you have. I love these big old places; so much character. That sweeping staircase – god, it is wonderful.'

'Connie, take Rita for a tour around. I will go and pour some drinks. What are you having?'

'A dry white for me, please,' said Connie. 'There is a bottle already open in the fridge.'

'Same for me please,' said Rita. 'Could I have some tonic in it, please?'

'No problem, I will be in the living room, OK?'

I went and got the drinks, wondering what Rita was doing coming dressed like that. She did not look like the Rita I had been visiting for the past few weeks. I knew what Connie would be thinking; I would be in for a grilling when Rita left.

The girls came back. 'Wow, Leif – your bedroom is bigger than all of my house put together, and I love that walk-in shower you have; my, you have made it nice.'

'Thanks, Rita,' said Connie. 'We have put a lot of work into it, but now we have it just as we wanted, our dream place – right, Leif? Be right back, I'm just going to check the lamb is cooked OK. You like roast lamb, Rita?'

'Oh yes, love it, thanks – hope you haven't gone to too much trouble, just for me?'

'No, we don't often have guests, what with work and everything, but I do love to cook, and tonight I have done one of my favourite dishes, Brittany lamb, with home-cooked baked beans, new potatoes and runner beans.'

She sounded like Fanny Cradock on one of her old cooking programmes.

We had a great meal, washed down with a nice merlot and fruits of the forest cheesecake to finish. The night went well – it had been a lovely evening with two gorgeous women; what more could a man ask for?

'Well, thank you so much for a wonderful evening,' said Rita. 'I have thoroughly enjoyed it and, thank you, Connie, for such a fantastic meal. That lamb was out of this world; where did you get the recipe from?'

'I found it in a French recipe book years ago. I love the way the juice from the lamb runs through down into the white beans and tomatoes, along with the garlic and rosemary; it does not take much doing on my part.'

'What beans do you use, and how do you get the garlic and herbs to infuse?'

'I always buy haricot beans. It is easy – just slice the garlic into slivers and push them into the joint using the blade of your knife as a guide; same with the herbs – only use fresh herbs, and push them down all over the joint. It's quite simple, really.'

'God, look at the time – I must be off. I've got to be up early in the morning as I am going down to Hereford to see my parents for a week. Mum's not been too good so I said I would go down. Thank you so much again.'

'No, thank you for coming,' I said. 'You've been great company. I will be in touch in a week or so then, and we can go over a few things I have prepared, regarding the MP thing, OK?'

'Yes, no worries. OK, I am off.'

She hugged Connie, kissed me on the cheek, and was gone.

Connie never commented about her – she just went into the kitchen and started to load the pots into the dishwasher. We went to bed, still no word. I finished my whisky, then followed her upstairs. Connie was already in bed reading a magazine.

'You are not saying much; what is wrong with you, something bothering you?'

She put the magazine down and looked up at me, frowning. 'No, why would there be anything wrong with me? You did not tell me that Rita was a fucking film star. A frumpy librarian was how you had described her. No wonder you were quick enough to nip round to her place for cosy chats about the fucking parliament – give over, you lying bastard.'

'Lying, what have I been lying about? I never said anything about her.'

'No fucking wonder you never said anything, Leif, the woman is a goddess. She is beautiful, and don't tell me you don't fancy her. I won't believe you – even I fancy her.'

I just laughed.

'Don't fucking laugh; it is not funny that you lied to me. Why?'

'Lied? How did I lie? I never told you anything about her, only how brainy she was and how she can remember things. How come I am getting this aggro? I have done nothing wrong. Just a minute – you are jealous of her the way she looks. Tonight was the first time I had ever seen her with her hair down. It was the first time I'd seen her in make-up; it was as much a surprise to me as it was you. Believe me, I have done nothing wrong – we have done nothing wrong. She is just a friend, and hopefully an employee.'

Connie's head nearly spun off her shoulders. 'A fucking employee? Oh, when was that fucking decided?'

'Not at work – I want her to be my agent or my personal assistant if I get in as an MP. I think she will be a great help to me down in London.'

I was digging myself a deeper hole here; it was not the right time to be telling my wife I intended to work in London with Rita.

'No fucking chance, mate! You are setting her on as a PA to work away from home, staying in London, with all it has to offer? No way, Jose, not a fucking cat in hell's chance.'

'OK, answer me this then. If Rita had come tonight with her hair up in a bun, a tweed skirt, and a flowered blouse and cardigan, would you be taking the same stance? No, you wouldn't – but she comes dressed, as you say, looking like a film star, and the shit hits the fan. Just because she made an effort to look beautiful, and yes, I agree she did. Still, I have no intentions of it being nothing but work; she has already told me she will not leave her job at the library to come to London with me. I have not even asked her; Rita is quite happy doing what she is doing now.'

'Oh, this gets even better. You're already planning to take her to London if she goes with you – you've already got it in your tiny fucking brain that you want to take Mary fucking Pippins back to London.'

'You mean Mary Poppins out of the musical, not Pippins.'

'Don't get smart, Leif; you know what I am on about. How did you think I would react when she turned up looking like that? You know she is a beautiful woman – you have been sneaking away from work to spend all day with her at her place, not getting home until late sometimes, and you expect me to think nothing is going on. Give over, do you think I am fucking daft?'

'Connie, come on, think about it. Do you honestly think I would have suggested that you meet her if we were having an affair behind your back? Now just think about it?'

'Hmm… but you must admit I did wonder what you were getting up to. You don't have the best track record; I know all about your past. Don't forget, you would fuck a hair-lipped rat in your younger days; just look at Holland, for example.'

'Oh, that's right, bring that up again; I have not ventured away since we have been married, now have I?'

'That sounds good – oh, thank you very much, that's really nice of you.'

'You know what I mean. Now, let's just drop the subject; nothing is going on between me and Rita – end of, OK?'

'OK, then. I'm sorry. Come here – give me a kiss.'

'That all I get after all the earache – a kiss?'

'Let's see if you are up to it.' She got out of bed, slipped her nightie off in front of me, and lay back on the bed. 'Now, come on, Leif; I will show you how sorry I am.'

CHAPTER 30

LEIF

Good and Bad News

The following day I was up early and went round to see Mum. She was looking a bit under the weather.

'You OK, Mum? You look crap.'

'I am OK, considering. I have been better. I suppose I had better tell you the truth. I have been suffering from breast cancer for quite a while now, but did not want to worry you, what with you working away from home all the time.'

I just stood and looked at her; I had no idea she was or had been ill. 'But, Mum, you should have told me – I am your only son. I should know what's going on in your life as much as mine. You are too good at keeping secrets; just look at Dad's tattoo, for instance.'

She started laughing. 'Wow, that's going back a bit. OK, and another thing while we are at it – confession time.' She stood up and walked to put the kettle on with her back to me. She spoke in a whisper, 'I have had a breast off.'

I got up off the chair and took her in my arms. 'What? When? Oh, fuck... I don't believe it! I can't think why you have kept this a fucking secret from me for such a bloody long time?'

'I told you I did it to protect you.'

'You even let me go on holiday. For fuck's sake, you were wrong.'

'If you knew, you would not have gone, you would have been worrying. Look, shit happens – there's nothing we can do about it; just get on with it. Oh, one other thing, our weddings are booked for next March.'

'Weddings, what do you mean our weddings? Who else is getting married that I don't know about?'

'It is at the church down Sculcoates Lane off Beverley Road; he is doing a double wedding – there are not many vicars will do what I am asking.'

'I thought it was going to be a register office do? Once again, why all the secrecy – and why a double wedding? I am already married – remember Connie?'

'OK, I suppose I might as well tell you now we are at it. I had been pen pals with a girl in Australia for a long time – Annette Brooksbank. She passed away, then her daughter Maya took over the writing. I found out she was coming over to Hull to get married in the town where her husband was born. He has no relatives that he knows of in the area; his mother came from Hull, but always wanted to come "home" to get married. Satisfied, now you know it all?'

'All right – it seems like a fucking expensive way of getting married, but who am I to talk? Everyone to their own thing. If it pleases you, OK, no worries.'

'Just a minute – I have a photo of her. It's upstairs; hang on.' Christine went up and returned with the picture.

'There you are – she is a bonny girl, isn't she? She looks just like her mother. I lost her photos when we moved. I haven't a clue where they went.'

'I can't remember you ever writing to anyone in Australia; you never mentioned her when I emigrated. Why didn't you give me her address? I could have gone and said hello.'

'I did not write to her for a long time. When I was at school, the English teacher had started it as an exercise, and we just carried it on. Annette then moved, and we lost touch, then she started writing to me again. She had lost my address, or something – anyway, we got back in touch. It's such a long time ago; I can't remember all the details.'

'Don't worry, no need to give me a reason. I was just asking, that was all. I think it is a great idea.'

'Thanks, babe. I love you. They will share the cost of the wedding – don't worry about the extra expense.'

'No, don't worry, it was your idea to have the double header; it is the least I can do for them. Let this Maya know it will be my wedding present to her and her hubby, whoever he is.'

CHAPTER 31

LEIF
Big Mac

I was on Hessle Road and I decided to call into Rayners for a couple. I spotted Bill Meadows, an old mate from school, got a pint and went over to say hello. While we were yarning, Big Mac walked in. He was still wearing his old red and white spotted Kromer cap and Union flag neckerchief – I had never seen him without them. Having said that, I used to wear one; it was a sign that you were different from the other tradesmen. A breed of their own, stovers were even worse, the guys who worked on the pipelines.

'I have to go,' said Bill. 'Our lass will go barmy if I'm late taking her to her mother's. Hate the old bitch, but that's life. See you later, Leif – we must have a session one afternoon, OK?'

Mac nodded at Bill as he got up. He never said much; just sat down near us.

'Hiya, Mac, how're things – OK?'

'Awrite, mate – how you doing, son?'

'What's with the sunglasses? You are inside now. You posing or what?'

'I had a flash and my eyes are still a bit sore – forgot I had them on.'

'Oh, OK – what are you drinking?'

'Gie us a wee swally.'

'What?'

'A wee swally a'beer, a pint of mild.'

'Oh yes, I remember. Be right back. How's your lass, OK?'

'Aye, no bad. What's happenin', big man?'

'Oh, not a lot; I'm OK. Be back in a sec.'

I came back with the beers; Mac had changed his sunglasses for his spectacles and was reading his crumpled up *Daily Mirror*, looking at the racing page.

'Here you go, all the best.'

'That's a stoater.'

I had known Mac a long time and could never understand some of the 'patter', as it is known in Glasgow, or the words he used. I had picked up on a few, such as stoater, meaning fantastic or excellent.

He took hold of the pint glass; it disappeared, hidden by the size of his hand wrapped around it. He must have been a big man in his younger days.

'So how's things with you, OK?'

'Cannae complain. Still here, living and breathing – only just, mind.' He laughed and started coughing.

'See you still got that cough, mate; you should do something about it.'

All the years I had known Mac, he always seemed to be coughing. It had never got any better, maybe even worse.

'Aye, they used to supply us with a pint of milk a day when I started my apprenticeship in the Fairfield's yards in Govan. It never seemed to do me any good.'

'Why did they give you milk?'

'They reckon that aids the deslagging of hazardous substances.' He was trying to put on a posh English accent. 'They say that it promotes the production of mucus. More mucus equals faster discharge of the fume particles. Which means you cough the shit up; in my mind, it was a load of pish.'

I used to think it was a bloody awful job when I served my time, with small scars on my wrists and burned holes in my T-shirts. No way was I going to be a full-time welder.

'I cough even more when I have been working on galvanised steel; they call it galvo poisoning – bloody awful stuff. I get scunnered after working on that, even wearing a mask don't help. Mind, at my age, I don't suppose it matters. You don't see many older men still working in the game; they are either dead or suffering from COPD. If it's not your lungs, it's your bloody eyes that get worse; I needed glasses at thirty by the way.'

'Are you the oldest in your shop still on the tools?'

'Aye, laddie, no many of us left.'

'I don't think I have ever asked you this – how come you came to England, and why here?'

'It was way back in the Sixties. I had served my time and saw the light. I was fed up with all the union strife in the yards. It was pure pish, man! Forever out the gate. I decided to follow the work about on the sites, worked in the Liverpool area – that was as bad as back hame – then on Saltend once, and yon side of the river in Immingham. Met the wife, and never left.'

'You liked travelling from job to job?'

'Aye, the money was good – had a great time, like sailors, a girl in every port, but it was time to settle down, I suppose. I never thought it would happen, but I have never regretted meeting wee Mary. Anyway, my turn, son – what are you having? Fancy a wee swally – whisky is it?'

'No thanks, Mac, just a bitter will do, thanks all the same.'

He went off to the bar coughing up that mucus again. This time he spat it into his handkerchief, making sure no one could see him. He needed to see a doctor.

*

A few weeks had passed; I had been away working out of town. We had some problems on one of the sites so I had gone down road for a few pints in Rayners.

I was sitting yarning with Jimmy Young, an old workmate of Big Mac's, and he told me that he had heard Mac had gone into hospital with his chest; it seems he had started coughing up blood.

'When did you find that out, Jimmy?'

'I have been away for two months on a job in Germany, only got home yesterday. It was before I went away, and as it's August bank holiday, I don't go back until Tuesday. I will find out more then. Our lass told us he had been at work, but that was not unusual. He hated losing money, always used to say, "No good being off work when you feel crap – might as well get paid for it."'

'How old is Mac, do you know?'

'Not sure – must be the late fifties, maybe early sixties.'

'Bloody hell. Thought he was older than that.'

'Yes, that's what you get burning rods all fucking day. No way would I do it; you don't see many old welders, that is for sure.'

We had just finished talking about him when Gwen, one of the barmaids, came on shift.

'Hey Gwen, have you heard how Big Mac is? You live near him, don't you?'

'Hiya, Jimmy – yes I do; he has been in hospital again, for a few days, but I believe he is home now. Haven't seen Mary to talk to but Enid, her next-door neighbour, was in the snug only yesterday for her weekly cream stout ration; she told me he was home.'

I thought I would go and see him see how he was.

'Gwen, have you got his address and phone number? How old is he? Do you know? We were just wondering.'

'Yes, he is fifty, I think, same as my old man, born 1945. Here are their address and telephone number.'

She handed me a note. Fuck me, only a year older than me? Jesus!

'Thank you, Gwen; much appreciated.'

I went home at around three and called their number.

'Hello, Mary here; who is calling, please?'

'Hi, Mary, it's Leif, and a friend of Mac's. I did not know his real name. 'How is he? I have been away and just heard he was unwell. I thought I would give you a call.'

'Oh, that is so kind of you, Leif; he will be chuffed when I tell him you rang. He is not too bad considering he has to take it easy for a bit.'

'Mary, can he have visitors? I wouldn't mind coming to see him – that's if it's OK, of course?'

'Oh, yes, that would be lovely; any idea when you want to come round?'

'Whatever suits you. I'm not working for a couple of weeks; what about Monday, or are you busy with it being bank holiday?'

'That would be fine. I have to go to see my aunt – she is in a care home in Hessle. I usually go every Monday and Friday, if you can be here for about eleven. That will fit in well. I get the ten past bus outside Rayners. Is that OK?'

'Great – look forward to meeting you, Mary; heard a lot about you from Mac.'

'Now that sounds a bit dodgy, knowing the big man.' She laughed as she said it. 'Hope it was only my good points?'

'Oh yes. See you on Monday, then?'

I found the house down Cholmley Street, off Boulevard across the road from Reuben's barbers shop. I rang the doorbell; no answer. I rang it again, and then it opened.

'Hiya, you must be Leif – thank you so much for coming. Mac is in the middle room. We have put a single bed in there for him; he's finding it hard to climb the stairs.'

Mary was not quite what I expected; she was a lot younger than I imagined – mid-forties maybe? Short, slim, not a lot of make-up, blonde ponytail – she was lovely.

I followed Mary into the room, not knowing what to expect. What met me was not how I knew Mac; he had a yellow look to his skin and lost a lot of weight since I saw him last. He had his eyes closed, but he opened them for a second; they were yellow as well, a jaundiced look, I think, is the correct term.

Mary looked at me and knew by my expression that I was shocked. She smiled and touched my arm.

'Mac, wake up, love – see who is here to see you; it's Leif. Come on, love, wake up.'

Mac opened his eyes and looked straight at me. 'Well, now then, big man, how are ya, son? Thank you for coming.'

'No problem – heard you were a bit under the weather. Thought I would call round.'

Mac lifted his hand for me to shake; what used to be a big, firm grip was now like shaking hands with a skeleton.

'Don't look so shocked, son, it's OK; I have the big C, so don't even ask. I have accepted it; Mary is struggling a wee bit, but that's only natural – we will get through it.' He had a look on his face which meant that we both knew it was a lie.

I was speechless; it was the first time I had been in this situation and did not know what next to say. There was a silence. I looked behind me, and there was a blue budgie in a cage, looking at a mirror, talking to itself in a Glaswegian accent. 'Fuck 'em, Wee Mac! Fuck 'em, Wee Mac!'

'Aye – took me a long time to teach Wee Mac that, but it was well worth it. People think budgies are wee dafties; just goes to prove. Anyway, I am going to be the first one in the family to die of the fucking disease; a family of big strong men, all shipbuilders going back a hundred years or more, and it has to be me.'

I kept the conversation going on the same lines. 'So what did your father do for a quid?'

'He was a riveter. As I say all my relations are, going back as far as the mid-1800s. I'm not sure about before then, but my great-grandfather Andrew was a shipwright in the new yard at Fairfield Farm.'

He looked relaxed; he was enjoying talking about his forefathers. I could see the pride on his face.

Mac went on. The first ship to be built in the new yard was the Macgregor; other fifty-nine ships followed in the next sixty-five years.

'Tell me more, Mac. By the way, what is your full name? Everyone just relates to you as Mac. What is it?'

'Michael Mackintosh – named after my grandfather who was born in 1877. He worked in the yards, and he did very well; finished up with a great job, by the way.'

'Why, what was his trade?'

'He was a millwright, but he got a stoater of a job. Has ye ever heard of the Fairfield Titan?'

'No, what is that?'

'Ye never heard of the great Titan? The biggest crane in the world at the time it was built in 1911. It could lift two hundred tons. Well, he got the job of driving that for a wee while. One of his stories was how he worked on the HMS New Zealand in 1912. I bet ye didnae know that ship was a gift to the UK from New Zealand?'

I was loving hearing about his ancestors; it was great hearing about the past.

'Go on, Michael, tell me more.'

'Away with ya, stop taking the piss, or I'll no say any more.'

'Sorry, Mac, tell me more about your family; what was your mother's name? Have you any brothers or sisters?'

'I had two sisters, Elizabeth and Mary, named after my mother, but they were older than me. I was born in 1945; they were born in 1940 and 1941.'

'Are they still alive? Do they still live in Glasgow?'

'Naw, they have both gone. Mary emigrated to New Zealand and died, must be ten years, I suppose. Lizzy died – young emphysema, think it was. I was still at school; Mum ne'er got over it.'

'I remember you telling me you left the yards after getting pissed off with the unions and strikes; what was that all about ?'

'Oh, that, aye – they had had a fortune pumped into the place over the years. One was called the Fairfield Experiment, supposed to bring in new ideas on improving productivity and industrial relations; now there's a good fucking name for ye – industrial relations, I knew what would happen and got out.'

I could see Mac was getting tired, and it was time that I left, but I had told Mary I would stay until she got back.

We nattered on about things in general, and Mac then closed his eyes as if he was thinking. He said, 'It never got any better; it was re-named again in 1977 to Govan Shipbuilders. I havnae been back, still got relations cousins and that, but we were no a close family.'

He nodded off; I did not disturb him, just sat by the bed. He looked so peaceful. It was funny; Mac had hardly coughed, not like he used to.

I heard the front door open; it was Mary back.

'Hiya – has he been OK, Leif? Ah look, he's asleep; that's all he seems to do nowadays.'

'Mary, Mac has told me what is wrong, but I see he isn't coughing as much. Well, not like he used to, last time I met him in Rayners.'

'No, Leif, the cancer has spread. It's in his liver now; that's why he is jaundiced; his liver has packed in.'

I did not know what to say. I just sat looking at Mary; I felt so useless.

'You don't have to say anything, Leif. He hasn't got long; the specialist told me it was more months than years, he said if Mac had gone to see his doctor a long time before and had X-rays, they may well have been able to have treated him, but he kept it a secret. Well, not so much a secret. He just kept saying it was a welder's cough, just part of the job.'

'So sorry, Mary, I had better get going. I will give you a ring next week and come and see Mac again, is that OK?'

'Yes, thank you, Leif. Our son Andrew is in Sydney. He emigrated five years ago. I haven't told him yet. They didn't get on; that's why he left home and then went to Australia.'

'I did not know you had any children. Mac has never mentioned your son; I think you should tell him, Mary – after all, blood is thicker than water, and Mac is his father after all.'

Mary looked at me with tears in her eyes, shaking her head. 'No, he isn't,' she whispered. Mac knows it, that's why they never got on. Mac could never accept that I had been unfaithful. I was lonely, Mac was working away, and I was out with my girlfriends and met this old flame in Ferryboat in Hessle – but anyway, that's another story. I have never told anyone before; you must be a good listener. You are so kind, Leif.'

I put my arms around her; she laid her head in my chest, tears flowed, and I felt so sorry for her. 'OK, Mary, I'm so sorry.'

She looked up at me, took a big breath, sighed, and nodded.

'Thanks for coming, Leif; once again, I appreciate you being here.'

Wow, that was a way to finish a conversation. I left, promising Mary I would ring her.

*

Then on Tuesday morning of the following week, the phone rang.

'Hiya, Leif, it's Mary – Mary Mackintosh, sorry to bother you.'

'That's OK, it's me who should be apologising. I promised to ring you and was going to today. How's the big man? Is he OK?'

There was a silence coming back to me down the line. 'I'm sorry, Leif – Mac passed away in his sleep on Sunday night.' Her voice was croaky. I was about to answer when the phone went dead.

The following day I rang Mary, just had to see her make sure she was OK. I felt for her after what she had told me. Mac had not been the husband everyone thought he was after he found out about their son Andrew.

OK, Mary was out of order, if that's the correct terminology, being unfaithful – it's not so much the doing; it's getting found out, and let's be honest, it was a one-off. Mary didn't impress me as being someone who would play away, but you just never know. As she said, he was away, she was lonely; ex-boyfriend, right time – it doesn't take much. I'd had my share of married women in the same situation; who was I to criticise?

'Hi, Mary, it's me, Leif; I just thought I would give you a call, see how you are doing. Have you anyone to be with you, relations or anyone?'

'Oh, hiya, Leif, thanks so much for calling. Yes, I'm sorted, thanks. Mum has been round; she has been good, considering. Things are going OK – the undertaker is coming this morning about the funeral, so once that's sorted I have to take the death certificate into the registry office; I think I have to do that before the body can be released, or something like that. I'm hoping the undertaker will give me more information; I have never had to do anything like this.'

It went quiet, then I heard her sobbing.

'Mary, can I come round and maybe sit with you a while for a bit of company? But only if you want me to, that is?'

'Oh, that would be lovely.' She sniffled again. 'Yes, please come round. Be nice to see you again.'

I had a quick shower and went round to their place.

'Hiya, Leif, please come in – so nice of you to think about me.'

I hugged her and kissed her on the cheek. 'You sure you are OK? Anything I can do for you, just ask. What time is the undertaker coming, do you know? Would you like me to stay when they arrive, to be with you? I don't mind.'

'Would you? That would be wonderful. Mum can't come today; she goes to bingo this afternoon, and no way will she miss that.'

Fucking bingo – her son-in-law had just snuffed it, and she couldn't miss a session to be with her daughter. What sort of mother was she?

'I know what you are thinking, but we have never been close. When I was a young girl, Mum disowned me; we did not get on. I know it sounds sad, a mother and daughter not getting on. Still, I was always a bit wild when I was younger, always out at parties, and a few boyfriends – more than I care to remember. I always had a thing for older boys. Mum and Dad did not approve; I left home when I was twenty-one, and had a decent job – that is one thing they did approve of, the fact I had a good education and finished up with a good job in Yorkshire Bank. Then I met Mac; this really pissed them off because of the age difference, he was more than twelve years older than me, but that was after I had bought my place.'

'Wow, so you bought your own place, then?'

'Yes, this house. I did not want to leave the area, as Mum and Dad live at the top end of Kings Bench Street, and these houses, although old, are very well built. This one came on the market, and at a good price. It was empty as the previous owners had both passed away; they had no children, and it was left to the estate, so I got it at the right price.'

Mary had changed; she was talking as if nothing had happened – the crying had stopped and, although her eyes were still red, a different woman was sitting in front of me.

There was a knock on the door.

'That must be the undertakers.'

Mary went to open the door. I heard a voice; it was soft, gentle, more of a whisper yet, loud enough for me to hear. 'Good morning, Mrs Mackintosh, I'm Henry from Appleyards; we have an appointment. So sorry for your loss; may I come in?'

'Yes, of course, so kind of you to come – please, this way.' They came into the front room and Mary introduced me. 'This is Leif, a friend of my husband's; he has just called round – it's OK to talk.'

'Hello, Leif, pleased to meet you. Shall we press on, then? I will be as fast as I can. You realise why I have come this morning; we have quite a lot to discuss; I have one or two forms that need completing, nothing too hard. I fill in most of the details and just need a bit of information; is that OK?'

'Yes, no problem, Mr Appleyard. I am ready; please continue.'

'Please call me Henry – it's much nicer if it's less formal. Now, we offer a package, which can cost whatever you want to pay from a few hundred to thousands. That is entirely your choice; we do not try to influence you in any way. First of all, how many cars do you think you will need – extra to the hearse, of course?'

'Oh, only one; there is only my parents and me. My son is not coming. Yes, one will do.'

'What about flowers? Here is a brochure of what we can supply; it is entirely up to you.'

'Oh, I don't know – what do you think, Leif? This one? I think just one on top of the coffin. He wasn't a flower man, never bought me a bunch in his life, Yes – just this one.'

'What about a casket? Would you like to pick one out of the catalogue, or would you like to come down to the parlour and choose one? There are photographs in there after the flowers.'

I was amazed. I had never been involved with this ritual; Mum was still alive, and I was only young when my old man died.

'Can I ask one thing, Henry? Do you pay VAT on funerals?'

Only on certain items, Leif, but in general, our bill and the burial or cremation cost will be VAT-exempt. However, the following fees are not exempt, and VAT will need to be added on these items at a rate of twenty per cent: they are the flowers, wreaths, announcement cards, headstones, plaques and other commemorative items. The coffin or, in your case, the urn is included in your costs. Any advertisements or articles put in the obituary column of the *Mail*. The cost of the wake if we organise it and finally the hearse and car hire, the cost of the drivers, are included in the funeral package. Do you want any order of service sheets printed, possibly with a photograph of Mac on the front?'

'No, thank you, it won't be necessary.'

'Well, that is about it, Mrs Mackintosh. You will go to the doctor's and collect the death certificate. We believe a post-mortem is not required as your husband had been ill. You will need a few copies – the registrar will provide them, at a cost, of course; we will need one. Have you any insurances, etc.? You will need one for each of them, one for your bank and any other mortgage, that sort of thing.'

'Yes, I know; I work in a bank. Thank you so much for coming. I will drop the certificate off when I get it; no problem.'

'Then I will be off; once we get the relevant documents, we will book the crematorium, etc.. It should take about a week from getting a certificate.'

'OK. I will see you out.'

'No, don't bother; it's fine; goodbye, then.'

'Well, that did not take long, did it? Fancy a cuppa or a beer, or maybe something stronger? Mac loved his single malts. Fancy a dram?'

'No, thanks, Mary – bit early for me. Tea will be fine; white, one sugar, please. You get sat down. I will make it; stuff shouldn't be hard to find. What do you want?'

'I'm having a dram; you're not going to let me drink alone, are you, Leif?'

'OK, just the one, then. Any ice in the fridge? I can't drink whisky without ice.'

'You don't put ice in single malt; that's sacrilege. Didn't Mac teach you anything? Maybe a dash of water, but never ice – my god.'

Mary disappeared into the kitchen and came back with two drams, a lot bigger than I would usually pour, on a tray with a small jug of water.

'Here you go. Well, let's drink a toast to Mac. RIP, big man – love you.'

We clinked glasses and took a sip of the spirit. It had a beautiful, mellow taste, not harsh like some I had tasted.

'Mmm, very nice, Mary. I don't usually drink spirits' – which was a white lie – 'but this is, as Mac would say, stoater, a great drop.'

Mary was relaxed now; we chatted for a good couple of hours about how she would manage now Mac had gone; I had not realised she was still working at the bank. She had gone back after her son had grown up and gone away. I drank more whisky than I should have, driving and all, but we were having a session.

We both must have fallen asleep, what with the drink and the situation. I woke up on the sofa. I don't remember even moving there, but Mary was asleep next to me, leaning on my shoulder.

I looked down at her; she was fast asleep. I tried to move her, and decided to carry her to bed, but then thought better of it.

I managed to hold her as I slid out from beside her. She muttered something about leaving me. I lay her down, putting some cushions under her head. She was now lying full stretch on the three-seater; as I was taking off her shoes, her skirt moved up her legs, revealing hold-up stockings. I had just taken the second shoe off when she woke up.

'What you doing?' she slurred. 'What you doing, Leif? Please don't go. I don't want to be alone; I'm sick of being alone. Please stay, please, Leif, don't leave me.'

'Mary, I must go. Come on, go to bed; you will feel better later. Isn't your mum coming back today, after bingo?'

'No, she is coming tomorrow, I fink.' Her words were jumbled; she was pissed, no doubt.

'Come on, I will make sure you are OK. Let's get you to bed.'

'Sounds good to me, the best offer I have had for years,' she laughed. 'Been a long time since a man took me to bed.'

I bent down and lifted her on her feet; she was limp and could hardly stand. She hung on to me, and I half-lifted her to the top landing.

I lay her on the bed; she was gone again. There was no nightie around in the bedroom; I assumed she slept in either a T-shirt and knickers or in the nude. No way was I going to strip her. I had only just met her – not even I would stoop that low. I decided to leave her in her bra and pants, but took off her stockings. She was fit, no doubt about that; her clothes did not show off such a beautiful body, especially for her age.

'No, Leif,' I told myself. 'Not even you could take advantage of a woman in this state, and a new widow at that; get a grip. What about Connie?'

I left her as I covered her up. She rolled over and said, 'Love you – night-night.'

I dropped the latch as I went out. I left my car; no way I was driving. I walked up Coltman Street and got a cab home.

Approaching Rayners, I decided I needed another drink, so I told the driver to pull over. I went into the bar and who was standing there, but Jimmy.

'Jesus, you look rough, Leif. Where the hell have you been?'

'Don't even ask – what a fucking day. You know Big Mac died, don't you?'

'Yes, they told everyone at work. Weird isn't it, as we were only talking about him want we the other day. Fuck me gently. You just never know.'

'Yes – I have been to see Mary; she is doing OK. It quite surprised me. Mind, I don't know her that well, but she seems very strong-willed.'

'Yes, she is a good-looking sort, that's for sure.'

'We had a few drinks – it just seemed right. I was only going to have a couple, and one thing led to another; it turned into a bit of a session. I fell asleep on the sofa, and had to put her to bed. And yes, you are right, she's a very good-looking woman under all those baggy clothes.'

'You put her to bed? You dirty bastard. How fucking low can you get? You would get under a snake's belly with a top hat on. Mac's not even cold yet, and you're trying to get into his missus's knickers – and what about your lass? If Connie were to find out, she would have your bollocks for breakfast.'

'Fuck off, Jimmy, nothing happened. I just took her clothes and left her in her underwear; she doesn't wear a nightie or anything.'

'How do you know she doesn't wear a nightie? You mean she sleeps naked?'

'I don't know; I couldn't see one in the bedroom, that's all. Fucking hell, what's this? The Spanish inquisition? Nothing happened – what do you take me for?'

'OK, OK! What you drinking? Mind, you look as if you have had enough. A pint?

'Yes, please. I needed a beer; too much whisky. One, and I'm off home.'

*

The phone ringing woke me up. 'Hiya, Leif, it's Mary; I am so sorry about yesterday. What happened? How did I get in bed, and who undressed me?'

'I will call round later. You OK, no hangover? I will explain when I get there, OK?'

'Oh, OK, what time will it be?'

'About ten-thirty, is that OK? I'm having some breakfast and a shower before I leave the house. I feel like shit.'

'OK, see you then. I need the same. Bye for now.'

She sounded OK in herself – quite bright, to be honest, considering we had consumed over half a bottle of Isle of Jura twelve-year-old single malt between us.

I arrived at the house about 10.45am, and checked my car out. It was still locked with no damage, which was quite pleasing.

I was about to knock on the door, and it opened. Mary was standing there in full make-up, and dressed to kill – with a low-cut blouse and tight jeans, she looked stunning.

'Wow, you look great; you sure it's the same woman I left yesterday?'

'Yes, this is me, same old Mary; just made an effort, that's all. Anyway, come in – don't stand there on the doorstep, people might talk, with me a widow, and my husband not even cold yet.'

'Yes, you are right.' I stepped inside. She hugged me, a little bit longer than you might expect, and kissed me on the cheek.

'So, Leif, what happened last night? What did we do that we shouldn't have done? How did I finish up in my bra and panties? Good job they were clean on,' she laughed, taking my hand in hers. 'We didn't, did we? Don't tell me we did... no we can't have. I still had my panties on?'

I could not believe my ears; Mary thought we had made love. How she could even consider that I would have taken advantage of a woman mourning?

'Mary, what do you take me for? OK, yes, I did undress you and put

205

you to bed, but it never entered my mind to do any more. Mac has just died – I hardly know you. How could you think of such a thing?'

'I'm sorry, Leif. Yes, you are right, but it's been so long since I had a man in my bed – any man, not even Mac; we stopped sleeping together years ago. I have been going without male company for that long now I just thought that, last night, well, just maybe I had succumbed. Please forgive me for thinking that way, but as I said, during my younger days, I was a bit what you might call easy; you know I don't have to spell it out, do I?'

'No, you don't.' I pulled her towards me, took her in my arms, and kissed her forehead. 'It's OK, Mary, I understand, but please think about what has just happened; let's just stay friends, shall we? There is no doubt you are a beautiful woman, and yes, under different circumstances, it could well happen, but let's not even think that way. You are Mac's widow, and he was an old friend of mine – let's not tarnish that friendship, OK?'

I got up to go, and we walked down the passageway to the front door. I opened it and stepped through, turning to say goodbye.

'Thank you, Leif, you are right. I'm sorry to have put you in that predicament, but it would have been nice.' She smiled as she closed the door.

A few days passed, and I had not heard anything from Mary. I didn't know if she felt guilty or just did not want to see anyone. Maybe she was now grieving?

I'd read in the paper when the funeral would be taking place. It was at the Chanterlands Avenue crematorium, and there was a decent crowd to see the big guy off. Mary had organised a celebrant as she was not religious in any way. I knew Mac had been brought up a 'proddie', or protestant; he had told me that.

I wondered why it wasn't a religious service. I intended to ask Mary when I got a chance to speak to her at the wake.

We had gone back to Cholmley Club; it was the place, apart from Rayners, that Mac used as a local, as it was only a hundred yards from his house.

As I walked in, Jimmy Young was standing at the bar.

'Good turnout, then, for the big man, Leif. You all right? I'm sorry about doubting you the other day, mate – my apologies.'

'That's OK, no need for apologies. Decent funeral, never been to one with a humanist instead of a minister; it was quite amusing, especially when they swear. Have you seen Mary yet? I did not stop to give my condolences and all that shit as they walked out. I had to be somewhere before I came here.'

'Oh, what? Another bit of fanny in tow, then? You have never changed. You would shag a hair-lipped rat.'

'Fuck off, Jimmy. Oh, there she is – catch you later.'

Mary walked over. She gave me a hug and a light kiss on the cheek. 'Thanks for coming, Leif; it was a lovely service, don't you think? None of that religious stuff, all angels and going to heaven and the like.'

'Hi Mary, how are you, OK? Sorry, I didn't ring you but I thought better of it. By the way, have you been in touch with your son yet, giving him the sad news?'

'Oh yes, I rang him last week; there was no real response. The only thing he said was, "Don't think I am coming home for the funeral – no fucking chance." That was about it, so I never pushed the subject.'

'Was that all he said? Seems odd to me; he must have some feelings for Mac – the hatred can't be that deep, can it?'

'Sorry, Leif, I would rather not discuss the subject, if you don't mind; you don't know what went on, so please, I don't want to be rude…'

I cut her short, as I could see she was getting upset; she was right, it was nothing to do with me.

'OK, sorry, didn't mean to pry anyway. One other thing, Mary, why no church service?'

'Mac told me he didn't want anything to do with any church. Being brought up in Glasgow, he had seen enough trouble between the two religions. He said that where he lived was a very sectarian area; half were Catholic descendants of Irish people who had come over during the great famine in the 1800s.'

'That's much like my descendants who had come over from Norway.'

'The other side of the area were protestants. What did not help was the two top football teams in the city, Celtic and Rangers, were created with religion as the base. Mac was told, or should I say it was accepted, that he had to support the protestant club Rangers.'

'So why the hatred? I could not just be because of religion, surely.'

'No, it all came out when Mac came to Hull and the hatred he that felt coming from both sets of rugby teams in the city. I know he could not understand why it should be when religion was never mentioned – just the hatred of red and white as against black and white. He once told me the full facts on how the clubs had started. I won't bore you with all that, but it turned him away from any form of religion.'

'OK, Mary, I understand. Anyway, it was a good turnout for him; you must be pleased?'

'Yes, I did not expect to see so many people here. There were some I had not seen for years. Oh, I see June, an old schoolmate over there. Will you excuse me?' She stroked my hand as she turned to walk away. 'I will see you before you go. We need to talk, OK?'

I never got the chance to speak to Mary again and was about to leave. I had been yarning with one or two of the lads who went in Rayners and knew Mac well, but it seemed that no one knew him that well to call him a real mate. He was just someone I had known a long time, similar to guys I used to see at the Boulevard. I stood with the same guys for years and never even knew their names. It was that sort of friendship.

But with Mac, we had somehow got closer recently, and then his sudden death hit me hard. I don't know why, it just did.

I had left the concert room and was in the hallway when I felt someone grab my arm.

'You're not leaving without saying goodbye, Leif, are you?'

It was Mary.

'I thought you were tied up talking; you were with your mother and father. I did not want to disturb you.'

'Don't you dare go!' she said with a look in her eyes that said more than she wanted to put into words, not there anyway. I could see she had had a bit too much to drink already.

She took my hand and took a step towards me, looking up at me.

'Mary, this is not the right place or time.'

'Then when is the right time? When can we make it the right time? Leif, I have had a miserable life, and Mac is now gone; he is no longer my husband. I am free. Do you know how much that means to me? I am a widow; he is no longer here to tie me down.'

'Mary, I think I should go before you say something we both might regret. Not here; come on, I must go.'

'Leif, no – that night last week when you held me in your arms, it felt so good. It was the first time for god knows how long that I felt like a woman again – to be held close, to feel the warmth of a man's body... you must understand, I want you.'

I could not believe what I had heard; I was stuck for words.

The front door opened, and someone I had never met before came through.

'What the fuck is going on here, Mum? What the hell are you doing in the arms of another man, and your husband, my fucking father...?

Mary cut him short. 'Oh my god, Andrew, what are you doing here? You were not supposed to be here. When did you arrive? Oh, baby!' Mary let go of me and ran to this stranger and hugged him tightly, kissing him.

'OK, Mum, let go; who is this guy? Who the hell is he? I changed my mind. I decided it was the right thing to do to come back for Dad's funeral. I know we did not get on, and I always argued with him. He did not like me for whatever reason; I always thought it must have been because I took over from him as the number one man in your life; he was pushed into second place. I could not take any more, Mum.'

Mary had regained her composure and sobered up a bit; it must have been the shock.

'Andrew, this is Leif, he is a friend of your dad's. He has helped me get through it since the death of your father. I was thanking him; it was the first time we'd had time to talk today, what with the service and everything. Come on – Grandma and Grandad will be so pleased to see you. They are in the concert room – go on and see them. I won't be a minute; Leif has to go.'

'Hope we meet again, Leif. I'm here for a week. We must have a beer, OK?'

'Yes, great – your mum has my number; give us a bell when you are free, be nice to have a chat.' We shook hands, and Andrew left us.

'Mary, doesn't he know that Mac was not his real father? Hasn't he got a clue? He keeps calling Mac Dad.'

'No, Leif – as I told you, Mac treated him like shit, and Andrew hated him, but I never had the heart to tell him the truth; let's just leave it at that, shall we? I must go now – I have a lot to talk about with Andrew, and I meant what I said. I want you; I think I am in love with you. I will leave you with that thought. Goodbye.'

She had to be joking; she knew damn well I was married. How did I get myself in some of these situations? But there again, she was a stunning-looking woman; maybe another time?

CHAPTER 32

LEIF

Big Day Getting Closer

We were looking forward to the wedding – it could not come quickly enough. Mum was doing OK. She did not say a lot,; she was not letting on what was going on with her. I had got her in a private hospital, and they were doing all they could with chemo and radiation treatment; we just had to hope for the best. The last thing we heard, they were happy with the way she was going.

The big day was getting closer. This fucking wedding was the only thing that was on anyone's lips; we could not hold a conversation without the subject coming up. Even at work it was, 'Are you ready for the big day? You must be happy for your mother? And who is this girl that is friends with your mother? Where is she from? How does your mother know someone from Australia? She has never been. How the hell did she come up with the idea of a fancy dress wedding?'

Even when I was going to meetings with Rita, she talked about it; you would have thought it was another Royal wedding.

Talking about Rita, things had settled down with Connie. She had accepted that nothing was going on between us. It was a good job; she did not know the truth of how I nearly did try my hand but had decided to stay loyal to her. If I had told her, she would never have believed it – or would she? The fact that Rita had led me up the garden path – was that just a lie from Rita, or would she have gone to bed with me? One thing was for sure – if I had ever seen her looking the way she did when she came over to our place for the first time, I may have been even more tempted.

Things had gone great with Rita after that night; she seemed a different person, and more relaxed. She became a regular visitor, and ended up great mates with Connie; they had started meeting up for coffee and shopping trips. I was pleased, really, as Connie was not one for going out on her own. She had turned into a bit of a stick in the mud since we had got married – she was worse than me; all work and no play.

I had a phone call from Einar, entirely out of the blue. I was watching TV, and Connie was out.

'How are you, son? Just thought I would give you a call to see how things are going with you. I see your company is doing well; I am pleased for you, son.'

'Einar, you don't ring me up after such a long time without having some other reason. I know you better than that.'

'I should have known better. I have one or two irons in the fire and have been thinking about spreading my wings a bit. Would you be interested in joining me again in one or two ventures? It may take a while to get it up and running what I have in mind, and it is somewhat different in some ways from our previous experience, although that would come into it.'

'OK – give me a shout when you know more. I am OK at the minute but wouldn't mind getting away now and again, if you know what I mean?'

'Excellent. Take care, son. I will be in touch, and will text you if I need more information from you.'

CHAPTER 33

LARS

Back in the Old Dart – Manchester, March 1995

We arrived at Manchester Airport on the Saturday before the wedding, and stayed in York for a couple of nights before going through to Hull.

Mum had arranged everything; there was nothing she had missed out on. All this and being very ill must have taken its toll on her. We had spoken many times on the phone during the previous weeks; it had been very hard keeping the secret away from Leif, but he had not got a clue. He had believed every word Mum had told him.

Since our last conversation, she had contacted the church. The vicar had got back to her and confirmed the dates, and he was more than happy to perform a double wedding. The reception was booked at the Lantern.

We arrived at the church early, and they let us go to a side room out of the way to get into our costumes; Mum did not have to guess my size, but why had she picked Batman for me? I suppose it was a good idea – the padded costume hid my build, and in the hood and mask you could not tell who I was. Then Mum and Billy arrived.

'Oh, Lars – it's so wonderful to see you again.' Mum hugged me and kissed Maya on the cheek; Billy shook hands with us.

'Hi, Billy, ready for it, mate? Been a long time in coming, what do you reckon?'

'I thought it would never come now I am sixty-eight. Who would have thought it? Still, if it keeps Christine happy... but fucking Friar Tuck, why this outfit?'

'Oh, stop moaning, Billy. We should have done this years and years ago, not just because one of us is due to drop off the bloody perch.' She turned and smiled at me. 'Never dreamt I would see my other boy again, never mind share the same wedding cake, hey, Lars?'

I just smiled. I could not believe it either. Mum and Maya had a lot in common; both had waited a bloody long time for their happy event, the one girls dream about.

'Right – here is the plan, Maya; we must go in and put our outfits on. I am a fairy, and you are Maid Marion.'

'Who is she, Christine?'

'Robin Hood's bird, you don't know? Oh, no matter, just put the outfit on. Then you and I will be standing at the front with Leif. Lars, you will be outside with Billy and Connie's son Martin – he is Leif's stepson. He will be dressed as Robin, and will be acting as if he is giving you away. I know this is not the usual way. Still, it is the only way it will work. I know it is usually the brides who walk down the aisle but, fuck it, we are doing it my way this time. OK, I know it is a bit of a shambles, but that is how we have planned it. Leif thinks he is giving Maya and me away.'

'What costume will he be wearing?'

'Robin Hood – it was the only other one in your sizes. He won't say anything; he will just stand there until you two walk up and join us. I have told him that we don't look behind us under any circumstances, that it is bad luck. It's an old fishermen's wives tale – a load of bullshit, but he will believe it if I tell him. He believes owt I tell him. He then just sits down. Hopefully, he won't realise Lars is the other groom. Lars, you try not to make eye contact with him, OK? Be kind of looking away from him – but under the mask, he won't be able to tell.'

CHAPTER 35

LARS

First Meet

'Yes, I did know I had a brother – but had no idea where you were. I was told you died at birth, and later that you had been taken away from Mum. I had no idea where you had disappeared to. Forgive me, Lars, if I seem a bit odd, but this is all new to me; as you can imagine, being brought up as an only child, things have always been about me. Christine is my Mum, and not to be shared with anyone else. I feel that you are an intruder; I still can't believe that you exist. Mum is over the moon about it, but me... well, I am fucking jealous. Sorry, mate, but that is how I feel.'

'Hang on, I will get us another drink; what's yours?'

'I think I will have a scotch, please; I think I am going to need one.'

'Here you go. My favourite – Lagavulin, the finest classic malt ever brewed. Well, I think so anyway. Right, where do I begin? Oh, just a minute, here's Martin. He has his own place now; I don't see that much of him. Hang on – Martin, come in and meet Lars and Maya officially.'

'Hello,' said Martin. 'Sorry I missed you after the wedding. I had to go and see someone; she was going home on the ferry, and I just had to go. So sorry.'

They shook hands and hugged. It was the first time they'd been able to meet, what with all the fuss of the wedding and all.

'Great to meet you, son; this is Maya, my new wife.' Lars smiled, having realised it must have been the first time he had introduced Maya as his wife. 'Maya, this is your nephew, Martin – Connie's son. Whoops – Leif's son.'

'Hello, Martin. My, you look like your mum. So pleased to meet you after all this time; wonderful to have you as our nephew.' Maya kissed Martin on his cheek.

'Yes, thank you; great to meet you both. Welcome to our family – I never, ever thought I would have an uncle and aunt in Australia. But, sorry – I have something I need to do; you will have to excuse me. Sorry about this, I'll catch you later.' He smiled and disappeared upstairs.

'Like I said, we don't see much of him now he has his own flat. He needed to get away from his mother's breast, needed to be set free. It broke her heart when he left home. But it turned out great. Martin works for us and he's doing really well. We're hoping he takes over the company for us one day; mind, that's a long way down the track. Where was I? Oh, yes – telling you the story about our father.'

'Leif, I deserve to know the truth. I was brought up in Australia by two people who I thought were my parents, only to be told later that they had actually bought me like some fucking pet dog. I know I am the son of my fucking grandad – Mum told me when we first met. You are taking the piss, mate – I deserve the truth.'

'Lars, it is not that simple – things happened that should not have happened… an accident at home that went wrong, It is a long story, mate; I do not like to talk about him. Some things are best left in the past. I am sorry, Lars, but that is the way it has to be.'

'OK, I can live with that. I won't push the subject, so let's just leave it at that. I am just so glad we have now got together, for now, but I hope you will tell me the truth, for surely it is my right to know?'

'Yes, I suppose you are right. Maybe later – but like you, Lars, I am the same. I cannot believe I have at last met my long-lost brother; it feels surreal just sitting talking to you, yet looking at myself – unbelievable. It seems unreal that I lived in Australia and yet never knew you existed.'

'Yes, that is when I found out I had a brother. I had been up to see Mum and Dad in Maitland, and they had a shitty on because they thought I had been up and not visited them; got a right razoo off them. When they eventually told me the truth, I did some enquiries and even hired a private detective. I found out about you working in Perth, and went over to find out anything I could on the bits of information I had been given. I visited Mel in Byron Bay. She had named one of her children after you.'

'I don't think it was mine, Lars. I am confident he is not mine, but I am humbled that she had thought of me when naming him.'

'Mel was besotted with you, mate; I do believe you meant everything to her. She was sorry she had turned you away when you came back from overseas. She felt it was her fault, and she had a guilt thing about her nan, which she regretted all her life.'

I was in tears as he told me. Lars put his arm around me and hugged me, like brothers do. I now had a complete family. I could not explain how I felt at that moment in time. My opinion had suddenly changed, from not wanting him in the family. He was right; he had a right to know everything.

'Just going back to the Perth trip, I found out about Donna and the tragic events up to her death. That was so sad; you must have been gutted, mate. I felt for you when Doug Perry told me about it.'

'You met Doug? How the fuck did you get on to him? Was it the private dick who found him?'

'Yes, he was good. Cost me a bloody fortune, mind, but he got some good leads. I found out I had been taken from Christine as a baby, and my parents were from Manchester.'

'I never knew you had emigrated.'

'Yes, we moved to Sydney. My father was in the banking game and he was moved around NSW. I hated it, and I always said I would leave home once I got the chance. I started playing rugby league as a boy and was luckily good enough for St George to pick me up.'

'Must have been a decent player, mate, to be good enough to sign for St George. Did you make the first team at all?'

With that, Martin came back in. 'Sorry, got what I needed. How long are you staying with Mum and Dad? When are you going back to Australia? I would like to invite you to my place for a meal – not them two, just you, they are always slipping in and out. Be nice for you to get away from them for a few hours, that right, Dad?'

'Oh, charming. When did you last have us round for a meal? Bloody few weeks, I know that?'

Connie walked in.

'Did you hear that? Martin has just asked Lars and Maya to his gaff for a meal.'

'Oh, that's nice; what night, Martin?'

'Not us, Connie, we haven't been invited. Fuck us; we have to feed ourselves.'

'Oh, that's an excellent idea; they will be sick of the sight of us. Well done, Martin. What a lovely idea.'

'OK, great, Martin – will look forward to it. It'll have to be when we come back from Europe, as we have to go there for a couple of days, so we'll catch up with you then?'

'Yes, fine. I have to go now; lovely meeting you both. See you when you get back.'

'He is a great kid, Leif; you must be so proud of the way he has become a confident young man.'

'Yes, we would never have thought it from the first time I met him, only seven years ago; bloody hell, they grow up so quickly. Anyway, we were talking about you and St George.'

'Yes – I wasn't a regular; they had some great players down there, one of the strongest teams in the comp. I played quite a few; that is how I met Maya – her father supported the Dragons. I was working as a bricklayer at the time we met, and that was it. Been partners ever since and built a fantastic business up with her. We have done OK in life; I believe you have been quite successful in your working life as well, that right?'

I remembered all that shit Mum had come out with about pen-pals. I needed to have a word with her about lying to her son.

'Yes, I have done OK – made few quid here and there. I've been in the oil game most of my life, and made the right contacts, been in the right place at the right time; you know how life pans out for some – just a lucky bastard, I suppose. You could call me a very, very rich man, but that is another story.'

'Please tell me about it, Leif; after all, we are brothers. I want to know everything about you, as I assume you do me. Or am I asking too much from you so early? We are only here a few days, and I would love to go back to Australia knowing as much as I can about you. Is that too much to ask?'

'I suppose you are right, but if I tell you, it is between you and me and the door over there, for no one knows about it – only two other people, Connie and the guy who helped me along the way. The thing I am about to tell you, I must ask you swear that you will never, ever tell anyone, other than Maya, and I would you rather you not say anything to her either, but if you do, she must be sworn to secrecy too. Do you swear, Lars? I must know.'

'Of course. Who would I tell that knows you, or knows of you, for that matter?'

'That is beside the point; it is a small world out there. Loose lips sink ships, OK?'

'Yep, you're right; I swear.'

'Right. A few years ago I met a couple when I was on a week's holiday down on England's south coast. They were Americans on vacation. They had hired a boat in Holland and taken it to the Isle of Wight. To cut the story short, they asked me to join them on their trip around the island. The only requirement was that we were naked when at sea. The only time we wore clothes was when we were in port, or there were other ships or boats where we could be seen.'

'Fair dinkum, mate – you're taking the piss, truly?'

'Yes, honestly. Anyway, I went along with it – why wouldn't I? I always fancied a bit of that nudist scene; it's great, mate, you should try it. It turned out that the old guy could not rise to the occasion, but the old girl loved the old sausage, as long as she could call his name when she reached Wigan.'

'Wigan, why Wigan?'

'That is another story; anyway, I finished up shagging her for over a week. It was a real adventure, I can tell you; I could write a fucking book about my life. Anyway, we have kept good friends over the years;

he has been my guardian angel many a time, and during the last twelve years or so, we have both made quite a few quid, god bless him.'

'Jesus, mate, what a story. I want to hear more of this; unfortunately, we have to go over to Switzerland to visit a crane manufacturer. We need more plant. I find it is far easier to negotiate with them face to face at their head office, not their branch in Hamburg, but we can't afford what we want. We will have to go to the bank and do not want to go into debt. We are ordering two new cranes, a 50-ton and a new 75. We want three, but I feel they may be out of our price range. Just have to wait. They are built to order, so we will have to see what they have to offer. We'll be back in a couple of days, OK?'

CHAPTER 36

LARS

Back from Switzerland

After our return from Switzerland we were sitting in Leif's lounge talking about our trip, telling Leif how they had a brand-new 100-ton that had been ordered. It seems the company who had placed the order had backed out, so losing their deposit; it was offered at a discount price if we wanted it, and they were prepared to ship it to Australia free as it was already booked to go on a ship next month to New Zealand.

Leif looked at me, pondered a bit, then said, 'I will lend you the money for it, but I want to be a partner in your company. You can have the money interest-free, paid back monthly. Alternatively, if you like, I want 33 per cent of every hire charge you get back from each project it works on, or a mixture of both. We can trust each other – I do not need a legal document, apart from one stating I am a director of your company. It's up to you. How much money do you need?'

I was struck dumb. 'Can Maya and I discuss it in private, Leif? It has come as a shock.' I looked at Maya.

'Yes, we appreciate what you are saying, Leif,' she said, 'but I would like to discuss it with Lars before we make a decision. We have another partner in our crane company and we would need to speak to him before we agree. It sounds good to me, but I have my business head on right now and need our other man's input. Is that OK?'

'No problem – take your time. Just let me know. I don't think I am on to a loser or I would not offer it, brother or not. It seems to me you have built up a thriving company and, having lived and worked in Australia, I know that it will continue to thrive. I want to be part of it – just ring your man and let me know tomorrow. What do you need? A million, or two? It's there.'

We were sitting in the living room alone. Leif had gone in to work, and Connie had gone to see some friends.

'What do you think about that? We need to get in touch with Bruce to see what his opinion is. We can't do anything without asking him. After all, he is in with us even though he doesn't do much now, with him being well into his eighties; he may not even knock the idea.'

'I don't know. I will go along with it, but Bruce has always been the cautious one. He has left us alone for quite a few years now, just taking his yearly salary out. I know he has never had an increase in the twenty-two years we have been together, which has always worried me, but yes – we must confide in him without a doubt. OK, what time is it now? It's 1.30pm here, so it will be late on back home; let's give him a ring. We will use their phone – Leif can afford it.

'Oh, hi – g'day Bruce, how are you, mate? Sorry to bother you so late on. Yes, thank you – we got wed a few days ago. It went well, and I met my long lost brother at last. Anyway, listen, Bruce – I've got something I wanna throw past you. No – I don't want any more money out of you. Listen, mate, talking about my brother, Leif – yes, that's his name – just listen. He has a few quid and wants to make an interest-free loan to the company to enable us to buy a 100-ton mobile crane on offer at an excellent price. In return, we can pay him back either monthly or whatever as a set figure, or he would take 33 per cent of the money we get back from hiring charges. Yes, until the loan is paid off. He has up to two million dollars… yes – that's what we thought. Jump at it – you sure? OK, mate, you don't want to think about it? OK, understand – we will go ahead, then. No he doesn't want any guarantee. I'm his brother, for fuck's sake. OK, cheers, mate – I will let you get back to bed; catch up when we get home.

'Well, you heard what he said – we should go for it.'

'When you think about it,' said Maya, 'a $2 million loan, interest-free with no guarantee, is unreal money. We would be fools not to bite his hand off; you could not get that anywhere else. We must tie Leif down to payment terms.'

'Whoa, hang on a second – sounds like we are taking advantage of his generosity. He is only doing us a favour, Maya; don't let's take the piss.'

'Lars, I don't intend to take the piss, as you put it. But we are in business. If we get an offer like this, we must take it. Two million would cover for all the three cranes we have purchased, and surely it makes sense if our bank at home came up with an offer like this. What would you do? Be honest now, mate. Even if we don't need that money, think of the interest we would get on the balance.'

'Let's discuss it with him when he gets home. He must have given it some more thought; he might even have changed his mind.'

'Hang on, Lars. He's just pulled up; give him time to get his coat off before asking him, OK?'

Leif walked into the living room. 'Hello, you two – or should I say g'day? What have you been up to? Have you given any more thought to my offer? I am genuine, and I think it would help us all. It'd help me lose a bit of money out of my offshore account as well as helping you out.'

'Funny you should say that, Leif; yes we have, and we would like to take up your offer. We need to do some final figures and cast it in stone. Would you want a contract drawing up, to make it legal? What terms do you want us to pay it back? You mentioned two options yesterday?'

'That is where I have been today, to see our legal team; they have looked at an option and come up with a draft of a similar contract we have with another company. Not the same, I will admit, as this one goes through our books, where yours won't; it will go straight into another account. I have one I can get at easier access to. It is in Switzerland. I move my money worldwide from the Cayman Islands, Isle of Man, Bahamas, and Swiss banks. I would want the payment to go into there. All we have to do is determine what is realistic – the maximum amount you can afford to pay on a monthly term, along with what would be the day rate or hourly rate you charge for the 150-ton crane, not including travel from site to site, just the day work for hours on site. You can give it to me in Australian dollars. If you want to send me a day worksheet that you issue with the crane and send it to me weekly, for I assume you hire out your cranes daily – are there many of that size crane in Sydney now, or would you send it elsewhere?'

'It would be predominantly in Sydney, or maybe Newcastle. To be honest, Leif, we have not even looked at the cost of it. We weren't thinking about purchasing one as big. But now you have made the offer, we can't lose on the deal. Can we get back to you on that?'

'OK, no problem; I know we can sort it out. When do you want the transfer of funds to take place? All I need is your bank details, and my bank will transfer them in a few days. Is that a deal?'

He put out his hand; I shook on it – $2 million in our bank account just like that. I rang the following day and got the crane for $US 456,100, a steal at that price. The crane was reserved in the company's name and they would put on our logo and name as part of the cost. I contacted my office in Sydney; they sent an email to our bank, which forwarded the money to their bank, and it was ours. It would be delivered in a month or so from leaving Germany. They would take care of all insurances and customs issues, and we had nothing more to do. Leif was now an LJM Engineering Pty director; once the payments had been made back, he had agreed his partnership would be dissolved. That was his security on his money. He had indicated that if we needed another cash loan at any time, then the same conditions would remain, with the rider that we were both still in the position of him being able to loan the finances and us being able to pay back.

We looked at the figures and decided we could actually pay him back in around four years, and by using his money, we could also buy the other two cranes we had ordered, plus another 100 ton, or leave the money in the bank.

The following day Maya came to me. 'Hey, I have been looking at those figures, and I think it would be better if we could pay Leif back in just over a year. We could afford that if we paid him back the full rental earnings. If we purchased the extra unit and over ten years, we would take in another $55 million just from those four cranes.'

'That is unreal. We just have to buy the other unit.'

I placed the order the following day as we decided it was not worth leaving the money in the bank. We could afford the other two cranes anyway; therefore, the 100 ton was a no-brainer.

'Got it sorted, then? Everything fixed up, mate?' said Leif with a big smile on his face.

'Yes; we paid the deposit of $45,600. We then pay the final balance once the crane arrives in Sydney. All done. I don't know how to thank you enough, Leif. It will certainly make a difference to our fleet. We have our eye on another one, but we will see how we get on with this one first. It's getting experienced all-terrain drivers that's the problem; it's not so much the plant as the operators.'

'You need some more Pommies over there, pal; there must be guys over here who would love to emigrate to the sunshine.'

'We could sponsor drivers – they need to get the right licences to work plant in NSW, but that should not be too much of a problem for experienced guys. We have done some rough calculations, Leif, and we believe that, all being well, we could have to money paid back in around three to four years if we give you some of our 66 per cent of the earnings.'

'Don't worry about that, paying me off; it does not matter. Even in ten years I won't give a fuck, mate – you are my brother. I have more than enough, let's be honest. If I can't help you out, who can I help?'

*

The following night we went to Martin's for an evening meal. His apartment was on a new complex built on an old docklands area called the Victoria Dock Village.

'Hey, this is nice, isn't it? All these new houses are like a subdivision back home, Lars. Imagine what these would cost – a few quid, you reckon?'

'Too right, babe – what's his address again?' Maya showed me the little map Martin had given her. 'There it is, look,' she said, pointing to a five-storey block overlooking the river. 'Number 326, there, look – two spaces.'

One had a red Ford Fiesta Xr2i parked up. 'Bloody hell, bet that little bastard flies,' I said. We pressed the intercom button and Martin buzzed us in.

I just about to knock when the door opened. 'Hello, great to see you both again. Come in, please come in; welcome to my home.'

The flat was a very nice-sized unit with a large living room and French doors on to a small balcony, with a fantastic view of the Humber.

'Lovely place you got here, Martin; how long you had it?'

'Just over a year. Dad loaned me the money to buy it for cash – we got a great deal; it came fully furnished and was the show flat for a while. Anyhow, enough chat – what would you like to drink? Beer or wine? I have red or white – a nice chardonnay, or an Australian merlot. I got it especially for you.' He laughed.

'I'll have a beer, as long as it's cold – not warm like you Poms prefer, please.'

'A chardonnay for me, please,' said Maya.

Martin came back with the drinks. 'Just make yourselves at home; there's not a lot to see but help yourselves. I have a bit to do in the kitchen; won't be too long.'

'Hey, this place is bigger than I thought,' said Maya. 'Look – there are French doors to the bedroom as well. Come on, let's have a look in there.'

'Stop being so nosey, Maya; hey, come on out of there, it's his private domain.'

Too late, she had gone in. 'Jeez, look – you wouldn't think this was a man's unit; look how neat and tidy it is. Everything in its place – unreal!'

'You are right, babe; I wouldn't live like this if I was single again.'

Maya had gone into the bathroom. 'Lars – come in here, quick,' she whispered.

'What's up? What are you doing? He will hear us! Now, come on.'

'No, look – two toothbrushes. He is not alone; someone lives with him. Let's look in the closet to see what she wears?' She slid the door open. 'That's odd – no women's clothes.'

With that, Martin appeared in the doorway.

'Yes, you are right, Maya, no women's clothes – but if you notice, some are a smaller size than mine; they are my friend's. He leaves them here when he stays with me. Anything else you want to know?'

'Sorry, Martin, for being so bloody nosey. We were just looking around; no offence, mate.'

'So you don't know about me then?'

'Yes, I do, Martin; your mother told me the other day about your homosexual tendencies. I knew, but Lars doesn't; I haven't told him yet.'

I stared at Maya. 'Haven't told me what? You mean you are queer, Martin?'

'No, Lars – not queer, as you call it. I'm gay. Yes, I prefer men's company to women's. That's it. I have told you. Does it matter what my sexual orientations are? You have a gay nephew – are you going to disown me? If you are, you may as well go now.' He opened his arms and smiled. Now we realised why he had asked us to come alone for dinner.

'Makes to difference to us, Martin; we have no opinions on the subject. Thank you for being so open with us.' Maya went over and hugged him, kissing his cheek and holding his hands.

'Right then, glad that's sorted. Come on, the food's ready – or, as you say, the tucker. Hope you like mustard with your chicken; bad luck if you don't.'

'That is gorgeous,' said Maya at the dinner table. 'I've never tasted anything like it'

'It is a French recipe. I got it when I used to visit a girlfriend's house over in France. I met her on holiday in 1987. I was almost fifteen, and she was seventeen; we became pen pals, and I saw Juliette a few times over the years. Then I met her older brother, Julian. He was nineteen at the time, and he rekindled my feelings for boys. I had dabbled a bit when I was younger, but didn't know I was gay until I met Julian. Then I knew what gay meant. It totally changed my life, like a new world had opened up for me. But that is another story.'

He looked away as if he was thinking of the French boy, and then continued. 'We were talking about the dish; it has chicken, of course, with leeks, onions, garlic, carrots, and thick chicken stock with three large tablespoons of Dijon mustard – it has to be Dijon. I will write the recipe down for you, Maya, before you go.'

'Thanks, babe, it was gorgeous.'

'I don't want to keep on about it,' I said, 'but I must ask you, Martin, how did Leif take it when you told him you were gay, or does he not know?'

'Oh yes, he knew, and was not happy, but he has accepted it now. I came out a year ago. I think they had guessed, as some of my friends are over-the-top gay, and Leif did not like them visiting his home. I think he was worried people might see them visiting; anyway, he did not like it. That is why they helped me buy this place when I was twenty-one – it gets me out of the way. Mum understood more than Dad, but that's a mother, isn't it? No matter what, you are always their baby.' He had tears in his eyes. 'Do you mind if we change the subject?'

'Yes, sorry to pry, mate – didn't mean to upset you.'

Maya looked at her watch, saved the situation, and said, 'Jeez, look at the time – we better get going. You got work in the morning, mate. I don't want Leif getting on at us about keeping you up late. It's been lovely visiting your place and thank you for your hospitality. One day we would love you to come to visit us in Sydney – stop as long as you like. Our house is your house, Martin.'

As we left, giving him a final hug, we went down to the car. We sat there, not saying anything until Maya broke the silence. 'What a beautiful young man. He's the first gay man I have ever met, and totally different from what I expected; so gentle and well-mannered. Must have taken some bollocks to tell Leif and Connie he likes boys more than girls. God, it is a funny old world, now, ain't it, mate?'

'You are right. Must be something in this gay thing, babe. I'm frightened to try it in case I like it.'

Maya punched my arm. 'You fucking galah! Trust you to say something like that.'

Over the days we had left in Hull, Leif took us round to places we'd not seen in the city. Connie and Maya went on shopping expeditions to York and Leeds while Leif and I went on the piss in King Edward, where we met Billy, who had unbelievably kept his mouth shut about my previous visit. I'd had never seen anything like it. Leif said it was so good to know that he had a brother and what a fantastic guy I had turned out to be, and that he was so proud that I had tried his hardest to find him and succeeded. We both vowed to stay in touch and visit each other often.

'Lars, what you got planned today? I would like you to meet Rita; she has been helping me by teaching me about British parliamentary history. When you meet her she will blow your mind, as she is a walking encyclopedia. I will ring her and arrange a meet at a pub not far from the library where she works, OK?'

'Yes, great – we had nothing planned, so that will be beaut. What time? We are going into town; we could meet you there.'

'OK. It is the Dram Shop; it is on the corner of George Street and Bond Street. You can't miss it; see you in there at say, one, OK?'

*

'Here it is – we have never been in here. Come on – looks a decent joint; bit old, mind – not like the bars at home.'

'Lars, we are not at home; that is the Pommie coming out of you. Haven't you ever noticed most of the Poms do that whenever you are talking to them? They always seem to want to compare, a bit like the Yanks; everything is bigger in the States. I will have a large chardonnay, please. I will grab a booth over there. They not here yet?'

'Hi, Leif,' said the barman. 'Not seen you for a while; how are things, OK?'

Here we go again, I thought; another one who thought I was Leif.

'G'day mate – pint of… er… what do you recommend?'

'Fuck off – stop taking the piss. You been back on holiday to Oz again? What do I recommend? Fuck off – you've been drinking Bass bitter since you were fucking fifteen in Engineers down Bean Street. It's me, Mike, you're talking to – and who's the bird? Does Connie know you are playing away?'

I just laughed. 'I'll let my brother explain when he comes in. I will have a lager and a large chardonnay, please.'

'Fucking brother? You haven't got a brother. You are a twat – you never change. OK, I will bring them over. By the way, she's not a bad-looking bit of stuff; you giving her one or what?'

Mike came over with the drinks. 'There you go, Leif.' He looked at Maya. 'Hiya, how are you, love? How long you known this twat? Take care, love, he is a right wanker.' He winked at me, and went back to the bar.

Maya sat there, gobsmacked. 'What the hell is he on about? What language was he speaking in?'

'Ignore him – he's an old mate of Leif's. He's known him from school, and he thinks I'm him. I'm getting a bit pissed off with it but I suppose it is going to happen. Here, look, they are here. What do you want, Leif? Er, Rita, isn't it? What's yours? I have just got ours. Here, go and get them – I can't face another inquisition from the barman.' I handed Leif a fiver.

Rita sat next to Maya and introduced herself.

'Hello, so pleased to meet you; when Leif rang me, I could not believe it. Isn't it wonderful, after all these years, finally getting together again? I don't know how I would feel if it ever happened to me.'

'Yes, we have known a while, but it has taken us a hell of a long time to get it organised. Did you know his mum got married a few days ago? We did a double wedding here in Hull.'

'Oh, how wonderful! No, I have been away for two weeks at my parents' down in Herefordshire. I'm sorry I missed it; he never said.'

'He did not know, that's why – it was a surprise. No one knew except us Christine and Billy, and the few people Christine had told, but without a doubt not that many.'

'As I say, I've been away, so I bet it has been a fantastic time catching up with each other and hearing about past and future times. Leif has had such a wonderful life and he's got a great future ahead of him. I suppose you know about him being a councillor and looking to stand for Parliament in the next General Election?'

'Yes, he did mention about the councillor thing but had not mentioned about being an MP. Wow, that is a hell of a thing. What is involved? Can I ask how you come into this? You work as a librarian, I believe?'

'Yes, I am at the Hull Central Library; been there a few years now. I studied at uni… oh, here is Leif back.'

'There you go, cheers, mate,' he said, handing the change back.

'I was just telling them about how you are hoping to stand in the next election, Leif, and they wanted to know how I came into it.'

'Yes, that is true, but we only have an hour or so, and if Rita starts, you won't get a word in. I asked her to help me as she has a photographic memory. I bet you can't ask her a question that she doesn't know the answer to; she has been helping me by teaching me the history and rules of the House of Commons. I am hoping she will be my PA when or if I get in.'

The hour flew by, and Rita had to get back.

'I must go; it has been lovely meeting you both – hope to meet again. Oh, by the way, Leif, I have come up with something and need to discuss it with you, OK?'

'Yes, no problem – will ring you tomorrow, OK?'

'Yes, great. I must dash – bye.'

I was dumbstruck; like Leif, I could not get over how knowledgeable she was.

Leif left to get back to work, so we went for a wander around the Old Town area, working our way to the city centre. Maya spent some more money on clothes at the Hammonds department store, before heading back to Leif's.

'She certainly was some woman, that Rita – what a brain; how on earth did you find her?'

'I told you about being a councillor, didn't I? And that I had won my seat as an independent. But I have been asked if I would be interested in joining the Labour Party and standing for election as an MP; I am not sure what to do, for there have been one or two splinter groups started up here that you may not have heard of back in Oz. One of them being UKIP, which began as the Anti-Federalist League, a Eurosceptic political party established in 1991 by a guy called Alan Sked, a historian. They opposed the signing of the Maastricht treaty. I have never agreed with the EU and as I have got older I could see we, the British public, were being ripped off, and I thought it would be better if we got out and started trading with the Commonwealth countries again, those we left when we joined the Common Market as it was then known. I do not agree with all of Labour's policies and was thinking about starting my own party. I thought of an obscure name like the GEUOOP Party – Get Us out of Europe Party, or GEUP, for short – stop fucking laughing.'

'You are taking the piss, mate. I thought the Monster Raving Loony Party was a fucking joke when I read that back home – but fucking GEUP? How do you expect anyone to take you seriously?'

'Listen, no matter what name I use, we need to get away from the big two. They are doing fuck all for the working man – the rich get richer, and the poor get poorer, and it has to stop. My ultimate dream is to be a minister, and I want to become prime minister –the first prime minister from an independent party if that could be possible. There is no real difference between the Conservative, Labour and Lib Dem parties. They all want continued membership of the European Union, they all want continued mass immigration, and I believe that they would be all out of touch with the vast majority of voters.'

'Why don't you get in with Labour, then once you are in, move over as an independent?'

'That idea has passed by me, and yes, it seems logical.'

'Use them like they will use you – once you don't toe the line, they will drop you like a hot lump of coal.'

The next few days passed quickly, and we were about to get ready to leave the UK.

'Well, mate, it has been wonderful to have eventually got back together,' said Leif. 'We can now live a normal life as two brothers can, even though we are thousands of miles apart. We are closer now than we have ever been. Let's not drift apart.'

'We have a saying that we often pass on to good friends – friends we have grown attached to over the years, and it is, I love you like a brother, mate. I will not say this, though, for you are my brother, one I lost through no fault of our mother but one of greed and downright evil. I will never forgive what my adopted parents did to us – never. They did not give a fuck how it would affect us in later life. Anyway, we must go. Thank you for a beautiful few days. Thank you, Connie, for embracing us into your house and friendship.'

Connie was in tears, as was Maya. We all hugged, and then we left, not knowing how long it would before we met again.

CHAPTER 37

LEIF

Bit of a Blow

I had got back in touch with Rita, and I was soon to discover that her attitude had changed considerably. I arrived at her house on that Thursday morning after Lars and Maya had gone back.

'Come in. Do you want a coffee before we start? I have been thinking about you and your wanting to become an MP.'

'OK, yes, please – just the usual… and why? You sound as if you have doubt in your mind. I am still keen on becoming –'

'I know – but it will be a lot of hard work. Leif, do you want me to be honest with you? I have always believed in you, but I do not think you have a chance in the world of getting in Parliament in Hull. Mickey Mouse has more chance of becoming King of England; just look at the facts – you know I am a statistics person.'

'Yes, but it is not based on stats; it is based on what I believe I can do for Hull. It has been Labour too long – we need some fresh ideas.'

'Leif, just think about it, please, before you go throwing a load of money at it, and that is what you are going to have to do. You say you want to stand for West Hull. Have you looked at the history of that constituency? They have not had a local man as an MP since William Wilberforce in 1780. Stuart Randall is from Plymouth, and he has been in the chair since 1983. It is a closed shop, Leif, now; let's just be honest with ourselves, shall we?'

'What do you think we or I should do? Just forget all about it? It has been my goal ever since I heard about the Triple Trawler Tragedy. What with that and then the Cod Wars, and the Gaul – something has to be done. The men have been fighting since 1974 when Iceland extended its fishing limits to 200 miles.'

'I try to understand, Leif, but that is a bit out of my remit, to be honest, and you may well be amazed. I do not know that much about it.'

'What? Amazed is not the word; you want to listen and learn, which will be a bit of a turnaround, but if I explain, it may bring it home to you why it means so much to me.'

'OK, let me go and get the coffee; it won't be a sec, OK?'

I could not believe my ears, Rita not knowing about one of the biggest tragedies ever to hit not only Hull but every fishing port in the UK.

'Right – where were we? Ah, 1974 and Iceland? OK, I am all ears.'

'It goes back to around 1950 when they reduced the limit from three to four miles.'

'What limit? What do you mean by limit?'

'International fishing rights have gone on for years. It means that trawlers other than Icelandic were only allowed to fish within three miles of the coast, and then in 1950 they extended it to four miles.'

'OK, I understand now; go on.'

'Then they extended it to twelve miles in 1958, which caused an uproar; in 1972 they set a fifty-mile limit.'

'But why did they do this the Icelanders? I mean, what difference did it make? How far you fished? The fish swim everywhere, don't they? They don't know how far from shore they are.'

'They were trying to preserve the fishing grounds; they believed that they were overfished and fish stocks were dwindling. You could understand it; Iceland has always said that it is more dependent on fisheries than any other country. About eighty per cent of its foreign currency earnings come from the export of fish and fish products.'

'Seems to me they were right, but 200 miles is a long way; maybe that was too far?'

'The argument just escalated with British trawlers going in the limits guarded by Royal Navy ships for protection; they had been hounded by Icelandic boats, whose tactic of cutting the nets of trawlers inside the 200-mile exclusion zone was a blatant breach of international law. Then the inevitable happened – one of the trawlers was involved in the ramming of the patrol boat Þór on December 11, 1975, when it was sheltering from a Force 9 gale off Iceland. It sparked a series of events that threatened Nato's future and left Hull, Grimsby, and Scottish ports paying a heavy price. Disputes over the fertile cold waters of the North Sea were not new: British fishermen had come into conflict with their Norwegian counterparts off the Icelandic coast as far back as the early 15th century. Although its navy was a lot smaller in size and firepower, the British warships were far greater. Iceland eventually played its trump card by threatening to close a tactically important Nato base at Keflavik and withdraw from Nato completely.'

'Wow, I bet the shit hit the fan there; the Americans would not stand for that.'

'Yes, you are right; with the Cold War in full swing and pressure being applied by the US, Britain had no option but to submit, although the manner of that pulling out of the dispute remains the source of some bad feeling. The other European nations had struck deals with Iceland which safeguarded their fleets, but there is a feeling that we had been hung out to dry.'

'I am not surprised – I would say well shagged, Leif,' she laughed. 'That is old Hessle Road terminology.'

'After the new limits came in, in 1974, the BFA or British Fishermen's Association, was introduced to help the UK's fishermen in lodging a compensation claim. They were told they would be looked after, that they would be retrained, and new industries would be introduced into the area, but it was a load of bullshit, nothing ever materialised. They then claimed for compensation of £1,000 per year of service capped at twenty years' full payment, regardless of rank, from skipper to deck-hand including radio officers and widows and dependants. Two guys who instigated the new association were Ray Smith and Ron Bateman ex-trawlermen. It seems arguments were rife, some treating the claim like a pay negotiation. But in my mind, it was not a pay rise open for arbitration. It was a payment for lost wages due to the government's

239

incompetence and a fear of upsetting the Icelandic government, who had threatened to make the Americans leave and take their ships and naval base with them.'

'You have certainly looked into this in some depth, Leif; I can see now why you are so adamant about doing something about it.'

'Yes, but it was not all plain sailing as the main delegation in the fight came from Hull and Grimsby. Grimsby had a variety of fishing grounds that had saved their industry from total collapse, but in the case of Hull, the industry was finished.'

'You mean the Iceland decision didn't hit Grimsby as badly?'

'No, they had lost thousands of jobs after the Cod Wars and were equal partners with Hull in setting up BFA, but they were mostly skippers of smaller vessels, where the Hull men were deepwater trawlermen. Having read a fair bit about it, there had always been a bit of a rivalry between trawlermen and the Grimsby mob, whose leading voice was a skipper's widow. They wanted more money for the skippers, rather than an across-the-board payment. Taking this stance did not help the cause, so to speak, and it must have been a detriment to the negotiating, which would suit the government as a lot of money would be at stake. They were not asking a lot, when you think that 900 ships were lost in the Barents Sea, Bear Island, Iceland and Spitsbergen, with a total of 8,000 men never coming back to their families – it was fucking disgusting.'

'I've listened to what you've told me, Leif. Do you mind if I do some research myself? I know one or two people who may know a bit more about this. Can you give me a couple of weeks to contact them and get some answers? But I still believe – and you are not going to like what I am about to say – but I do believe you are, to use another Hull saying, pissing against the wind in wanting to gain a seat in the Commons.'

A week later, I had been busy at work, which was a bit of a change, but I had concentrated on Cager's position, surprising everyone, including Connie, when I got a phone call from Rita.

'Hello Leif, can we meet again? I have found out a bit more on your fisherman thing.'

*

The following Thursday I met her at her home again, and was welcomed with a kiss on the lips. Now, that was something different. She had her hair down, and looked lovely in a pair of shorts and T-shirt; I'd never seen her look so relaxed.

'How did you get on then? Find anything out?'

'Yes. Hang on – coffee? Before we get down to it.'

'Why not? By the way, you are looking rather, what you might say, ravishing today – what's the occasion?'

'Give over – you are a married man; you should not be even looking. I just fancied a change of direction – this is the new modern me. I noticed that Maya, Lars's wife, looked so relaxed and younger than her age. I don't know – she seemed to have an aura of, "Hey, look at me" – do you agree?'

'Yes, but I'd not given it much thought. A lot of Australian women are like that; must be the outdoor life. Most of them are brought up wearing nothing but shorts and T-shirts and they live in swimmers all the time, especially those living on the coast. When I was there, I noticed the kids never seemed to wear shoes; either bare feet or thongs – sorry, flip flops – at the most. Anyway, I love the new look, it suits you. By the way, are you not wearing a bra?'

She blushed. 'Is it that obvious? No, I thought I would get away from the restrictions in the house anyway. Does it show that much? Are they sagging?' She cupped her breasts, lifting them at the same time.

'No – they look quite nice, if I am honest, very nice indeed. Anyway, let's get on with why I am here – and it's not to discuss your tits, as much as I would like to.'

She smiled and punched me on the arm. 'Yes – right, then. I found a report from the NAO, or National Audit Office, on the compensation scheme to former Icelandic water trawlermen and it follows an earlier report from the Parliamentary Commissioner for Administration. The Commissioner's report highlighted three areas of maladministration. This NAO report looks at the value for money issues.'

'Who told you this?'

'I have friends in the right places now. Listen, or we will be here all day.'

'OK, I will shut up, but don't make it too hard to understand.'

'The background to both reports is that the UK government made agreements in the 1970s to end the Cod Wars with Iceland. UK vessels could no longer fish in Icelandic waters, which led to the decline of distant water fishing. Trawlermen were not entitled to compensation according to the interpretation of employment law at that time, but did you know that this decision was challenged in 1993, only two years ago?'

'No, I didn't, sorry,' I said, pulling a face like a schoolboy butting in.

Rita looked over her glasses, shaking her head. 'It seems that, in response, the Department of Employment set up an ex-gratia scheme to compensate former trawlermen who had not sought redundancy at the time of their original dismissal. Trawlermen further challenged this scheme because it did not consider that many of them had often changed vessels and employers. Were you aware of this that some men have already been paid out?'

'I knew that some had been paid out, but not all of them. I don't think that the department knew enough about the fishing industry, particularly its structure and working practices, to draw up a workable scheme. Only about half of the men's claims had been paid and underpaid at that.'

'Yes, you are right. No one seemed to realise that the loss of the Icelandic water fishing industry in the aftermath of the resolution of the Cod Wars of the 1970s had an intense effect on whole communities.'

'The scheme was to provide compensation for the livelihoods lost due to the government s action that made the collapse of the industry. Lots of complaints followed after the way it was handled.'

Rita stood up with a severe look on her face. 'That is what I believe – the scheme had been devised too quickly. I believe that they should look at what has been already paid out and start by giving some ex-gratia compensation payments and a proper examination to all relevant issues; any changes to such schemes should be properly publicised and explained.'

'That is why I feel I need to be at the front line to push this through.'

'Leif, you do not need to be an MP to push this. You already have what is required in your mind; it is getting it through to the local MP – let him do the lobbying and drive it through. It is his job to.'

She sat down again. 'I did speak to a couple of people in London. They told me that Stuart Randall has already been making noises in the right places. He has started to work with the BFA to establish a compensation scheme for trawlermen thrown out of work following the final Cod Wars.'

'I need to think about what you are saying; this would be a hell of a turnaround for me. It was my goal to go into politics.'

'I can't decide for you. I just feel you can do more good staying on the city council and trying to change some of the attitudes on there, but there again, that is up to you.'

I gave it some more thought, and Rita was right. I got in touch with the relevant people and advised them that I would not be standing for election.

CHAPTER 38

LEIF

Worst News Ever

O ne thing I was going to do was make sure that the ex-fishermen got what was duly theirs, after governments had refused the rights of redundancy. The men were classed as casual labour; the fishing industry was fucked, for want of a better word. Since the EU had let other countries fish in our waters, the Icelandic Cod Wars had taken place. The top dogs in Brussels gave the trawler owners compensation for scrapping the vessels, but nothing to the men.

I was still going to fight their corner even if I was not going into the House of Commons, for I believed they should be paid a minimum of £30,000 each in compensation; there must have been at least 5,000 men eligible to receive it, though a lot would have died waiting.

I had been on the phone to Lars nearly every week. He was doing OK, and had a big party when he got home. The new cranes had arrived, and payments had started going into my Swiss account, not that I even thought they wouldn't. He was still bubbling about finally finding his long-lost brother, and so was I, to be honest.

I was at work when the phone rang. 'Hello? Oh, hi, Billy – what's up mate? You sound bad. You been on the piss again? What? The doctors said what? When? OK – what ward? OK – I am on my way.'

I got to the reception at Hull Royal A&E. 'Mrs. Smith – Christine Smith – she is my mother; she has been brought in.'

'Just a second, please. Yes, she is still in the assessment ward.'

I went along this long corridor that seemed like fucking miles – nurses everywhere, people on trolleys, people in wheelchairs, just waiting. Fuck, I hated this place.

I spotted Billy. 'Hey, how's she doing? Where is she? What's wrong?'

'She started feeling bad middle of the night; she had been a bit offish most of the week but kept saying it was indigestion. She had a pain in her right-hand side but kept saying it would go away; they are doing some tests on her now. They said she might need a scan, just waiting for some specialist to come down – a consultant gastroenterologist. I think that is how you say it? Whatever that is, they need him to see Christine before they can make a decision.'

'When did she have her last check-up on her cancer? Do you know, she has not mentioned it; it must be due.'

'Yes, I think she said it was in a few weeks, but it can't be that. She has been OK for a while now. Mind, she would not tell me there was anything wrong even if there was.'

Billy was right about that. She certainly knew how to keep a secret.

With that, a nurse came to see us. 'Mr Smith, your wife will be kept in; she needs some tests doing. She will be going up to a ward as soon as we get a bed available.'

'Can we see her? Is she going to be OK? She is, isn't she, nurse?'

'We will know better after the test results come back. She is sleeping now; we have given her something to help her rest. You can go in and see her – we have put her in a cubicle. Come, I will show you.'

I could see Billy was starting to panic; he wasn't the only one. It did not sound right to me, not that I knew, but consultants, tests, something to help her sleep… not good.

We got into the cubicle, and Mum was sitting up asleep, not lying flat, but at an incline; she looked peaceful enough, but her skin was tinged with yellow, as if it was a lousy tan and was wearing off.

'How long has she been that colour, Billy? It doesn't look right to me.'

'Oh, a couple of weeks at one time. She looked like she had been on a bender. Her eyes had a bit of yellow in them, but it went away. It started not long after the wedding. I thought she had overdone the drink, but you know your mum – "Oh, it will be fine." It was, and it went away, but she has been moaning about her side for a few weeks now.'

We sat there on either side of the bed, not saying anything, just look-ing at Mum. We had tried talking to her, but she was out of it. The nurse came back in.

'She is going up to ward H100. To honest, Mr Smith, there is nothing you can do; you may as well go home. She is comfortable and sleeping.'

'No, I will stay. I am not leaving her.'

As the nurse started to walk away, I followed her to the nurses' station.

'Excuse me, nurse, I am Christine's son. Can I have a word, please?'

'Yes, I can't tell you any more than I have told your father; she will be out of it until the morning. I would go home and bring some of her nightwear, as she may be in a few days, and she will like her own toiletries, change of underwear, that sort of thing. Can you bring all the medication that she is taking, please?'

I went back to Billy. 'The nurse told me we might as well go; they need all her medication, and a change of clothes, toothbrush, shampoo, all that stuff.'

'I'm not leaving her. Will you go? You will know what to bring. Ask Connie to go with you. She will know what's needed.'

I had forgotten about Connie; she did not even know what was going on. I never told anyone in the office where I was going. She wasn't at work, and I had not yet called her. It was gone nine o'clock. I looked at my phone – six missed calls, and I had turned the ring off; this meant bother.

'Hey, Connie, I know – you don't have to go on; I'm sorry. Forget the tea, listen – it's mum, she is in Hull Royal... we don't know yet. Will you shut the fuck up and listen? I'm sorry... but just listen, we need to go to Mum's and pick up some of her stuff; she might be in a couple of days. Billy won't leave her, and I haven't a clue what to bring. Can you go over to Mum's? I have got the key and will meet you there in, say, fifteen minutes; OK, see you there.'

Connie sat outside waiting for me, with a face like thunder.

'Why the fuck didn't you let me know what was happening? I was worried sick. I have been trying to ring you all fucking day; why didn't you answer your bastard phone?'

'I know, I'm sorry – I had to turn the ringtone off in the hospital.'

'Liar – you're up to something; I can tell by the look on your face.'

'For fuck's sake, Connie, not now; let's just concentrate on Mum, can we? What stuff will she need?'

We got the bag with what we thought would be needed. We did not have to look far; all the medication was in one cabinet. I had not realised Mum was on so many tablets – once again, another secret.

'You go home; no need for you to come back if you don't want to. Mum is sedated and won't be talking. I will get Billy and bring him home; he can stay the night with us. Don't want him left alone. Can you make sure the spare bedroom is ready for him?'

'Yes, OK, will do. Sorry about before, love.' She kissed me on the cheek.

'OK, no problem, it is me that was wrong – we can talk about that later; Mum's important now, OK?'

The phone rang at about seven-thirty.

'Hello? Yes, speaking – yes, he is here – just a second.'

I handed the phone to Billy. 'Here – it's the hospital.' He went the colour of bad shit.

'Hello, yes? OK... when? This morning? Why? What's happened?'

I could tell he was beginning to panic again; his eyes were filling up.

'OK, thanks, we will be right there; thank you for ringing. Bye.'

'What is it, Billy? What's happened?' said Connie.

'She is going into theatre this morning. She needs an operation – something to with her liver; she has had a scan this morning, and they have found something.'

'What have they found? What are you talking about, Billy?'

'They did not tell me, Leif, just that it was urgent, that's all.'

We got back to the hospital and into the waiting room. They asked us to take a seat; it was hectic – people everywhere. How they worked under such stress, I couldn't imagine. It must have been half an hour before Billy came down to meet us.

'What is happening? Any more news, Billy? Did you find out what was going on with Mum?'

'Did you bring her medication? They need to know what tablets she is on. I always thought that they could automatically get your records.'

'They are in the bag with her other stuff.'

He looked totally in shock, and just stared into space as we talked to him. We were not getting any sense out of him. I left him with Connie and went up to the ward. The door was locked; I tried to catch someone's attention when this young nurse came up behind me.

'Can I help you? Are you looking for a patient? How can I help?'

'Yes, my mother has been sent to this ward – Mrs Smith, Christine Smith. Her husband is down in the main reception area, but I think he is in shock. I can't get any sense out of him. I wondered if I could speak to someone, please?'

'Hmm… let me see. Follow me in, but please go in the waiting room on the right, OK? I will try and get someone to talk to you.'

It must have been fifteen minutes before this older nurse came in.

'Mr Smith?'

'No, I am Leif Askenes, her son; Smith is her married name. What is going on?'

'OK, well, Leif, your mum is not very well. She has cirrhosis of the liver, and has gone down to theatre to do a drain; there is quite a lot of water retention around there and, to make things worse, she has a tumour on the organ. The idea is to try to drain off the fluid in the hope we can remove the tumour. We knew she'd had previous problems, and it was thought the cancer had gone into remission, but I am sorry to say it has come back, but moved.'

'What does that mean? Can you be honest with me? What is the prognosis, if that is the right word?'

'We do not know yet, and we will know once the surgeon has cleared the way. I'm sorry, that's all I can tell you. As soon as I get some news I will come back to you. Do you want to wait in here or go back down to main reception? You are quite welcome to wait here. I can get one of the nurses to bring your father back up if you want.'

I headed back down to the others in the main waiting room, and the oncology surgeon came back.

He gave us the news.

CHAPTER 39

LEIF

Ring Sydney

I rang Lars in Sydney, but I'd forgotten about the time difference. If you ever want to know what time it is somewhere, ring them in the middle of the night; they will always tell you. The phone rang for ages, until Lars finally answered.

'Hello? Who the fuck is this is? It's three-thirty in the fucking morning. Who is it?'

'Lars, it's me, Leif. Sorry, mate, but I had to ring you. I've got some bad news; I don't know how to say it, but Mum is not too well – she's had a relapse.'

'Hang on… what did you say? My head is not clear; just a minute.'

I heard him put the phone down, but he did not hang up.

'OK, now start again; you say Mum is crook again. Why? What's happened?'

'She is back in Hull Royal; it's the cancer – it has spread. I'm so sorry, mate, I don't know what to say.'

There was silence at the other end, then Maya came on the phone.

'G'day mate – what's up? Lars is in fucking in bits here; what have you said to him? I can't console him; what the fuck is wrong? He is moaning something about his Mum – what has happened?'

'Hi, Maya – yes, it's Mum. She is back in the hospital, and it is not great news; she has not got long. The cancer has spread, it is in her liver, and there is nothing they can do.'

'Fuck me, mate – when you say not long, what have the doctors said?

251

Years, months? How long is not long?'

'Weeks – I spoke to him yesterday, and he explained something about a system two specialists had developed. It is based on some scoring method called Child-Pugh; I don't know how it works. He gave me this sheet explaining it; listen – I will read it out to you. "The Child-Pugh score is determined by scoring five clinical measures of liver disease. A score of one, two, or three is given to each measure, with three being the most severe." He told me that the clinical measures are A, B or C, with A, five to six points, being the least severe liver disease, with a one to five-year survival rate of 95 per cent. Class B, seven to nine points, is moderately severe liver disease, with a one to five-year survival rate of 75 per cent, and Class C, ten to fifteen points, is the most severe liver disease, with a one to five-year survival rate of 50 per cent. Mum is class C, the worst it can be; they have said everyone is different, but she might not even have a year. I am so sorry to have to tell you over the phone, but I just had to let you both know.'

'That's OK, babe, will call you later today. What's the best time to catch you? It's just gone three here; what time shall I call you?'

'Er, there is nine hours' difference. It is 6.30pm here; ring us later to-night, around about seven your time, and it will be ten in the morning here – we may have some more news, OK?'

'OK, babe. Bye for now; better get back to him. He is curled up on the floor sobbing like a bloody kid, poor bastard.'

I never got much sleep, and was up early. I rang the hospital, and they said Mum was awake and not too bad, but her belly had swollen, and they were talking about putting a drain in again to release the fluid.

We went back to the hospital, and sat in the waiting room outside the oncology ward.

'Hello, Mr Smith?'

'No, I am her son – this is Mr Smith,' I said, pointing at Billy, who was in bits. 'How is she, doctor? She is going to be OK, isn't she?'

I just knew by the doctor's look that this would not be good news.

'I am sorry, but cancer has spread. We took some blood last night, and it is not good news, I am afraid. We did not do the drain. Sorry but your mother is –'

I cut him off. 'You mean she is going to die? How long, doc? How long?'

'She has gone into a coma. She is not in pain; her blood pressure has dropped. I am afraid she has not got long.'

'Can we go in and see her?'

'Yes, of course. I am so sorry.'

We went into the side room. Mum was lying there so peacefully. She did not look ill; her skin was yellowish but it looked more like a decent tan than jaundice. I sat at one side of the bed, and Billy was at the other. We held her hands, and talked to her, telling her how much we loved her, and how much she meant to us. Tears were rolling down Billy's face; his nose was running like a child with a bad cold.

The heart monitor was on, but it was getting slower; a nurse came in, and smiled as only nurses can do in situations like this. I thought it must be terrible for them every day having to live through such sadness and sometimes great joy; how they did it I would never know. She turned off the machine, smiled and nodded.

Then Mum seemed to take one last deep breath. I looked at the nurse. 'Has she gone?'

She put two fingers on Mum's neck and nodded. 'I am sorry, yes.'

I looked at the machine. It was two flat lines. The nurse had turned off the sound, but not the screen; she was right – Mum had gone.

Billy broke down, tears streaming down his face. He lay on her, and would not let her go. 'Come on, Christine, you will be OK; come on, babe, talk to me, Christine, Christine, baby.'

Mum's eyes were still open, staring into space. I could not stop looking at her, just hoping against hope that the nurse and the machine were wrong, waiting for mum to smile just one more beautiful smile – but no; nothing. I was looking into the eyes of a dead person.

I pulled him away. 'Come on, Dad, it is no good. Mum's gone; we must go.'

The nurse took us back into the small room; the doctor came in to give his condolences, then his buzzer beeped, and he had to go. Another patient needed him.

We waited half an hour or so for the death certificate to be signed before we could leave. It all seemed so irrelevant, as though it was just another death. To those working, I suppose it was. Another person who did not make it, and they'd tried, but it was not to be.

Connie was with Martin in the main waiting room. We didn't have to say anything; they could tell Mum had gone from our expressions.

I rang Australia as soon as I got home. Connie had gone up for a shower, and Martin had gone back to his place. I was alone, with a large whisky in my hand. It had to be done.

'Hello, Maya here? How can I help?'

'It's me, Leif.'

'G'day, mate. I can tell that it's not good news by the tone in your voice; hang on, I will get him.'

'Leif.' There was a silence.

'G'day mate.' Lars's voice was croaky. 'Well, how's Mum?'

I could tell he knew but didn't want to hear the news. 'Lars, I'm sorry, mate, there's no other way of saying it – Mum's gone. I'm so sorry.'

'Oh, fuck, when? I knew as soon as Maya said it was you, that it would be bad. Did she suffer, mate?'

'No, she went to sleep. OK, she had medication to stop the pain, but just slipped away. Billy and I were by her side. So sorry, mate, that you could not be here.'

'How long before the funeral? I will book a flight as soon as I can; we will be there. Just let us know. Will it be quick, or do you have to wait long in Hull?'

'I don't know, mate. Will let you know as soon as we have seen the funeral directors.'

There was a brief moment when he never spoke, then I heard Lars crying. I'd never felt so useless all my life; I just wanted be there and hold my brother tight.

'Just let me know when it is, please. I will start to look at flights, but whatever, we will be there, and, thanks, Leif, I love you so much.'

'OK, mate, I love you too. Take care now. Bye.'

I put the phone down. I was numb; I never thought I would ever feel like I did that moment. I had never been as close to a person as I was right then. Thinking of all the years I had missed not having a brother or sister to grow up with, it had never bothered me until now. I just started to cry, and I could not stop – tears flowed down my face; my nose was running. My life changed right then.

I contacted the local Hessle Road funeral director. I wanted the best for Mum, and she'd always wanted a horse-drawn hearse. But whenever someone died 'on road', that was the ultimate respect that families tried to pay their loved ones – a hearse drawn by two black horses, and an abundance of flowers.

'It must be lovely to go out that way,' she would say to me. 'I just wish I could afford to do it when I go.' Well, now she would be able to have the best send-off ever.

There was no autopsy as it was apparent what Mum had died of. The paperwork was completed; we had to register her death and get the certificates, then the directors could collect her body, bring her back to their place, and do the business.

It had been a week before we could go and make the funeral arrangements, and it was going to be another two weeks before we could have the horse-drawn hearse; they had to bring one in from out of town, and it was fully booked up.

We had to pick a coffin. They were all laid out in a showroom, and it like choosing a new car. The cost was unbelievable, given that you were going to burn it; talk about money going up in flames – this was the ultimate. We chose an oak one; I liked the cherry one, as the wood was a bit darker, but Billy loved the oak. We only needed two cars; one for me, Billy, Connie and Martin, and the other for Lars and Maya, with room for two others. They used old Austin Princesses, which looked like the poor man's Rolls-Royce.

CHAPTER 40

LEIF

Date Set

I rang Lars the following day.

'Hi mate, it's me, Leif – how are you doing, OK? Listen, got a date for you. The funeral is set for Friday, April 28, which gives you a couple of weeks to organise your flight.'

'No worries, we can fly midweek. We will try and get a flight for the Monday, to arrive on Wednesday the week prior to the funeral; it should not be too much of a problem. I will ring today and get one booked. Even if I have to fly first class I will get there, or should I say we will get there.'

'You sure you're all right, mate? At least you sound a bit better?'

'Yes, I'm OK. I've got over the shock. I'm not looking forward to the day, but, hey, that's life, mate; we are all going to die one day, nothing so sure. OK, I'll let you go; I will book flights in the morning. If you don't hear from us, you know everything is OK, and we will ring you next week.'

'You want me to pick you up from the airport? Where are you flying into, or don't you know?'

'No worries, mate, we will try and get flights into Manchester and hire a car for a few days. We will be able to stay as long as you will have us – we're not really busy at work. Mind, we've got a big crane bill to pay off.'

'Fuck off, that's the least of your worries. I look forward to seeing you again soon, bruv; love you, mate – bye.'

I had tears in my eyes when I talked to Lars; god, it seemed strange when I said, 'Love you, mate.'

*

Lars and Maya arrived as planned on the Wednesday afternoon. It was late afternoon. I got a call at work from him at the airport saying they would be in Hull around seven, depending on the traffic.

'That's great, mate. We have a room set up for you and a few cold beers in the fridge; we will wait for tea for when you get here.'

'No, don't worry about a feed, mate. We will grab something on the way over on the motorway.'

'Like fuck you will, eating that shit? No – we will wait until you get here, and no arguments.'

The doorbell went around six-thirty.

'G'day, how the fuck are ya, mate? Great to see you – and you, Connie,' he said, looking around my shoulder. 'We did not think it was going to be so quick us coming back, but anyway – you both OK?'

'Yes, fine, thanks. Come in, come in, leave your bags in the car; get them after a beer and some grub down you. You must be famished after your journey; who you fly with, Qantas?'

'No, we managed to get some seats on Singapore – great airline, food and service unreal, mate. Bloody slept most of the way here – great flight, hey, Maya?'

'Yes, spot on – but he still bloody snored most of the trip. Might have been all the bloody free grog he drank.'

'OK, come into the lounge. I will grab a couple of beers, and we will fill you in with what happened with Mum.'

'I will go upstairs and talk to Connie,' said Maya.

I came back with two beers, and handed one to Lars.

'OK, mate – now tell me the bad news; how did it come on so quick, or did Mum know and it was yet another secret she kept to herself?'

'I am not so sure, mate, but she had made plans and had a written letter locked in a drawer in her dressing table; she had told Billy about it even before the wedding, so I think she had some idea. Still, you know what she was like – very deep at times, and could keep secrets for years;

just look at us two, for example. Billy was sworn to the mystery, and he was fucking terrified of Mum anyway; he would not say anything. He told me about the letter and the plans Mum had made for after she had died. I asked him for the letter, but he said he had destroyed it, and that was what she wanted – in the letter, she'd said that once he had read it and carried out her wishes, he had to burn it.'

'Fuck me, mate – it's a wonder she did not tell him to eat the bloody thing. Talk about James Bond stuff.'

'Yeah, you're right there. Anyway she was taken bad, and it happened so quickly – once it's in the liver you are more or less fucked, for want of a better word, and it was not long. Luckily she went to sleep; she'd been given a strong dose of morphine. Then she went into a coma and never came out of it.'

'How is Billy now? When will I see him? I want to catch up with him before the funeral if we can. I don't just want to meet him there; it's not right, blue – we need to catch up beforehand.'

'I will ring him in the morning; he has been on the pop since she died. He spends most of his time either on his allotment or in Rayners. We could go and have a beer with him one afternoon; that might be best. What do you reckon?'

CHAPTER 41

LARS

Passing Time

We had been back a couple of days, and Leif came up to me.
'Hey, I've got you a present, mate,' he said. 'Remember the book you were reading when you were here for the wedding? Well, I found you a copy in a little second-hand bookshop down the Hepworth Arcade in the Old Town. You want to go in there, mate – there's loads of stuff on Hull and its history.'

'I will do – whereabouts is it? Remember, I don't know Hull that well. Is it near the indoor marketplace, behind the big church?'

'Yes, that's it – you can get into it either from Silver Street; you know, the street that is at the end of Whitefriargate, or through the market, or off Lowgate – it's worth a visit. There is an old joke shop in there as well – you will love it. You can spend hours just looking through the window.'

He handed me the book; the corners were turned up, and it had been well-read, that was for sure, but hey, I had my very own copy now. I was choked.

'Gee, thanks, mate. I will treasure this; I looked for it when I got home but knew I would never find a copy.'

'Pleased you like it – you do, don't you?'

'Fucking oath, mate.'

I could not get over what an incredible insight into the world of the fishing industry this book was. It explained how it had started back in the 1800s when fishermen came up from the south of England, mainly

Brixham and Ramsgate, and how they had been pushed aside for places to keep their boats in the different docks in the city. That was until the fishing industry was given sole use of the dock named after St Andrew, which opened in 1883. It was initially built for the coal trade, but this did not come about, much to the good fortune of the fishing industry. It also explained how the Albert Dock transfer coincided with the introduction of steam trawlers, leading to the end of sailing boats, or smacks, as they were known.

The girls came down. 'Hey, look at this Maya – the book I was telling you about, the one I could not get at home. Leif got me a copy, look.'

'Hey, very nice.' She looked at Connie, rolling her eyes.

'OK, come on, let's eat. I'm starving.'

'Yes, you're right, Connie; come on, put that book down, Lars. You have plenty of time to read that later.'

We had a great meal, and a few more beers, and I was starting to feel tired. Maya had to tell me to go to bed.

The following day I was sitting in the lounge, and Leif came in.

'Fuck me, mate, you are reading the letters of the pages. How far you through it?'

'I started again, mate; as I told you, I had only browsed through it before, and now I have got properly into it, it's fantastic.'

'Great – it will be able to tell you more about Hull than I ever could. Well, the critical bits anyway; Hessle Road and what it is all about. It will give you an idea of what makes us people from around this area different from anyone you will ever meet anywhere in the world. I may be biased in what I say there, mate, but this community is something different, or it was when the fishing industry was at its height. You will see why I am so intent on putting things right somehow. Anyway, I won't bore you with that; it's too fucking early to get on my pedestal. I will leave you to it; got to go into work this morning.'

'OK, Leif, catch you later. I would love to take a look at the dock if we have time?'

'Yes – not much to see now, though. It was decided to move the fishing industry to a new home on Albert Dock in 1972, and three years later, St Andrew's Dock was closed to shipping. I'm not 100 per cent sure of that, but I know it was filled in 1985 to build the shopping centre. Oh, by the way – about seeing Billy. I rang him, and we will meet him in the pub tomorrow, OK?'

'Just the two of us?'

'Yes, just you and me. We'll leave the girls to plan what they want for the funeral, and we'll piss off for a couple of hours and have our private wake with Billy.'

*

I went into the Old Town to look for the little book shop Leif had mentioned, and found it with no problem; what a great little place it was. Jane, the lady who ran it, was so helpful. They had a great selection of books on the history of Kingston upon Hull, to give it its full name. What I couldn't understand, though, was why there as a West and North Riding, but not a South, in some of the older books.

'Excuse me, can I ask a question, please?'

'Yes, no problem; what is it?'

'I am Australian.' I immediately realised that sounded foolish; it was apparent by my accent. 'I noticed that the term Riding is mentioned in quite a few of these books; what does it mean? Was it as far as someone could travel on a horse in a particular time, or is that stupid?'

'No, not at all. I get asked the same question quite often, but it's nothing to do with horses. The word comes from the Viking "thriding", meaning a third. Before county reorganisation, Yorkshire had three Ridings: North, East and West. The area was split up by the Vikings when they first came over. There is a region known as South Yorkshire, but that wasn't created until 1974.'

'Oh, thank you – I never knew that. It's funny, as I have Nordic blood in me. My ancestors came over in the 1800s during the great famine.'

One book I found very interesting was called A History of Hull, written by Gillett and MacMahon. It was a great little book, but the only problem was it was already sold. Jane said she could get me another one, but it might take a week or so. I told her I might not be here, but I left her Leif's number. 'I can post it to Australia if you wish,' she said.

I declined the offer, saying, 'Maybe I could get it when I get home?'

I was looking through the books and found one about whaling in Hull.

'If that interests you,' said Jane, 'why don't you visit the Maritime Museum? It's not far away; you must have seen it in Victoria Square. It's in the old Dock Office.'

'OK, thanks, I will go there now. Will it be open, do you know?'

'Yes, every day, as far as I am aware, and best of all, it's free.'

I left the shop; I must have been in there an hour or so. Jane was so lovely. I bid her farewell, and she thanked me for visiting her little shop.

I found the museum, and there were a few people about – mostly tourists like myself. I saw a sign on the wall saying it had been built in 1872 and was the former headquarters of the Hull Dock Company, which operated all the docks in the city. A museum guide strolled over. 'Hello, can I help you in any way?'

'Oh, g'day – how are ya, mate? No, just browsing – I was advised to come over and take a look, as I am interested in the fishing and seafaring history of Hull.'

'Oh, can I ask why? You are Australian?'

'Is it that obvious? No corks on my hat.'

'No, forgive me – it was your accent that gave you away. We get quite a lot of Australians and New Zealand people in here. We have had quite a few players come to both the rugby league teams over the years from your part of the world, and most of them and their families seem to visit the museum.'

'Oh, right, I see. Well, I am British by birth, but my parents emigrated to Australia in 1946 and took me with them.' I did not want to go into too much detail; it was too hard to explain.

'OK – anything I can help you with, just ask. That's why we are here.'

'I know a bit about the fishing industry, but I was looking at a book, and whaling was pretty big in these parts, I believe?'

'Yes, that's right. Deep-sea fishing replaced the whaling industry. It is said the first whaling ships left Hull in 1598, after the discovery of Greenland by a Sir Hugh Willoughby.'

I could not believe some of the dates people quoted when discussing history here. Australia had nothing compared with Britain or Europe, where history was concerned.

'In 1618, the king at the time, James I, gave an island in the Arctic ocean, Jan Mayan – between Greenland and Norway – as a fishery station to Hull's merchants,' the guide continued. 'After this period, there was a decline in the industry until it was revived by Sir Samuel Standidge, which organised a small fleet of whalers in the mid-1700s. Then, in the early nineteenth century, there was a surge, around the years 1818 to 1820, when sixty-four vessels were sailing around Greenland and the Davis Strait. It was a dangerous occupation – at least one ship a year was lost, but the money was good.'

'You know all this without looking into a book; how is that?'

'It's my job. Apart from that, you are asking about something I have always been very interested in, as my father was a fisherman, but his grandfather was a whaling man and his father before him, so I had to know about it – it was handed down to me.'

'Fair dinkum. Your ancestors were whalers? Strewth!'

'Oh, yes, you are an Aussie,' he said, laughing.

'What type of ships did they use for whalers?'

'They were sailing ships with three masts, each mast having three sails attached. You can see one or two paintings over here; look, one of them is of the Mary Frances. The vessels were very well-built; one of them, the Truelove, was in use for eighty-four years and was 109 years old when it was taken out of commission. They were double-hulled with the timbers trebled on the bow, a bit like ice breakers, to smash their way through the ice. But the actual catching of the whales was done from small rowing boats. You must have seen the famous film *Moby Dick*, surely? They were caught using a harpoon. Once the men had harpooned the whale, it would attempt to escape by swimming away and often diving. The boat would be dragged along until the whale would slow down with exhaustion. Often hours would pass. It was then it would be killed using long lances or spears being stabbed between the ribs.'

'What type of whale did they catch?'

'The one that was the favourite prey was the Greenland right whale, so named as it was classed as the "right" whale to catch, due to it being slow, and not as dangerous as, say, the sperm whale. Also, when killed, the carcass would float, which made it much easier to get back to the mother ship.'

'How long were they away at any one time?'

'The season only lasted through the summer months. The government paid a bounty, as long as the vessel sailed before April 10 and returned in time for Hull Fair in October.'

'Can you imagine being away all that time on a ship without seeing or landing anywhere? Must have been terrible.'

'Yes, life aboard the whalers was hard – the food was just about unfit for human consumption. They fed on seals' hearts with liver, or wild bear meat. Boiled deer flesh was another delicacy often on the menu.'

'How many men were in the crew? Were they big ships?'

'With a crew of up to fifty men, the quarters were cramped. One whaler wrote that he had never seen blossom or fruit on trees during his time at sea – more than seventeen years. He missed eight and a half years of his children growing up.'

'Did they ever get trapped in the ice?'

'Yes, quite often, and if they did not get out, they could be stranded for up to a year, or, even worse, the vessels were crushed and sank. As bad as it was, a thousand men sailed from Hull every year, but the decline in the numbers came about due to the rise of the Americans and other countries increasing their fleets – there were too many hunting not enough whales.'

'What did the crews do for relaxation?'

'Have you ever heard of scrimshaw artwork?'

'No, what's that?'

'Scrimshaw is scrollwork or engravings and carvings done on bone or ivory. There aren't many elephants in the Arctic, but an abundance of whales and a by-product of the whale is bone and teeth. The sailors used to take pieces of bone or cartilage and carve elaborate engravings in the form of pictures and writing on the surface.'

'When did Whaling finish in Hull, then?'

'It began to decline, and by the mid-1850s, there was only a small number of ships in the fleet. The last successful voyage of any whaler out of Hull was in 1868, and that was the Truelove. Is that OK? That sums up a little of the times of the whalers in Hull. There is lots of information on the pictures and postings around the walls; I hope I have helped you. Oh, and we have the most extensive collection of scrimshaw in Europe, so make sure you take a look at it.'

'Thank you so much, er...?'

'Alex, the name is Alex.'

'Hello, my name is Lars; pleased to meet you.'

'Just another thing – has Hull always been one of the biggest ports in the UK? When did it all start?'

'Fucking hell, mate – a long time ago. From earliest times, the Haven (Old Harbour), the lower portion of the river Hull as it flowed toward the Humber, was the main gathering place for vessels to load and unload their cargoes. As numbers of boats increased and vessels became larger, they found it difficult to negotiate the crowded waterway. When St Andrews Dock opened on September 24, 1883, at the cost of £414,707, which was a lot of money in those days, there was what they called the Old Dock, which opened in 1775, and it was renamed Queen's Dock in 1854. In 1930 it was closed and filled in, and became what is now Queen's Gardens.'

'Why did they change its name?'

'After the visit to Hull of Queen Victoria and Prince Albert. There has been a load of docks closed down in modern times. Humber Dock was opened in 1809 but closed down in 1969, and became part of the marina in 1983. Not far from there Junction Dock opened in 1829, and it was renamed Albert Dock, the same time as Queens Dock. That closed in 1968 and became what is now Princes Quay shopping centre in 1991.'

'Jeez, mate – unreal. All those docks in more or less the city centre.'

'And there were more – Victoria Dock opened in 1850, and that closed in 1970. It was eventually filled in, and a new village was built on there in 1988 at the cost of £63 million. Railway Dock, which was opened in 1846, later became part of the marina. Then we come to William Wright Dock, named after the chairman of the Hull Docks board in 1873. Alexandra Dock, which opened in 1885, was built by the Hull and Barnsley Railway as the eastern terminal for the coal exports, along with timber imports from Scandinavia. Riverside Quay opened in 1907, followed by King George Dock in 1914, which at the time was the first fully electrified dock in the UK. Roll-on, roll-off shipping came in around 1965 with a direct route to Rotterdam and later Zeebrugge. Along with all the docks, we also had a jetty built to service Saltend chemical plants to the east, near Hedon in 1914. That is just about it, mate. Not bad memory, eh, for an old guy?'

'No, you certainly know your stuff! I must be going. Thank you, Alex. I appreciate your time.'

'No problem. I love talking about it; that is what we are here for. Goodbye, Lars, you are a good listener – and have a pleasant holiday in Hull.'

CHAPTER 42

LARS

Private Wake

We walked into Rayners, which was an old fishermen's pub, all bare wooden floorboards, and photographs of Hull trawlers on the walls.

'Bloody hell, Leif – this place is massive. I've never been in a pub with such a long bar.'

'Yes – back in the day, this was one of the busiest pubs on Hessle Road; a bloody gold mine. It is said it has one of the longest bars in the north of England. There were twelve barmaids on during busy periods at four pump stations.'

'Fuck me; it's huge.'

'That's not all – the back room used to be one of the best concert rooms, always full of women – some not so respectable; that is all I will say on that subject. But wherever you find seamen, you will find girls who, shall we say, like them a lot – and their money.'

There were quite a few in for a weekday afternoon. Billy was with a few of the old bobbers he used to work with. Now that was all gone. There were some real hard cases in there, most of them built like brick shithouses with hands like shovels, and one or two broken noses.

They were standing at the bar on the right as you walked through the entrance. Billy did not see us at first; he was holding court, telling some yarn. You could see he had been drinking too much – his face was bright red.

'G'day Billy,' I said. 'How the fuck are ya?'

'Fucking hell, Lars. Great to see you, mate, welcome home.'

'Sorry for your loss, mate – so sad about Mum.' We hugged, and Billy broke down. There was a deathly quiet come over the pub, maybe some did not know Mum had died, but it was unreal. It was like someone had turned off the volume.

'That's OK, thank you, Lars. I am hurting inside, but I know she is at peace; it's for the best.'

His mates gathered around him, hugging and consoling him; he was in tears. I felt so sorry for him.

I was introduced to Billy's mates – four of them; Ted Jackson, who was the oldest at seventy-five, Kenny Walters, aged seventy, Tommy Richardson, sixty-five, and Paddy McGuire, who was only sixty. I had a chat with all of them, but Ted was the one I latched on to. He was the most relaxed guy to talk to but had a serious side to him, which must have been down to his age.

He stood at the bar with the rest of us for a while, but then went and sat down; his leg was giving him a hard time. I went over and sat with him.

'G'day, again, Ted – mind if I join you, mate?'

'No, get sat down, son. Old leg's playing up – can't stand too long.'

'Can I get you a beer, mate? What are you drinking?'

'Oh, very nice of you – pint of bitter, please, be great.'

I went to the bar, and had a chat with the youngest of the barmaids; not a bad sort either, I wouldn't have minded giving her one, that's for sure.

'Here you go, Ted, bitter it is. You always drink in here, Ted? This your local watering hole?'

'Yes, us bobbers had to go down to the fish docks every Friday afternoon to collect our pay packets, and we used to meet up in here for a quick pint after. Lots of great memories in these walls, son; yep, some great memories. What you been up to today?'

'I went for a stroll around the Old Town and then went into the Maritime Museum in Victoria Square. Very interesting – I learnt quite a lot about the history of Hull, especially about the whaling industry.

How the fishing industry kind of took over from that when it fell away.'

'Yes, one or two of the lads I know had relations on the whaling ships. I believe one of Tommy's was a bosun; you should have a yarn with him about it.

'Yes, I will do it later, but I wanted to have a word with you. Leif tells me you used to be one of the bobbers way back; how did they get their name, do you know?'

'No one is certain where the name bobber comes from, but some say it derived from it being very cold in winter during the night and some of the workers on the quayside. They would sometimes bob or jump up and down to keep warm, but no one has ever asked me that question before. Come to think of it, don't think any of my Chinas would have either.'

'China's? What does that mean, China?'

'You never heard of a China? A pal, or a mate as you Aussies call them. I've used that word, oh, as long as I can remember.'

'How long did you work as a bobber, Ted? Did you start as a boy?'

'No, I started as a barrow boy when I was fourteen. I left school on a Friday and started down dock the following Monday morning – no wonder I am fucked. It was too hard graft for a boy with the bobber gangs; I did not get a job with them until I was twenty-one. I was a fish filleter from being eighteen or nineteen, then got the chance of a start with them, and jumped at it.'

'How did guys get jobs as bobbers? Was it through being a family member, or did you have to be chosen?.'

'It was a bit of a closed shop, a lot of families involved – you had to be in the know to get a start. If you belonged to one of the better-known families, then you stood a better chance of getting a regular book sooner than others. It was also an advantage to be a bobber's son.'

'Leif told me about the family thing and that there were a few prominent families like the Plattens and Davises. He also mentioned the sporting connection; I read that in a book he has given me. Can you tell me any more?'

'The Plattens were probably the largest family gathering on the dock, with twenty, but the Davis family, with six, and the Watson family, with seven, were two other well-known clans. Charlie Platten was the union rep. Then there were three more called Charlie. So you see, they had it tied up. Another one came along, called Ken, and he was there until he got made redundant. He did well for himself; the kid became a solicitor, even lectured at Hull University in corporate law – not bad for a fucking old bobber. He once told me, as I knew him and his family quite well, that the reason he went to be a bobber was based on money. There was no comparison – £25 per week as an engineer as against £50 as a bobber. Regarding sportsmen, obviously the bobbers were mainly Hull FC supporters, but the bobbers also had a good football team in what was known as the Thursday League; their main rivals were the Fire Brigade. When the two teams met, there were real fireworks with many a game having to be abandoned.' Ted chuckled to himself as he said it. 'As far as rugby league was concerned, now, you might be interested in this; they tell me you played a bit back in Oz, that right?'

I nodded.

'The bobbers had the Bedford brothers – two big lads who both played professionally. Arthur played for Hull FC, and Ted played for Hull KR. Arthur lived in Redbourne Street, that's down Rosamond Street, just across the road, not far from here. Two other brothers played for the dark side at Rovers in the 1950s, Charlie and George Young. Another sporting star was Peter Morrison, who lived in Sefton Street. He was a professional boxer, who had about thirty-six fights, I seem to remember. I do know that he boxed in the Olympics. They reckon he was a great prospect. Still, some say he went too far, too fast.'

'What weight did he fight at, do you know?'

'Featherweight. I think he turned pro around 1949 – it was a long time ago. The name Albert Fielding rings a bell; I think that was his first fight, but I know he started OK. He won his first five fights, but lost in a title fight against Roy Ankara, who went on to win a world title, I believe. He took a bit of a pasting. Then the British Boxing Board of Control suspended his licence to box, and he came down the dock as a bobber. He comes in here now and again with his wife Dorothy, but I think he goes more in St Andrew's Club.'

'This is amazing; tell me more. When did the bobbers first get organised as a company?'

'The bobbers were never an individual company or organisation but were employed by the Hull Fishing Vessel Owners Association. However, the bobbers were in existence well before the Second World War and probably as casual labour was taken on by individual trawler owners as and when required.'

'How were the gangs chosen, and who decided who was in each group?'

'There were sixty gangs each comprising ten men – one weigher out, one swinger, four below men, one fifth man, one barrow man and one on the winch. These gangs were permanent and once made up they would remain the same unless someone desperately wanted to change. I was assigned to gang 16 and stayed there for nine years until I moved to the freezer gang, unloading freezer trawlers for the last three years of my career as a bobber. Unloading freezer trawlers was all-day work – nine to five with a similar pay scale as wet-side bobbers. The pay was based on unloading a specified tonnage per day of fish albeit in frozen blocks, but once the bobbers got used to the system, they could unload double the specified rate and so earn double pay and quite often unload the catch in two days and have the rest of the week off! On the other hand, at Easter on the wet side, it was common for work to finish on one trawler and then unload another trawler and get a double day, which was quite lucrative. The bobbers were mainly west Hull-based as there was no transport to work by 2am. Are you sure you want to know all this shite?'

'Yeah, it's my past, mate – don't forget. I never got the chance to listen to stories that I would have been brought up with; it's fucking unreal, mate.'

'OK, son. I love talking about it. Anyway, during the fish discharge or landing, the fish would be contained in pounds arranged below deck. The pounds could accommodate shelves for laying out the more expensive fish such as haddock, Norwegian cod, halibut, etc. These were known as shelf fish, and would command a better price at the fish auction. Other types of fish such as coley, some types of cod, and less favourable types of fish would be laid out in the pounds without a great deal of separation by boards and was called bulk, which was cheaper to buy. It was hard, back-breaking work, especially down in the fish room, working in a confined space. Each fish had to be manually moved and lifted, then swung back onshore. The swinger and the winchman would get a rhythm going; this was a joy to watch, and the skill of these two men made life a hell of a lot easier. As the fish came ashore, the weigher-off emptied the contents into a ten stone kit, which had been placed on the scales ready to check the weight. While all this was going on, the barrowmen would be taking the full kits to its location on the dockside. There was always a spare man who could do all of the tasks at hand, ready to take over should the need be. Often, if they were doing well, the foreman would let us nip off to Cullen's coffee shop for a mug and a banjo.'

'What is a banjo?'

'Oh right, course – you being a fucking Aussie, you've never heard of it; this was a breadcake dipped in pork dripping.'

'Did you work in all weather? Was there any cover to help keep you dry when you were working?'

'Now, how could you cover us up? There was a bit of cover on the dockside. But it depended on which way the wind was blowing. With the basket on a winch, which was worked off the deck and pulleys, it was impossible to put any shelter up, and all the hatches had to be open to lower the basket down inside the hull of the ship. Do you know, only once in all the years I worked on the dock did we ever miss a day's work, and that was in the winter of 1947, during the big freeze as it was called. When there was a severe storm blowing, and the swinger could not see the men on the quayside, they had to cease work. We worked through every type of weather imaginable from freezing cold in winter to hot summer days when they worked with their shirts off – them up top, not the lads in the hold; it was still fucking freezing in there.'

'What happened after the trawler had been unloaded? Where did the vessel go? Did it stay there?'

'No, once the catch had been landed, the trawler would be towed across the dock from the wet side to the dry side where it would be replenished with supplies including coal/diesel, food, etc., and ice. The vessel would be moored next to the icehouse. Here the ice was pumped into the now empty fish pounds, nearest to the focsle at the front of the vessel. This made it easy for the crew to be able to take baskets of ice and spread it on to the fish, which would be either in bulk pounds or on shelves for the shelf fish. All the fish had to be segregated into their different types once below deck to make landing it easier.'

'How did you know if you were required to work? When did they tell you, and how?'

'The union office in West Dock Ave displayed a board in the window from 4pm every working day, including Sunday, to confirm the gangs required as this was the only method of communicating the requirements. However, many an old bobber made some pocket money, by going to get the information at 4pm, and relaying it to his customers by knocking on their doors or putting a note through the letterbox.'

By this time, the other three guys had joined us. They had been drinking all day and needed to sit down before they fell down. The conversation went on, with the others chipping in their twopenneth, as the Poms say.

CHAPTER 43

LARS

Navy Rum

'**G**lad you guys have joined us. I was yarning with Ted here about the bobbers and the life you guys had – fucking hard by the sound of it. Anyone want another beer?'

They all accepted my offer, but it was 'top shelf time'. They all requested a dram, and Navy rum was now the drink of the day. I joined them – fuck me, it was beautiful. I'd never tasted anything like it.

I continued my interrogation. I just loved listening to these old Poms. They had so many great stories, and so much history between them.

'Was it a set wage or work to any bonus system?' I asked. This time Kenny joined in.

'We had a set wage for landing a trawler's catch, with each gang having a quota of 300 kits per trawler. It gets complicated in terms of a bonus payment. An example would be a trawler coming to land a catch that had, say, 1,200 kits on board, then that would need at least four gangs and 300 kits each. If the trawler landed 1,200 kits or less, then we would get their basic pay. However, if it landed just a few kits more, and it should have been five gangs, then the four gangs would share the "missing" gang's money. If this came about, it was called a buster. In summer, when fishing was right, there were times when there was not enough workforce, and the trawlers were assigned fewer gangs, so busters were quite common. Although starting at 2am, the harder the bobbers worked, the quicker they got home, so quite often a bobber could be on his way back home any time between five and six o'clock.'

'Was it like the dockers? You got a standby pay if you did not work like dinting, as the dockers called it?' Now Tommy was listening, and he came back.

'There was a kind of dinting used when there was a surplus of labour or a shortage of fish being landed, and in the winter months, we might get two or even three dints each of which was less than a working day's payment. There was a catch to this system, though. If you dinted during a week and slept in on another day, you lost all the dinting payments for that week. Sleeping in was common, but usually on Fridays when we had done four good days or nights, some would deliberately sleep in, resting on the fact that four days' pay was good enough. The casuals would be used to fill in the gaps, so everyone got a bit, no need to be greedy.'

He went quiet again, deep in thought. Tommy was standing rubbing his chin as everyone was bringing up other comments. He remembered what he was going to say.

'No one has mentioned this yet, but every now and again there may have been a latecoming vessel that would be met by some of the lads. They would rig their gear up, and then it was towed alongside ready to be unloaded, and its catch would then be sold last. This often happened in the winter months when a vessel was delayed steaming home due to bad weather; I just thought I would mention it.'

'Yes, good one, Tom,' said Ted.

We were all talking more or less on top of each other. I heard Ted telling Paddy that he had mentioned Ken Platten and how he had kind of jumped ship and got out while the going was good.

Then Paddy joined in. 'After Ken moved to unload freezer trawlers, it was all-day work, nine until five, with a similar pay scale as wet side bobbers. The pay was based on unloading a specified tonnage per day of fish all in frozen in blocks, but once the bobbers got used to the system, they could unload double the specified rate and so earn double pay and quite often unload the catch in two days and have the rest of the week off! However, while he was on the freezer gang, it became apparent due to the Cod Wars and the fact that freezer trawlers were the future that the scheme operated by HFVOA was overmanned. The trade union operated a last in, first out scheme, and as the last in and youngest bobber, he knew he was certain to be selected for redundancy. Ken decided to rely on his educational qualifications and apply to Hull University to take a law degree. The fucking trade union did not lift a finger to fight for its members. I remember on his last day's work, he was asked by some of the freezer gang what he was going to do, so he told them. It provoked a discussion among the gang about what some of them were going to do. One said he was off to become a brain surgeon, and another said he was running for PM, while another claimed he was going to work for the Bank of England, and so it went on. Piss takers, but it lightened up the atmosphere; that was what it was like – great craic.'

'I know I may be asking a lot of questions, but as an Australian, we never had anything like this job. The wharfies are the dock labourers, and I know quite a few of them. I just want to be able to tell them all about this job; great talking points down at the pub on a Friday arvo. What happens after all the fish has been loaded on to the quay?'

Kenny answered that one.

'The sales began at 8am. The cod and oddments all other species of fish sale started at Stand 204 at the Iceland end of the market with the haddock starting at the other end at Stand 1.'

'Who did the salesmen work for? Was it a kind of cooperative?'

'No, each trawler owner had their permanent salesman; you can imagine the turmoil if there were five different companies trawlers in at the same time. The sales used the Dutch auction style, where the price started high and worked down.'

'A Dutch auction, how does that work? I have never heard of it.'

'Do you know fuck all?' replied Tommy, shaking his head. 'I believe it was in the 1600s – it began when traders from the Ottoman Empire brought tulip bulbs to Holland. The marketplaces were a bit of a shambles. So the Dutch auction was invented to get traders in and out with what they wanted as quickly as possible and at a high price. The sellers would begin at a price at which they knew there would be no demand, and then lower the cost at a known increment.'

'Increment? Fucking hell, where did you dig that word from? You never learnt that at school, phony bastard,' said Ted.

'Fucked if I know – somebody must have told me. I don't think I have ever told anyone,' said Tommy, laughing.

Ted came in again; he had been quietly sipping his navy rum, and was getting a bit of a glow on now.

'Quite often, the buyer would whisper in the salesman's ear his price or even slipped him an amount written on the back of a tally. Once the salesman reached the price, he just said, "Sold ten kits, naming the buyer," and then would start again selling the remaining kits if there was any.

'For example, the salesman would start high depending on which fish he was selling. Lets us say £10 or 200 shillings. He would drop the price in increments, say 10 shillings a time. This is only an example, not cast in stone, working his way down until someone shouted "AT." The purchaser quickly said how many kits he wanted of that forty, say ten – and the salesman then returned to the original starting price for the remaining until each block was sold.

'Once the sales were over, the barrow lads would take the kits of fish back to the stand or workplace where the filleters were waiting to process the fish and get it into boxes, ready to put on either a lorry or into railway wagons and be delivered all over the north of the country. They tried their best to get the kits back as quickly as possible, for often it was known that the odd kit would go missing, usually by mistake. Still, a lot was simply pinched. This was often the case with highly priced fish like plaice, hake or lemon soles; they disappeared like the Bermuda triangle. Once gone, they were never traced.'

'Really? Was there much of that going on? Could be quite a good earner, I should imagine.'

It was Tommy's turn to tell me about this.

'Yes, like any kind of industry, there will always be people who look for a quick buck. I know of one guy who made a living out of stolen fish; he was a filleter buyer for a guy who had a chain of fish shops. He would stand in the crowd as they walked down the market as a sale went through. He used to buy the odd kit, not a lot, as they did not need that much. As he purchased his lot, he would put his tally on top of the fish, marking them. Hanging back, he would wait until the crowd had moved on, then change tallies in a couple of kits. He had a ready-made market for the stolen goods. It was said that he did that much of it he had one or two of the bobbies on the dock getting backhanders, to keep their eyes closed or look another way when he was getting his bounty of the dock.'

Paddy chipped in.

'Yes, I know the same bloke, but filleters stood working through all sorts of weather; at times it was that cold they could not feel their hands. Often one slip of the razor-sharp knives and it was down to the bone and they'd not even known they had done it. The big merchants could afford to lose the odd kit or two.

'Everyone wore wooden clogs due to the often frozen floor; it was terrible due to the water and pieces of fish; it made the footing treacherous.

'What if they did not sell all the fish? Say there were too many trawlers in all at the same time – what would happen to the excess fish?'

Ted took over again.

'It would go to what we call fishmeal at a low knockdown price, to be used in fertiliser. I saw days when excellent-quality fish went to the fishmeal factory because of the glut on the market. The fishermen hated this; it meant a loss of earnings – it made the settlement pay poor.'

'You talk about the fishermen with warmth in your voice. Did you ever want to go to sea, or was it out of the question?'

'No, my father would not let me go,' continued Ted. 'Like a lot of lads in my day we wanted to go to sea – for the adventure, and the way the fishermen were treated like heroes when they came home every trip, but it was a hard life. My old man had done it, and it was hard in those days in sailing ships before steam came in. He always said no son of his would risk his life to put fish and chips on anyone's table. In those days, you did not argue with your father, or it was a clip round the ear. Nineteen days away, and then you got home. Sometimes if you were lucky you could jump off the ship and take a taxi straight home, or even two taxis – one for a few of the blokes and the other to take their kit bags home. The married men mostly went home to their families. The majority all lived in the area in terraced houses, two up, two down. They used to buy chocolate bars out of the bond and give those to the children – it was often the only time apart from Christmas that kids ate chocolate. One or two friends might call round for a drink or two, then it was an early night for more than one reason or another,' he smiled.

'The following morning,' said Paddy, 'it was up early to get down the dock to pick up your fry of fish – a tradition where each member of the crew would be given three fish each, to feed their families. Then, at around 10am, all the crew would meet at the owner's office to find out how much they were going to get paid out of the catch. Not only that, but it was the time you found out if they wanted you back for another trip. Often men were told they were not wanted, possibly because they had not performed well enough.'

'Has Ted explained what it was like fishing?' said Kenny. 'I was at sea for five years before I had enough and got a shore job. Fucking hard graft, mate.'

'No, Kenny, he hasn't. I read a bit about it in the book Leif had, but not that much detail. I'd love to hear your version.'

'Right, then – when fishing at sea, most of the crew would be busy on deck gutting the fish before putting it below deck in the fish room. Here a couple or so of the crew would be busy icing the fish after placing it on to shelves or into bulk pounds and making it secure using more boards across the pound. All the hatches would be battened down to avoid seawater enveloping the fish room, except for one hatch from which the fish could be passed down to the fish room crew. Before any fish could be put in the pounds, the ice had to be broken up and dug out; this was the mate and a deckie learner's job. They would be up to the waist in ice, making ready to build up the racks. It was about twenty-five feet from the floor of the fish room to the underside of the deck. Each fish would be laid on its belly, on a bed of ice, special care taken for the shelf fish, and they would be stacked head to tail like we used to sleep in beds when we were kids. Remember that, Ted, when we lived down Connies Terrace, all four of you in one bed with the army coats for a blanket. They were the days, eh, mate? Then more ice was placed on top of the fish followed by one of the aluminium trays, and this was repeated until that pound was full. Then you'd start again from the floor, making sure that all the same species of fish were put together.'

I could not imagine what it was like having to work in those conditions, with the ship rolling and swaying in heavy seas, climbing up those racks trying to handle dead fish, laying it out like some undertaker, taking care not to damage the precious cargo.

'Cod livers would be saved, and usually, the radio operator would be charged with boiling these down into oil and this would also be sold off when back in the dock. The boiler was often inside the focsle and it smelled bloody awful, especially to any crew berthed there. The quicker the trawler caught and processed the fish, the better price it would obtain on the market and with fewer expenses to be considered. If the catch was well presented and made a reasonable price, it was common practice for the mate to give the foreman a backhander.'

'Backhander? You mean a tip.'

'A fucking tip? He wasn't a fucking taxi driver. Hey, lads – you heard him? A fucking tip.'

My head was spinning. Ted came in again.

'If the man says he wants another trip, he signs on and pays the ship's runner what we call a backhander; you might call it a bribe, for he might need the runners to help if ever he needs to find another ship in the future. It is then on to the pay office to get his settling money off the cashier. Paid up, they were off to the pub for two days of drinking, eating, keeping the wife happy, and sleeping – then the circle started all over again. It was no life, and I am truly grateful to my father for not letting me go, but if these warriors did not do it week in, week out, 365 days of the year, I would not have had a job, nor would thousands of people in Hull. That is why we think so much about our village in the city, Hessle Road; we are a different breed, son, a different breed.'

Talking to these guys was a privilege; you could see the love in their eyes. I felt humbled to have some Hessle Road blood in my veins, for at that moment in time, I also felt different.

Tommy was standing at the bar again; I wanted to ask him about the whaling scene.

'Hey, Tommy, got a minute, please?'

'Yes, sure; what's up, mate?'

'I was telling Ted earlier about me being in the Maritime Museum today and was taken by the amount of information on the whaling industry. He said to me that you had relations years ago who worked on the ships, that right?'

'Yes – one of my uncles sailed on them for over ten years during the prime years 1815 to 1825. Mind, I only know the stories that were handed down through the generations, but the gist of it was that it was a bloody hard life. They were away six months of the year, April to October, or so I have been told. Most of the whaling took place around Greenland, but over time it spread to the Davis Strait and Baffin Bay when ships were often trapped in the pack ice. I don't know how true it is, but the stories that 800 ships were lost between 1818 and 1899.'

I left Tommy on that note, as I could see he was getting upset thinking about it, and went back to sit with Ted.

'See you had a word with Tommy. Did he tell you about his family and whaling? I think one of his relations was on the Diana when she went down in 1869.'

'Oh, he did not mention that.' I thought I had touched a nerve, so I changed the subject.

'When I was in the museum today, I asked about trawler fleeting, and one of the museum guys, Alex, suggested I should ask in here if anyone knew anything about it. Do you know, Ted?'

'Bloody hell, where on earth did you dig that one up from? Never heard that subject mentioned for years. Yes, I know a bit as I knew one or two lads who sailed in the three ships. Hamlings owned them; they were notoriously bad sea ships, and were nicknamed slush-buckets, so it would have been suicide to secure them together.

I am confident that the fleeting trial went ahead in the summer of

1969 and lasted about four months, I think, but the method was never adopted for many reasons. I can recall that we bobbers had difficulty unloading the metal crates, and the trawlers could not rely or predict on getting back to a good market as they always tried to do. Add this to the extra time and expense of three ships, and the coming of freezer trawlers made it an unpopular option.

'I know the word was that they thought were going back to the 1920s when they had what was called the Gamecock fleet, which also sailed out of Hull, I seem to recall. Now, this was before my time, but some of the old men in my day used to tell stories about them – 40 or 50 steam trawlers, six carriers and one hospital ship, made up the fleet. They sailed together, and operating orders were signalled by the Admiral on his flagship. The fish was gutted on board; imagine the number of seagulls that would be hovering about. The men then packed the fish into boxes and sent them over in rowing boats to the carriers. The rowing boats then picked up new boxes from different carriers. Many men were either lost or injured as it was hazardous to work on a heavy sea; these little rowing boats could easily be swamped. That is why they took a hospital ship. Most of the fish they caught was herring. It had gone on for years, I think it began in the 1840s – I know it was the 19th century; not much more I can tell you, son.'

I had sat there listening to Ted's tales and was mesmerised by his wisdom. How these stories were handed down from generation to generation was beyond belief.

'Can I buy you a drink, Ted? You must be gagging after all that talking.'

'Why yes, please – I'll have another dram; thank you, Lars.'

I returned with his drink. 'Do you drink in Rayners all the time, Ted?'

'Oh, yes. Its real name is the Star and Garter, but they call it Rayners because of an old landlord who had it for years. It was used to be a Hull Brewery pub a long time ago; it was bought out by Northern Dairies in 1971, and then by Mansfield in 1985. I used to drink the dark mild in here when it was Hull Brewery, but that went downhill, and now I drink this Riding bitter, which is not too bad.'

'There are that many different beers over here. I have noticed quite a few. It is not the same in Australia. We've only got Tooheys and Tooths in NSW, XXXX in Queensland, and there might be one or two in other states, Swan lager in Perth and Victoria Bitter in Melbourne, but nothing like here.'

We spent the rest of the afternoon drinking and talking about Mum; a couple of the guys knew Peter, and they spoke about how he must have died. They said that he was, as they say in Hull, a 'bad'n'.

The memory came flooding back to me; I was quite moved to think that the mystery had died with my mother, and would die with Billy, for he never mentioned it again, not once after that fateful night back in 1957.

CHAPTER 44

LEIF

Billy Spills the Beans

Lars came over. 'Billy was just telling me about the night our father – or should I say, Peter – died.'

'Why, what did he tell you?'

'Oh, just that he must have fallen in the river pissed on the way to his ship. You'd never mentioned that, Leif. Why have you never told me that before?'

'Sorry, Lars, it's too painful. I've always tried to block it out of my head, but at least you now know the truth now.'

We hugged – maybe too many beers. I thought we had better go before something else came out from Billy.

'Just another one, and we will go. I want you to tell Kenny about when you played for St George; he is a rank black and white – he will love it.'

'No, we had better go.'

'Too late – I have ordered them.'

'OK, no worries.'

'Hey, Kenny come here – Lars wants to tell you about him playing for the Dragons in Sydney.'

'That right, Lars? You must have been a decent player to play for them – they had some great players.'

'Yes, mate, I played a bit, mostly reserves but I did make the first grade. You are right; some fantastic footballers wore the famous red V.'

'You play with Gasnier? He was some fucking player, that kid. I watched him play against a joint Hull and Rovers team back in, er, 1959, I think it was, at Hull City's ground, Boothferry Park. Him and a guy called Wells.'

'Harry Wells, you mean used to play for Western Suburbs?'

'Yes, that's him – what a partnership, built like a brick shithouse, that Wells. It was the first time I ever saw two centres playing inside and outside, instead of left and right. Wells just took them on, then put Gasnier through a gap, cut us to ribbons, and Gasnier was that fast, we had no fucking chance. I just remembered the date – October 26, 1959, played under lights – the first game I ever saw under floodlights; 29-9 was the score.'

'Bloody hell, mate, you got some memory there, blue – how the fuck you remember that?'

'I don't know... it's just in there somewhere. I only tend to remember the good things in life, mate – can't remember my wedding anniversary.' He laughed. 'Anyhow, it has been great meeting you son. By the way, I can't tell you apart; talk about identical – you are the best I have ever seen.'

We were just about finished. Billy was staggering around and started singing the Hull FC song Old Faithful with Kenny. It seemed like the rugby talk had set them off; it didn't take much.

'Come on, I will call a cab,' I said. 'Billy can come home with us and stop the night at our place. Billy,' I shouted as I grabbed his arm. 'Come on, Dad, time we went home – we have had enough, and you certainly have. Now, say goodnight.'

We dragged him out, got into the taxi, and set off home; Billy was half-asleep on the back seat with Lars, and he kept going on about how Mum had kept secrets from him, but she had told him lots of them in her letter. 'I can't tell you now, you know, Lars, – I will tell you after the funeral. He must have repeated himself two or three times about revealing all tomorrow.

'Come on, get out – don't let Connie see you in that state, or you will sleep in the fucking garage. Now, stand up straight.'

'I am OK, just leave me be,' he slurred, and staggered towards the front door.

The door opened before we even tried to get in.

'What the hell do you think you have been doing?'

Don't women ask some stupid questions?

'G'day, Connie. Just had a few beers with the boys.'

'Get your arses in here – tea is ruined. And what's he doing here?' She pointed at Billy, who was swaying as if he was on the deck of a trawler in a force eight gale. 'Get him inside, and put him in the other guest room... actually, no – just put him in the office on the sofa; don't want him pissing the bed again.'

'He is OK – he's just had a few too many, that's all, Connie. His wife has just passed away – my mother. Have a bit of heart; we were just having a wake for Mum.'

Connie shook her head and left us to it.

The next day we were up late, which was not surprising considering the amount of beer we had drunk. I decided I would have the rest of the week off.

'OK, let's go. Come on, Lars, and you, Billy. We are going down the dock to show Lars what is left of it and try and describe how it used to be, see if we can place what was where.'

'He should be at home. That is where the funeral is going from; we all have to be there,' said Connie.

'Don't panic; there is plenty of time. I will drop him off after looking around the dock area. We can still get on to Bullnose; that's about all that is left. Let's take that book with us, Lars. It has some great photos showing trawlers coming and going. At least you will see the river and lock gates even though they are all silted up.'

We left without any more comments from Connie; she went upstairs out of the way. She was outnumbered, three to one.

*

'Right – here we are, we can park here and walk along the front up on to Bullnose.'

We set off, with the filled-in Iceland market to our left; you could see the Lord Line building in front of us. It was a beautiful day, sun shining, seagulls still flying about as if the fish market was still on the go. There weren't as many as there used to be – hundreds used to live on the rooftops of the buildings, which saved them from predators – but it set the scene for Lars.

We arrived at the lock gates, which were all silted up, but you could still walk across the top of them as workers did many years ago, moving from the dry side to the wet and vice versa, when the swing bridge was in operation. Sadly, that had also gone now; it had been filled in, and there was tarmac road in its place.

In the book I had given to Lars, there was a poignant scene of a young boy and his dog watching as the Arctic Warrior moved out of the lock and headed up the Humber, possibly with his father on board, hoping for a safe return. It took me back to my days as a boy when this area was our playground and we met relatives coming home. We hoped we could jump on board and sail through the lock gates with them, dreaming that it was us who had just come back safely and were ready to meet our families. I had a bit of lump in my throat. 'OK – had enough, you two? Shall we call it a day? You get a feel for it, Lars? Can you understand how it is in our blood?'

He turned and looked at me; there were tears in his eyes. It had undoubtedly touched his heart. That old saying came to my mind. 'You can take the lad out of Hessle Road, but you can never take Hessle Road out of the lad.' He had never lived here, but, by hell, it was in his blood.

'My fucking oath, mate – I never thought it would get to me, but fair dinkum, it bloody well has, mate; unreal.'

We got back to my place and started talking about old times again.

'Oh, one thing I have been dying to ask you,' said Lars. 'There was a young girl up at Surfers. Stephanie Longbottom was her name – good-looking sort.'

'Fuck off, never! I only spent one night with her; she was only a kid, eighteen, I think? What a beautiful thing – one of the best fucks I ever had. How the fuck did you meet her? Unbelievable. Come on, tell me – she has a kid called Leif as well?'

'No! I drove into a takeaway joint one night, and she was serving. She thought I was you. Well, one thing led to another, and we ended up in the cot. After we had finished making love, we lay back, just enjoying the moment. She kept comparing me with you. Funny, same as Mel used to. Suppose it's rare that a girl gets the chance of rooting twins – and identical ones at that. She mentioned a couple of things about how you used to nibble at her bottom lip as you kissed. She was going to tell me something else. We got interrupted, and she never got round to it. I never thought any more of it. One thing she did mention was about you saying stuff she could not understand as you rooted her. Muttering other girls' names like Cass, Kally and Leigh, as you were just about to shoot your load. Anyway, all my life I have suffered from premature ejaculation, and Maya made me see a therapist about it. She advised me to think about something other than rooting when giving Maya one. She even told me her old man had the same problem; he used to think of footy teams and name them as he went along – and that's when I realised they weren't girls' names, they were English rugby grounds.'

'I had the same problem. I lost my cherry to a girl from Pontefract when we were on holiday in Withernsea, on the coast. I can't believe I'm telling you this, but I used to come too fucking quick. I started to think of all the rugby league teams and their grounds as I was shagging, which cured it, that's for sure. Fucking unbelievable – we are identical twins, mate, right down to the old dick.'

We both laughed and then hugged once again.

CHAPTER 45

LEIF
Last Goodbye

Mum had requested that it not be a religious service as she was not a great believer. She always used to say if there were a god, he would not let children suffer, as many did all over the world – the one he was supposed to have built over seven days, and on one of them he did fuck all.

She had written in her letter – the one she had told Billy to open on her death, with strict orders that he told no one what she had said – her last list of things to do. Mum had also organised the celebrant, the woman who would carry out the service, and only the Lord's Prayer was to be said. There were no hymns, just the songs that meant something to her, the songs she had loved all her life.

As we left their house, people stopped along the street as we passed; some men took off their hats and bowed their heads. It was so moving to think strangers could be so friendly towards someone they might never have met. It was a slow ride. I thought to myself that she would have been so proud – her last farewell, riding in a carriage with two black horses, her coffin decked in flowers… what a way to go. We had stopped in traffic, and were sitting there, looking at the coffin in front of us, not speaking – but the silence was broken when my mobile rang. Fuck; I thought I had turned it off. I ignored it, but it kept on ringing. It stopped, then almost immediately a text message came through.

I sneaked a look; it was from Einar Hegdahl. Four words – 'Ring me, it's urgent.'

293

Connie was looking daggers at me; why had I not turned off my phone?

We arrived at the crematorium. The large chapel had been requested, which was Billy's idea. He thought there would be many people wanting to pay their last respects to her, a proper Hessle Road funeral, and he was right.

As the procession pulled into the drive, there were people still walking up to the building. It was heaving; I'd never seen so many people, most of whom I did not know or recognise.

No black was what she wanted; people were asked to wear colours and no formal wear, and if the women wanted to, they could put their hair in headscarves. Only a couple of the older generation had done that as a sign of respect.

My phone sounded again; this time, it was a text message. I sneaked a look. 'Ring me NOW, it's urgent.' Another look of disdain from Connie.

We walked into the chapel. The congregation had already gone in, which was something else Mum had requested. She had said she did not want people to stand outside getting pissing wet through while she was covered up.

As we walked into the chapel, they played one of the songs my mother loved, – The Most Beautiful Girl, by Charlie Rich. I smiled to myself. That was the right choice. Mum was placed on the plinth in front of us. One of the pallbearers showed us to our seats on the front row.

Mary, the celebrant, began the service. 'Good afternoon, everyone, and thank you for coming to bid your farewell to Christine.'

'Christine Smith was born Christine Askenes on May 23, 1930, the only daughter to Hans Askenes and Elizabeth, sister to Olaf and Arkvid. She had a different childhood, being brought up in a family whose ancestors were brought over during the great famine in the early 1800s. They had settled in Hull after stopping off here on their way to the USA,but decided to end their journey here. Having fallen out with her father, Christine ran away from home, to Blackpool. Why there, no one seems to know – but in 1946 it was a long way away; there were no motor cars or motorways in those days. She went to stay with her aunt Freda, who had a B&B in Blackpool, where she met Peter Daniels and fell in love, and then fell pregnant. On June 27, she had twin boys, Leif and Lars. Now, here I must change the story a little, for Christine was led to believe that Lars had died in childbirth. As we can now see, he is alive and well and with us today, and we welcome him and his wife Maya having flown over from the other side of the world.'

She paused for a second, looking at Lars and smiling.

'After giving birth and the trauma of losing Lars, she decided to come back to Hull, but still at loggerheads with her father, she found accommodation with Peter. They all lived happily, Peter getting a job on the deep-sea trawlers, but sadly after eleven years of married life, Peter had an accident and drowned in the river. Christine, once again on her own, brought up Leif, and after a while found another man in her life, Billy Smith. They fell in love and settled down to a happy life on Hessle Road. On this note, we will listen to another piece of music, again chosen by Christine, and once again it's the silver fox himself, Charlie Rich, singing, There Won't Be Anymore. This song is on one album Leif bought her for her birthday back in 1975. Written by Charlie, it describes a guy telling his girlfriend he won't be writing to her again. Christine wanted this song to be dedicated to Lars and Maya. Because it was through her writing to Lars, after he had found her, that made her family whole again.'

I could hear another text arrive on my phone. 'RING ME,' was all it said.

'I told you to turn that fucking phone off,' Connie whispered.

'It's Einar. He wants to talk urgently.'

'I don't give a fuck who it is. You are at your mother's funeral, for god's sake, have you no respect?'

'He doesn't fucking know that,' I whispered back.

'I will call on Lars to say a few words on behalf of Christine's family.'

Lars stood up and went up to the podium. 'G'day. Well, what can I say about a woman I only met a few months ago? A woman I did not know existed until Leif had visited home, in that case, Australia, and visited a town my adopted parents lived in, Maitland. He had been spotted in a pub, which is no surprise.'

The crowd laughed, and you could see everyone nodding in agreement.

'It was through her planning and keeping secrets, which she was bloody good at, that we came over to get married alongside her and Billy. It was the proudest moment of my life, but the downside was that Mum was crook – sorry, ill. I didn't have long enough to get to know her as my true mother. I won't go on. I had more to say but... sorry.'

Lars rejoined the family, tears running down his face; there wasn't a dry eye in the place.

'Thank you, Lars, for those wonderful words.'

My phone beeped again; another text. Connie gave me that look again, 'Turn the bastard off,' she whispered. I nodded my head.

I was in tears. The ceremony had got to me; I needed to get out. I felt like I would be sick, and was feeling faint. One of the people who worked at the crematorium noticed me and came over. 'You OK, sir, can I help?' He took my arm and guided me to a small room, sat me down and went to get some water.

I took the opportunity to ring Einar.

'Einar, what do you want? I am at my mother's funeral. Yes, it was sudden. What do you want that is so urgent? What? You are kidding me, you want what, to take over what? Are you sure? Yes, I know Excel. I use it a lot. Yes, I will ring you later. Of course I am interested. Bye, Ein – yes, I will ring you.'

The man returned just as I put my phone in my pocket. 'There you are, sir.'

I took the drink, got up, and went back into the main chapel. Connie was looking like she could rip my head off.

'I want to add before we come to the committal that Billy and his family would like to thank everyone for coming today, and you are all welcome back at Rayners on Hessle Road where refreshments will be served.'

The congregation was asked to say the Lord's Prayer. Then Mary gave the 'Ashes to ashes, dust to dust' committal, and it was time to leave Mum for the last time. Mary picked up her folder, walked over to the coffin, bowed her head, turned, and walked towards the exit.

The last piece of music began – but this time it was not a recording. It was the sound of a piano coming from upstairs in the gallery – it was our song, *Save the Last Dance for Me*. Then a voice sang out – a beautiful woman's voice.

I looked up at the balcony. I could not see her, but I knew it was her. It was Jenny; she had come to Mum's funeral to sing for her. I looked at Billy. He nodded and whispered. 'Your Mum had kept in touch with Jenny over the years. She had asked her to come and play at her funeral.'

Another secret. That was it. I just fell apart, broke down. Connie held my hand. She had never met Jenny, and did not know what my feelings still were for my first love, but hey, that was history. No need to bring it back today. It was Mum's farewell.

I walked up to the coffin with Lars and Billy; we held hands, touched the wooden casket, and said our last goodbyes, tears flowing down our cheeks. 'Goodbye, Mum.'

We stood back from the casket; our mother, lover and best friend had left us. Now only our memories remained of the most wonderful woman you could ever meet.

With Jenny's voice singing out, the curtains began to close; god, it was the hardest thing I had ever done.

When we turned to leave the chapel, the congregation had left. The three most central people in Mum's life remained, no longer dependent on the woman who, forty-six years ago, had given birth to two of us and made the other the happiest man in the world. The phone in my pocket vibrated; it would be Einar, for sure.

THE END

COMING UP...

If you enjoyed reading the Askenes Trilogy, look out for more adventures of the twins in Keith's next novel, *You're My Best Friend*, due to be published in 2023.

Lightning Source UK Ltd.
Milton Keynes UK
UKHW041126070622
404006UK00002B/462